RISKING LOVE

JANIE MASON

Copyright

First Edition: November 2013

Web Site: www.JanieMason.com

EPub Edition ISBN: 978-0-9860687-0-6

Print Edition ISBN: 978-0-9860687-1-3

Dedication

To my Debut Sisters, for encouraging me to write the book I wanted to write. To Marcia, for your endless support and friendship. To Stephanie and Lisa, for your editing suggestions. To Kat, for sifting through the mire of my e-mails to write my back cover copy.

To my daughter, Rachel, for nailing my vision of this cover. Love you.

And as always to David, who's at the heart of every hero I write.

Chapter One

Southern Ohio, 1852

Apprehension skittered up Lucy Neels' spine as she halted the horse cart in front of Thomas's cabin. *He always stays close to home when runaways are here.* But even though Wink had barked enthusiastically from his perch next to her, their neighbor still hadn't emerged to greet them.

Sitting still as the scarecrow guarding the farmer's neat rows of corn, she looked out over the clearing. The rustic cabin appeared as peaceful as always, and the aromas of sweet honeysuckle and rich earth mingled with the reassuring message of a robin's song.

You're overreacting. It wasn't as if fiendish eyes glowed from the shadows of the woods. Yet she caught herself rubbing her forearms through the rough sackcloth of her coat.

"Thomas?" she called. If he was in the barn he should have been able to hear her. And surely he would have heard Wink.

Lord, please let him be alright. The thought of Thomas—a negro man living precariously close to the Ohio River, with a slave state beyond—getting caught helping runaways, made her frequent nightmares even *more* terrifying. Had he been caught last night? Arrested? Or maybe even kidnapped and dragged south by slave catchers even though he'd bought his freedom years ago.

She took a slow breath and once again scanned the exterior of the cabin and the new barn he'd built to replace the one that had collapsed from last year's snows. Both bays quietly munched grass along the fence rail inside the corral, which meant Thomas hadn't ridden to town. She climbed down, her gaze tracing the edge of the cornfield and the woods separating his property from hers. Nothing.

Wink had already finished watering his favorite tree stump, leapt onto the porch, and was now dancing an impatient jig outside the cabin door. She should be comforted by his behavior, with his tail wagging faster than gossiping tongues at a town social. But she wasn't.

Something's happened. She pulled her basket from the back of the cart and stepped up onto the porch, the weathered floorboards creaking with each deliberate movement. Although she had nothing to fear from either the law or southern slave catchers, her leg muscles tensed as if readying to flee. She heard a faint call.

"I'm in here."

The fist gripping her stomach relaxed as she charged inside. Wink was at the older man's bedside in two shakes, shamelessly seeking affection. Lucy hurried across the room, dumping her basket of provisions on the scarred table. Her gaze went to the branches secured along the length of Thomas's left shin.

She knelt alongside her dog and lowered her voice. "What happened? Did you run into trouble?"

He gave her coppery, brown dog one last pat and offered her his hand. "Some." The crease between his brows deepened. "But clumsiness is the only reason I have this broken leg. We'd lost the men chasing us..."

Her spine stiffened. Despite the summer heat and two layers of cloth, chills raised gooseflesh along her arms.

This was the first close call Thomas had ever had since he'd become involved in the Underground Railroad.

"I tripped on a tree root climbing out of the stream and fell over a big stone. All that running and then I get careless when we're almost here. It's a good thing I had help."

"Are your passengers in the barn?"

"Yes. There's a woman about your age, her twelve-year-old girl and eight-year-old son. As a matter of fact, the boy just hopped out the window and ran to the barn. I wasn't willing to bet it was you even though I thought I recognized Wink's bark."

Lucy relaxed her grip on his hand and sunk back onto her heals. She examined his homemade splint. Thomas had learned to read since he'd bought his freedom and knew a considerable amount about doctoring.

"How bad is your leg?" she asked.

He grimaced. "I'd say I'm going to be laid up for close to a month."

"Only a month?" She gave him a narrowed glare. "That doesn't seem like long enough for a broken leg to heal."

He patted her hand. "Child, it's not like it snapped clean in two. You'll see, it'll be right as rain in four weeks or so."

"Or so," she mimicked. "But how are you going to get your passengers to their next stop?" Another wince crossed his face and she lifted her hands away from the bed. "Did I bump your leg?"

"No, no. It's just that...well...I never wanted to ask for your help."

Thomas had never wanted her to become directly involved. Even supplying extra food for his passengers had been at her insistence.

"Lucy, the woman is expecting." She saw the same sorrow in his coffee-colored gaze that had drawn them together two years ago. Bleak memories settled over her like a sodden quilt.

"Although her time's supposed to be a month away, she's having labor pains. The boy says they seemed to have stopped this morning, but that baby might decide to come if she doesn't stay off her feet and rest. Would you be willing to hide them at your place until I can walk?"

Bile burned in the back of her throat and she swallowed it in a gulp of heartache. "Thomas, I don't—"

"Please, child. With me laid up I can't take care of her, and if that baby comes, she's going to need help with the birthing. More than those children of hers can provide." Thomas squeezed Lucy's hand and his dark gaze pleaded. "I know it's a lot to ask."

It was. Oh, Lord, it was. Her chest pounded and she leaned forward to rest her cheek on their clasped hands. Thomas knew her sorrow well and said no more, granting her time to grieve.

A baby. Two years had passed, but suddenly she was swept back to the pain and regret of her miscarriage. After her husband's death she had managed to carve out a new life, but jealousy and longing still had her avoiding mothers with babes in arms. How could she survive taking an expectant woman into her home and, God help her, delivering the child?

Wink nudged her, bringing her back to the here and now. She met Thomas's gaze and let her tear-filled eyes say the yes her lips couldn't form. She blinked the moisture away.

"You helped me when I needed it most. I would do anything to repay you."

Promise delivered, her stomach roiled. What if she got caught hiding runaway slaves? She could be jailed, or issued a fine so large she'd lose her farm.

But she owed Thomas her life.

"You don't owe me a debt, child. The Good Lord put me on this earth to care for others. Simple as that. But right now I can't care for that scared family hiding in my barn."

But not even his assurance could change the facts. Thomas had nursed her back to health. A colored man tending a white woman as closely as he had her, could have been reason aplenty for some to string him up from the nearest tree. But that hadn't stopped him.

As much as she wished she could drive her cart home and pretend he didn't need her help, that he wasn't in this predicament, she owed Thomas.

Lucy took a fortifying breath. "I'm headed into town with eggs and to pick up supplies." She swallowed against the churning in her belly and painted on a false smile. "I'll just buy extra."

He patted her hand, but his ragged, whiskered face betrayed wariness.

"I know it'll be hard."

"But I'll do it," she said, tamping down regret. Best put an end to this conversation and get a move on.

The corners of his eyes crinkled with his smile. "Alright. Now be careful what and how much you buy. And don't do anything out of the ordinary or it will raise suspicions."

"Don't worry. Mr. Anderson doesn't pay me any mind, and his wife has never been one to pry."

Trying to ignore the weight of foreboding on her shoulders, she stood and began a mental list of supplies. More flour, corn meal, coffee... "Wait," she said as another crucial detail popped into her whirling brain. "What about you? I can't leave you here by yourself."

"Oh, I can get along." His unconvincing tone paired an averted gaze.

"Thomas Washington, you're lying to me as surely as you're lying in that bed. I need to get you over to my house so I can take care of you. There won't be time to bounce back and forth between our farms."

"Now, child, you know you can't do that. It wouldn't be fitting."

But providing meals was a far cry more impersonal than the care she had needed two years ago. Narrow-minded folks could still be found north of the Ohio River, but Lucy really didn't think they would attack a white woman for emptying a chamber pot. And anyone who thought that her cooking and providing a bed for him was improper could just go to the devil.

Besides, it wasn't as if she would spread the word about their arrangement. If the situation hadn't involved runaways, she would have asked Sheriff Tate to keep an eye out for trouble. He had proven himself an ally after Emmett's sudden death. But with slaves at her place, Lucy couldn't risk the sheriff stopping by.

"The boy, James, could stay here to help me." Thomas pushed himself up on one elbow and grimaced. "He can fetch and tote whatever I need."

Lucy wasn't convinced an eight-year-old could adequately care for an ailing man, but apparently they'd managed well enough last night. She fetched the basket of food from the table. With so much to think about, she'd trust that they could make due until she figured out how to move Thomas. But first she needed to get the mother and daughter to her place.

"Alright. For now. The sooner I can get..." Lucy set the basket next to the bed and straightened. "What are their names?"

"Emily is the woman," he supplied. "And her girl's name is Rosalee."

"Alright, the sooner I can get Emily and Rosalee hidden at my place, the better." She started for the door, eager for activity to crowd out worries. "Should I check on them?"

"No, James says his mama's resting comfortably, and you're already running late. Stick to your routine. We can't afford to draw any unwanted attention." She opened door. "Wait until dusk to come back. You know the way through the woods and the darkness will cloak you."

A shudder ran through her as she nodded. Although the darkness provided an added measure of safety, he'd forgotten that for her, nighttime made it more difficult to know trouble was near.

Lorenzo "Renzo" Ross peeled off his wide-brimmed hat and slapped it against his thigh, sending up a small cloud of dust. A farmer's wagon rolled past, adding another fine layer of dirt to the acre's worth already imbedded in his skin and clothes.

A young girl's squeal drew his attention as a boy chased her down the boardwalk growling like a lion and holding fingers curled like claws. Down the street new arrivals to Rush Crossing retrieved bags as they were tossed down to the coachman on the ground then disappeared inside the hotel. Another man with stacked boxes propelled his handcart in the direction of the Ohio River, where a massive sidewheeler gleamed in the noonday sun like a gingerbread palace.

Renzo ran a sleeve across his brow. Frustration, paired with the blazing sun, fizzled what was left of his determination. He turned back to the greasy-haired livery boy who'd remembered Elizabeth.

"You're certain it was them?" Renzo couldn't understand why the small traveling party had passed up all the riverboats in Wheeling to board one in Rush Crossing, Ohio, a town with a main street not much longer than the drive of his parent's summer estate outside Philadelphia.

"Yup, two maybe three days ago" His informant wiped his nose with the back of his hand. Although the young man probably hadn't bathed in a month, Renzo took comfort in the fact that the stable looked well-kept and prosperous. His horse deserved some pampering after the journey they'd had.

"Do you remember the name of the boat?"

"Nope. Actually I think there might have been more than one that day, but I was too busy to walk down for a closer look."

So much for demanding an explanation from his fiancée, or rather his ex-fiancée. Renzo shook his head. It still felt damned strange to think of Elizabeth as being married to someone else. Although the Hargroves had insisted that becoming Mrs. Lorenzo Ross would be their daughter's dream come true, he'd realized, too late, she'd never been as forthcoming. Obviously his bride-to-be had been as unenthusiastic about their engagement as he, especially since she'd secretly married some mystery fellow and taken off.

And as if being jilted wasn't bad enough, the mind-numbing conversation he'd overhead between his parents still had him reeling. Betrayal ate at him, crumbling any desire to forgive his father. How could he have lied to him all these years? Renzo wished he'd taken the time before leaving to ask his brother if he'd known the truth.

He inhaled slowly.

A whistle from the steamer pierced his thoughts and he looked back. Ladies with parasols strolled along the upper deck, no doubt spreading gossip from previous stops along their journey. Elizabeth could disembark at any number of cities between here and New Orleans and he'd lost the will to follow up at any of them. But he sure as hell wasn't ready to go back and confront his traitorous father. Mrs. Hargrove's near hysterical request to return Elizabeth to the bosom of her family, along with Renzo's own temper, had gotten him this far. But no further.

Boots crunched on the pebbled ground as the boy spun and walked away.

Renzo called after him. "One last thing, did they seem to be getting along?"

The boy's brow furrowed.

Does he not understand English? Renzo shook his head and closed the distance between them, lowering his voice. "Did she seem at all frightened, or intimidated by her...her husband?" Pride, rather than jealousy, made him hesitate at the word.

The boy's sudden cackle startled Terra into whinnying. "That fella's the one I feel sorry for. Not that she wasn't purdy as a picture, but from what I saw, she jabbered non-*stop*. If you hadn't shown me that likeness, I'd think you was asking after someone else."

Elizabeth talking non-stop? Aside from discussing the weather, she'd rarely had much to say to *him*.

The young man gave him a sock on the arm as if they were boyhood chums, leaving a stamp of grime on his sleeve. Ah, well, the shirt was marked for someone's rag bag anyway. All that remained in his saddlebags were some underclothes, his coat and the cravat he'd removed in deference to the heat. And his revolver.

The lad backed up, waving his thumb over his shoulder. "I've got to get back to work before the old man starts hollering. You want me to take your horse?"

He gave a quick nod. Until he decided what to do, he wasn't going anywhere. He tossed his saddlebags over a shoulder and handed over the reins.

"Give him a good rub down," he said as they walked away. Terra was still out of sorts over his unexpected train ride from Baltimore to Wheeling.

Renzo rocked his hat onto his head and pulled the miniature back out of his bag. Elizabeth's likeness smiled up at him as if proclaiming him a fool. Her lips curved up in a way that could melt the hearts of men, but something in those cool green eyes mocked him for riding even a quarter mile past the city limits after her.

Why the hell had he bothered? In truth, when he'd found out she'd left, his first instinct had been to rush to church and thank the Holy Mother. A significant reaction since he hadn't accompanied *his* mother to church in years. But Mrs. Hargrove's insistence that she would suffer an apoplexy if her sweet daughter wasn't rescued, along with his bitter argument with his father, had been enough to get him to set out after her

Over the miles his anger had swelled and receded like the tide. But now, after muddy roads, flea-infested inns and questioning scores of people, all he cared about was a meal and a clean bed. A hot gust of wind blew down the street, reminding him to add a cool bath to the list. Coughing, he tucked the picture back inside the saddlebag and scanned the storefronts for a restaurant. Patsy's Bakery wasn't far and surely would have something to take the edge off his hunger. If Patsy would let him in the door. He set down his bag and tried to dust himself off.

By now the whole damned eastern seaboard knew he'd been jilted. He shouldn't have agreed to the engagement. He hadn't had any interest in marriage yet. In courting and wooing. But his parents had insisted that a wife and family would give him the sense of direction he seemed to lack. His indifference had made the match seem like the best thing. Then Elizabeth had sent everyone into a tizzy by taking off.

Funny, knowing she'd had the guts to do it made him think she might have been more interesting than he'd credit for.

He heard another long whinny from Terra. It had been one hell of a week and the horse could be as particular about his handling as Father was about the amount of starch in his shirts. At the thought, his jaw tightened. This debacle *had* provided a damned good reason to put some distance between them, and he still wasn't ready to go back.

Had Elizabeth somehow found out about his father's lies? Was that why she'd run off with someone else? He might never learn what had made her cry off at such a late date, but he was determined to move on. Forget it.

Easy enough, in theory. But he wasn't ready to go home. He'd be the one in control this time. *Let the old man sweat about it for a few weeks.*

He hitched the saddlebags on his shoulder and

started toward the bakery at the center of town. If Mr. and Mrs. Hargrove wanted their daughter found, let their high-and-mighty son, Charles, track her down. He'd bet the prominent banker knew more about her disappearance than he let on.

Renzo was finished chasing her. Finished with women, at least the marrying kind. Before he'd agreed to this farcical betrothal he'd sampled a variety of ladies, all of whom expected nothing more complicated than a lusty romp between the sheets. This disaster was a sign. He wasn't destined to find a love match. His brother's healthy marriage had already produced sons to carry on the Ross family name. There was no reason why he shouldn't resume his previous habit of enjoying *un*wedded bliss.

He made his way up the bowed treads to the boardwalk, calculating how long it would take him to eat and bathe. It had been hours since breakfast, and he hadn't fully bathed since the morning he'd left. But when he spotted some spools of ribbon on a hanging dowel in a dressmaker's window, it reminded him of how his mother had chattered about some such frippery she'd purchased for the wedding. His empty stomach knotted.

She'll be fine. When I get back home, everything will go back to normal.

His steps became more determined. He'd stay awhile, explore the area and when he was good and ready, he'd take a different route home. There was no hurry. And if enough time passed, society would be focused on some other scandal.

He nodded to an elderly couple as they passed, pinching the brim of his hat. It wasn't as if his presence at home was essential. His father and Roberto had the business was so well in hand, he felt superfluous at the shipping office. If his grandfather hadn't built Ross Shipping from the ground up, he'd have left the business long ago.

"Help! Somebody help!" A child shrieked from

ahead. He dropped his bags and took off toward the cries, his hat flying off somewhere behind.

The pig-tailed girl he'd seen earlier emerged from between two buildings. "Somebody help! Mark's on fire!"

Renzo leapt down from the boardwalk and sprinted past her into the alley, his heart pounding.

He spotted the boy waving his arm through the air, his sleeve aflame. "Ow, ow! Put it out!" he sobbed.

Renzo whipped his braces off his shoulders and pulled his shirt over his head. A second later he engulfed the boy inside the cloth, cutting off his cries. Renzo had battled enough dockside fires to recognize the scent of burned flesh but he patted the child's squirming arm anyway, more concerned with quickly suffocating the flames. The boy's sobbing began again.

Renzo lightened his touch. "I know, it hurts. But I've got to make sure the flames are doused." A moment later he pulled the fabric away from the boy's face. His freckled cheeks and nose were streaked with tears and dirt, but luckily the skin there appeared undamaged. The flesh on his arm would be another matter.

"Don't move." He turned toward the small crowd that had gathered in the alley behind them. A woman had taken charge of the crying girl, catching her muffled sobs in her skirts.

"Where's the doctor?"

"This way." A man in dirty work clothes waved his arm in a gesture to follow. Renzo picked up the boy, still tangled in his shirt, and headed toward the street. As they passed the hotel, a plump woman in an apron hustled out the front door. "Mark!"

She was probably the boy's mother, but Renzo didn't stop to let her catch up. The child needed immediate medical attention.

"Meet us at the doctor's office," he called over his shoulder. Less than a minute later, his guide started up a stairway on the side of a clapboard building. The sign at the base of the stairs read Dr. Benjamin Morgan.

"Doc!" His guide pushed open the door.

An elderly gentleman emerged from a back room. "I'm not deaf, Harold." But the physician's eyes narrowed as he spotted the child. He gestured toward the adjoining room. "Back here."

Renzo laid the boy down on a table and stepped back just as the woman called from the outer office.

"I'm here, Doc."

Doctor Morgan looked back at Renzo. "What happened?"

"His sleeve was on fire."

The doctor slowly peeled away the cloth to examine the wound. It had to hurt like hell, but the boy barely made a peep.

The boy's mother rushed in and instantly began stroking her son's hair. "Thank you, sir, for getting my boy here." She nodded once then returned her attention to the doctor's ministrations. "Be careful, Doc," she said.

Renzo smiled. He'd met too many society mamas whose histrionics would take precedence over comforting their child.

Dr. Morgan spoke to Mark. "Since I know Mabel wouldn't have you tending a stove, I can only think of one reason you'd be around a fire on a hot day like this. Were you sneaking a cigarette?"

Mark averted his gaze and nodded.

Morgan shook his head. "I figured. Children just can't seem to resist." The physician's gentle touch belied his gruff tone.

Mabel winced as she looked at the burns. "Mark's not as hearty as his older brothers."

Renzo touched her shoulder. "He seems pretty tough." He met the boy's tear-filled gaze, and winked. Damned good thing the lad wasn't overdo for a haircut or the flames could have quickly spread past his arm.

A sudden clatter had them all swiveling to look at

Harold, who had knocked some kind of framed certificate off the wall.

"There are too-damned many people in here," the doctor's voice boomed. "You two fellows, clear out."

Renzo pulled Harold with him. In the outer office Renzo spotted his saddlebags and hat sitting on a chair inside the door. Some kind onlooker must have delivered his things, instantly endearing him to this small town. He pulled his coat out of the bag, slipped it on and followed Harold down the stairs.

"Well, Renzo," Harold said after he'd introduced himself, "You probably saved Mark's life." The man mopped his brow with a faded bandana and shoved it back into his pocket. "Have you moved to Rush Crossing?"

Renzo bit back a laugh. "No. Just finishing up a hunting expedition of sorts and thought I'd rest up for a couple days." He glanced back up the stairs. "Do you think someone's gone for the boy's father?"

Harold shook his head. "Mabel lost her husband last year. Ed was a good man but he had weak lungs. Pneumonia took him."

That would explain why she'd come out of the hotel wearing an apron. A woman forced to work to support herself and her son. She might not want it, but he added sympathy to the respect he already had for her.

Renzo headed off once more in the direction of the bakery. Harold stuck to him like the grime caked on his skin. "That was nice of someone to go to the trouble of returning my things. Is everyone here so honest?"

Before the man could reply, two elderly women stepped out of the apothecary shop, glanced at his partially bared chest and singed him with withering glares.

"Obscene," one of them huffed before they flounced away.

Harold chuckled and pointed across the street. "Honest *and* Godly. That's why you'd better get on over to Anderson's to buy a shirt. Since Mabel hasn't had time to sing your praises, the respectable females of Rush Crossing might just see fit to have you tarred and feathered for public indecency."

Chapter Two

The overhead bell jangled as Renzo entered Anderson's Mercantile and looked around. The whole store would have fit in the dining room and parlor of the family townhouse. *What did you expect?* At least it wouldn't take long to pick out clothes. Then he could eat. As he approached the counter, a short, thin man hastily approached.

"Can I help you?" The man glanced between Renzo's bared skin and the wide-eyed woman behind the counter.

"I need some shirts."

"Yes, you do." The man gestured toward the back. "Please, come this way." Renzo hurried to follow, sorry to have caused any embarrassment. They passed behind the cover of a display of baskets.

The door's bell rang once again and he heard the woman behind the counter clear her throat. "Oh, g-good morning, Lucy."

"Good morning, Mrs. Anderson." The female customer's familiar accent snagged his attention. It was just like Nanny's. He turned back to look between the baskets.

With her straw hat hanging by its strings behind her back, he could see her profile. She appeared to be in her middle twenties and had a dark blond braid wound in a tight bun at her nape. Her dusty brown skirt, worn, dirty boots and faded coat suggested a life of labor.

A coat in this heat? He glanced at the shopkeeper, who was still busy sifting through a stack of shirts, then back toward the woman.

She lifted her basket up onto the counter. "Not too many today, I'm afraid." Her accent said she wasn't native to Ohio. No one else here spoke with the same drawl. Engulfed in her ill-fitting, rough wardrobe, there wasn't much to draw a man's eye but her comforting voice softened a corner of his soul that had hardened in recent months.

Mrs. Anderson transferred eggs from the woman's basket into another container. "No matter. We're always glad to get your eggs, Lucy. You must have happy hens because their eggs are always the largest."

He smiled. *Lucy. I like it.*

She handed Mrs. Anderson a scrap of paper and the woman gathered items from her shelves. Lucy pulled a slim novel from the pocket of her coat and opened it.

"Hmm," he said, more to himself than for anyone else to hear. He'd assumed any female with breath would browse the merchandise while she waited, but Lucy seemed more interested in her book.

And what is she reading? Poetry? A scandalous novel? He glanced around, not seeing any books for sale. Where did people get books in a small town like Rush Crossing? While Philadelphia boasted book shops, impressive private book collections, as well as Benjamin Franklin's The Library Company, Renzo would have assumed most households in the area were lucky to contain a Bible. Obviously he hadn't given this woman, or her community, enough credit.

"Here we are," Mr. Anderson said.

The woman's gaze tracked the man's voice, and eyes the color of a clear, summer sky rounded as she spotted Renzo. The cornered-hare expression made sense when he realized he'd stepped out from behind the baskets and stood there, indecently covered from the waist up.

Anderson tugged on his arm. "Sir, I must insist that you step back here with me. Our ladies should not be exposed to men in your state of undress."

Renzo ducked back behind the display. "You're right. I apologize." He must look unscrupulous at best.

"Here." Anderson non-too-gently shoved a white Fairlawn shirt into his hands. "This should fit."

But a desire not to stick out like the stranger he was made him set it back down. Despite having much nicer shirts hanging in his closet at home—hand-tailored to properly fit his shoulders—he picked up a blue work shirt from another stack.

"This one should do." He yanked off the coat, slipped the shirt on and began working the buttons. If he hurried, he could get to the counter before Lucy got away.

Mr. Anderson spoke up. "Will you be needing anything else? Perhaps some new trousers?" Was the little man trying to stall him?

"Later." Renzo gave up on last few shirt buttons, tucked the tails into the waist of his trousers, pulled his braces back over his shoulders and grabbed his things.

So much for acting calm. Lucy shoved her book into her pocket and began packing her purchases. She had to get out of here. Not only did she have preparations to make before she returned to Thomas's place, but who knew when that man would be coming up to the counter? The intensity of his gaze had stolen her breath. And he was so, so large. And muscular. And wickedly handsome. And prit-near naked.

Her cheeks warmed and a strange fluttering in her belly made her fingers fumble with the last of her supplies.

"Thank you, Lucy. See you tomorrow." Bess Anderson never forced her into conversation, and today she, too, seemed downright anxious for her to leave.

Lucy nodded and quickly lifted her basket.

"Can I help you with that?" The deep voice froze her sure a February blizzard.

It was him.

She knew it even before lifting her gaze to confirm the fact. Chills rolled up her spine as eyes the color of raw honey stared down from an intimidating height. She reached deep inside for every bit of gumption she could manage.

"No." She hustled toward the door without giving him time to reply. Was she rude enough to keep him from following? Even though the dark-haired stranger had offered a kindness and was handsome as the devil, she'd barely survived hell-on-earth with one powerful man. She wouldn't survive getting tangled up with another.

Just as she reached for the knob, the door opened. A trio of men blocked her escape. She'd never seen them, but their sudden appearance shocked her sense of self-preservation in an entirely different way than the stranger behind her had. The grisly-looking men wore well-worn gun belts slung low on their hips and their filthy clothes reeked of body odor. Her stomach clenched to keep from spilling its meager contents. As the second and third man fanned out behind the leader, an eerie danger filled the room. She fought the instinct to run.

They could just be farmhands. Drifters. But their hardened expressions told her they were much worse. Outlaws. Or...slave catchers.

"Ma'am." The tallest of the three fingered the brim of his hat, flashing yellow teeth as he spoke. His gaze traveled down and back up her body, and she pulled the front plackets of her coat together.

"Before you leave-" He shoved a paper at her. "We're having folks take a look at this."

She fumbled with her basket and had to let go of her coat to take hold of the notice.

ONE THOUSAND DOLLARS REWARD. Ran away from subscriber's plantation, forty miles northeast of Hillstown on the evening of June 22nd, a NEGRO WOMAN named Emily Tyler, a MULATTO GIRL, Rosalee, and a MULATTO BOY, James. The woman is of light color, dark brown hair, twenty-five years of age and is increasing. The girl is twelve years of age, light skinned, coppery hair, with freckles on her nose and cheeks. The boy is eight years of age, also light skinned, has brown hair and a wide gap between his upper front teeth. This is to forewarn all persons from harboring said runaways, as the law will be put in full force against all so offending. The above reward will be paid on the delivery of them to the subscriber. _____ Wilber T. Barnaby, Gilmer County, Virginia.

Taking a slow breath, she maintained her expression. Lucy handed the piece of paper back and resisted the urge to wipe her hand on her skirt. These must be the men who chased Thomas last night. While she would relish telling them how much she despised their kind, her common sense kept her from making these men enemies. It would only invite trouble.

"I don't know anything about them." A cold sweat dampened her palms and she squeezed the handle of her basket. Still blocking her way, the men studied her.

Please, Lord, let me be convincing. "I have chores to tend to so, if you'll let me pass."

The leader slithered to one side. As she passed the trio her skin crawled, and their combined stench made her stomach threaten to retch once more. One of the three whistled low, but no female with a lick of sense could ever find it anything other than revolting. As she crossed the threshold, Wink came immediately to her side from his spot on the walkway, growling at the vermin behind her.

"What a sorry looking one-eyed mutt. He sure must have pissed somebody off." The men laughed, and the accuracy of the stranger's comment sent more chills up her nape. But rather than respond, she made a beeline for her cart, feeling the slave catcher's gazes every step of the way.

These three are trouble. Renzo hadn't heard what the tall one asked Lucy as he'd handed her that piece of paper, but the way they were all eyeing her made him want to rip off a few heads. Normally he was an easy-going fellow, not quick to judge, but these three reminded him of bilge rats, gutter stench and shady dock deals.

He turned to Mrs. Anderson. "You know, I believe I'll take another one of these shirts and a couple pair of trousers." After flicking her gaze between her husband and the crew that stood staring after Lucy, she scurried to the back of the store.

Mr. Anderson took his wife's place, and Renzo leaned his elbow on the counter as if he had all the time in the world.

And I thought I was in desperate need of a bath.

The first man nodded to Mr. Anderson, then to Renzo. "We're after some runaway slaves."

Renzo's jaw stiffened. Slavery was immoral, and those who supported it or profited from it were soulless. "You boys must have taken a wrong turn somewhere. This is a free state." He'd love to pound each one of them into a pulp but the unfortunately the law wasn't on his side.

The leader of the three took a step forward and narrowed his eyes. "You must not have heard about the Fugitive Slave Law. Says that even up North, I can hunt down and return runaway slaves, and anybody caught hiding them or getting in my way is in for a shitload of trouble."

So these bastards stomped on whoever got in their way and resorted to intimidation and brute force. Renzo held his temper but ground his teeth. No matter how he felt about the injustice of the Fugitive Slave Law, he couldn't do a damned thing about it, short of entering the political arena. While that would have thrilled his mother, to his mind a career in politics resembled a death sentence.

No longer interested in feigning indifference, he straightened. "Now that you mention it, I believe I *have* heard of that unfortunate piece of legislation."

The leader looked momentarily befuddled before handing Mr. Anderson the same paper he'd shown Lucy. "I want to post this reward notice in your front window."

Anderson looked it over briefly before handing it back. "No, not in my store."

Good man. He'd add the most expensive pair of boots in the store to his order. Whether they fit or not.

"What's the problem?" The tall man's sneer and the way the other two had moved to appear like a small force at his sides were all meant to intimidate. "You wouldn't be harboring any runaways upstairs of this here store, would you?"

"Of course, not." Anderson puffed up as much a skinny man could, but his voice squeaked. Beads of perspiration dotted his high forehead. Renzo feared the man might pass out if this lot didn't clear out quickly.

Renzo laid the money for his purchases on the counter, adding something extra. "Send those other things down to the hotel for me. The name is Lorenzo Ross."

Then he met the head slaver's gaze. "Gentlemen, I believe the smartest thing for you to do would be to check in with the sheriff." He'd spotted the lawman's office as he rode into town. "I'll show you the way. Maybe he'll be willing to post your notice."

Or send you back to whatever swamp you crawled out of.

Suddenly one of the men ran and threw open the door. "Son of a-"

Chapter Three

Renzo followed them outside just in time to see the tail-end of a couple boys bolting in between buildings across the street.

The first man shook his fist in the air. "Next time I catch you two sniffing around my horse, I'll tan your hides." He hopped off the boardwalk to check his saddlebags.

"The sheriff's office is this way." Renzo went down the stairs and gestured for them to follow, glad to be up-wind. "No need to mount up."

No one bothered with conversation, and from the hurried steps of some of the townsfolk, people already seemed to be trying to avoid the strangers. Renzo hoped people wouldn't assume he was part of the merciless gang.

Outside the front door of the red bricked sheriff's office a thick layer of Wanted posters tacked on a board fluttered in the warm breeze. A hand-lettered, DEPUTY WANTED sign swung from a string over the knob as he opened the door. Inside, a pot-bellied stove dominated the far corner while a pot-bellied man sat sideways at a cluttered desk, his feet propped on a chair. The shiny pin on his vest labeled him sheriff, but the bulbous bandage on one foot marked him as lame. As the four men entered, he slid his gold-rimmed spectacles down his nose and looked over the top with an expression of pleasure.

"Come on in, gents. You're saving me from paperwork." The lawman pushed the stack of papers away. "I'm Sheriff Tate. What can I do for you all?"

"Name's Carl Mays." The trio's leader pointed a thumb over his shoulder. "Fred and Gil Greenley. We're after some runaways from Virginia. Almost had them last night, but they lost us along the river a mile or so west of town." Mays pulled the folded up notice out of his vest pocket and handed it to the sheriff.

Tate read the paper and returned it without the slightest shift in expression.

I bet he's one helluva poker player.

"Well, I sure do appreciate you boys letting me know you're in the area. That's real professional-like."

May's smile came off as more of a sneer. "We're the best there is. You heard any rumors about runaways or know any folks that you think might hide them?"

For the first time since they'd entered, one of the Greenley boys—Renzo hadn't really paid attention to who was Fred and who was Gil—came to life.

"How about that sweet thing we saw at the store. I've a mind to search under her bed." He elbowed his pug-faced brother in the ribs, and they snickered like a pair of dangerous simpletons.

Renzo took a step forward, his blood suddenly boiling.

"I don't believe the residents would appreciate you bothering any of the ladies in Rush Crossing." The two straightened for a fight, but the sheriff cleared his throat.

"Have you fellows taken a gander in a looking glass lately?" Tate's smile and tone were placating as he gestured toward a small mirror hanging on the wall.

"I suspect you boys have been traveling for some time. I'd imagine folks around here will be a little friendlier once you pay a visit to the barber and the bathhouse." He gave all the men a conspiratorial wink.

Renzo bit back any additional warning, respecting the way the sheriff had diffused the tension. Did slave catchers chase runaway slaves into this area often?

"We're not here to get friendly." Mays gave a disapproving gaze to his cohorts back to the sheriff. "We'll be round these parts until we find them or pick up their trail. And if I catch any of the locals hiding my runaways, I expect you to arrest them." Mays thumped one of his companions on the chest. "Come on. We've got some hunting to do." They pushed past Renzo and let the door slam behind them, rattling the glass.

"Now, my fine fellow," the sheriff said, "You're no slave catcher, so just who might you be?" Tate pulled his spectacles off, set them on the desk and folded his hands on the shelf of his belly.

"Lorenzo Ross."

"Ha." Tate slapped the desktop. "I knew it. You're the fellow who saved Mabel's boy. Harold told me all about it. The gout's got me pretty bad off, so do me a favor and come over here so I can shake your hand."

Renzo smiled, returning the man's firm grip with one of his own.

"Harold says you're planning to hang around for a bit to rest after your hunting trip."

No need to get into the particulars of that. "I was just on my way down to the hotel. I'm so hungry my stomach is ready to turn inside out."

"Well, by all means." Sheriff Tate grabbed a pair of wooden crutches propped against the wall. "Let's get you something to eat. You don't mind if I join you, do you?" Given the man's girth, Renzo wasn't surprised that the sheriff would change his mind about rising from the chair if it involved a meal.

"I'd enjoy the company." He also might be able to find out about the skittish Lucy.

"I'm glad you stopped in, young man. While I treat you to a nice steak, I'd like to hear about your hunting trip. And just how well you handle a gun."

Lucy set out for Thomas's place rather than pace around the house until dusk. She'd already started a mess of ham and beans, milked Agnes, and readied a corner of the hay loft for Emily and Rosalee. There was no need to delay anyway, since it wouldn't look unusual for her to bring supper to a friend in need. A jar of fresh milk, corn bread, fried chicken and half of an apple pie weighed down her basket.

The fragrant scents of the woods brought her peace and a dose of that was welcome right now. All afternoon she'd been unable to forget her encounters at the mercantile. First the three slave catchers. Then the beautiful man with the honey-colored eyes. And the certain feeling that they all presented some kind of danger.

The slavers were an obvious threat to the Tylers. But the danger the darkly handsome man presented didn't give her chills. Rather, it flooded her with warmth. She suspected he could captivate her without lifting a finger. As much as she hated to admit it, the man had awakened a longing inside her unlike anything she'd ever experienced. Breathtakingly well-formed, he had shoulders wide as an axe handle, a flat belly and a muscular chest. His near-nakedness had triggered a response in her so raw her defensive nature had immediately risen to do battle. But an afternoon of self-examination had forced her to face the shameful truth. She'd wanted to touch him. And when he'd looked into her eyes, it was as if *she* had been stripped bare. With luck he'd just been passing through and was already on his way.

Lucy rippled between two rows of corn and stepped into the clearing of Thomas's cabin. She made her way onto the porch in the descending dusk and tapped on the door.

"Come in." His relaxed tone told her all was well.

"Wink, you stay here." She leaned down and scratched the dog's jowl, whispering. "You keep watch. Good dog." She kissed his head and went inside.

By the light of the oil lamp, she made out her friend's broad smile. *His guests must still be safe in the barn.* She set her basket on the table.

"Are you getting along all right?" Somehow he'd managed to change into clean clothing since that morning.

"I'm fine. I'm more concerned about you." He gestured to a ladder back chair next to the bed. "How was your trip into town?"

Wishing he hadn't asked and too nervous to sit, she busied herself by unpacking the food and filling a plate with chicken and cornbread. She carried it over. "Would you like milk?"

Thomas balanced the plate on his lap and grabbed her hand before she could turn away. "What is it, child? You're avoiding something."

Resignation kept her from pulling her hand back. After all, it wasn't as if she could keep him in the dark about something so important. She met his gaze. "Everything's fine, but I did run into some strangers at Anderson's." She lowered her voice. "Slave catchers."

Thomas' grip tightened and his eyes narrowed. "Are you certain?"

She nodded. "They had a notice about Emily and the children. It said there's a thousand dollar reward for the return of all three of them." This time Lucy did the studying.

He stared over her shoulder, weighing the threat.

"I told their leader I didn't know anything about the runaways and left as quickly as I could."

After a moment he gave her hand a tiny shake then dropped it. "Well, there shouldn't be any reason why

they wouldn't believe you. Let's just pray they move on."
Then Thomas smiled. "I have a surprise for you." He
leaned toward the edge of the mattress, the dried husks
inside crunching beneath him. "It's safe, James. You can
come on out."

Lucy prit-near jumped out of her skin as a boy slid
out from under the big bed. He stood and gave her a
hesitant, gap-toothed grin.

I wish he hadn't heard about the slave catchers. She
crossed her arms against the urge to hug him. *They won't be
here long. Don't form attachments.*

"Lucy Neels, this here is James Tyler. James, this
is Mrs. Neels."

"Pleased to make your acquaintance, ma'am."
James bowed at the waist, straightened and then looked to
Thomas. "Did I do it right?"

Thomas chuckled. "You did it just right."

The boy spotted the plate of food on the bed and
his eyes widened. Introductions could wait.

"Why don't you come on over to the table and
have something to eat."

James looked to Thomas. "Sir?"

Thomas smiled so fondly at the boy that the sting
of tears burned her eyes. "Soon as you get back. First, take
Mrs. Neels out to the barn and introduce her to your
mama and Rosalee. Looks like it's dark enough now, and
they need to be heading over to her place." Thomas
looked at her. "You be careful. And don't worry about us.
You saw how James has a fine hiding place right here."

She nodded and James slipped his small hand into
hers, startling her. James had been hunted these past weeks
and he was giving her his trust. She made herself hold on.

"My dog is outside on the porch, but he's friendly.
His name is Wink and he'll protect us both." She said her
goodbyes to Thomas and they went outside. James
tightened his grip as Wink sniffed him from head to toe
and she wondered if dogs had been used to track them.

With a shudder she hustled toward the barn.

The darkness cloaked them in shadow, and she said a silent prayer that they would make it home safely. She was no longer just contemplating breaking the law. She was doing it, and her heart felt as if it was ready to pound its way right out of her chest.

A barn owl's screech made her stumble but she regained her footing. What direction had it come from? Moving on, she mentally cursed Emmett for the thousandth time. Thanks to his heavy hand, darkness made her the next thing to useless.

When they reached the door, she ordered Wink to stay outside and followed James into the dark interior. The smell of freshly hewn wood and the smooth movement of the door hinges made her recall the pride on Thomas's face the day he'd put the last nail in his new barn. He'd hired out the larger construction but had completed the finish work himself. Two times the size of her barn, it had more spaces for runaways to hide. A shiver ran through her at what she was about to undertake.

"Mama," James whispered. If Lucy hadn't been resting her hand on his shoulder she wouldn't have known exactly where he was. Then she heard a rustling from the other runaways.

"We're ready."

What direction had the voice come from? This wouldn't do. For the safety of all she was going to have to confess her shortcoming.

"James, let's go out the other door that faces the woods." Still holding his small shoulder, they crossed the dirt floor to the back door. As they slowed, she sensed rather than saw people close by.

"My dog will meet up with us outside, but don't be afraid. His name is Wink, and I promise, he won't hurt you."

"Mama, this is Mizz Neels, come to take you to her place."

"We're much obliged." Emily's voice cracked with what Lucy suspected was the dread of being separated from her child. She swallowed against a dry ache in her throat as she sensed Emily hugging her son.

"You take good care of Mr. Thomas and mind what he tells you." And with those words, Emily Tyler earned Lucy's deepest respect. Even though her life and the lives of her children were at stake, she was instructing her boy to care for Thomas. Perhaps confiding in her wouldn't be so bad.

"Emily, we need to go. But I'm going to need your help on the way." She wished she could make out their faces, but the darkness was too thick.

"I can only hear in one ear. In the darkness I can't tell where sounds are coming from. While I know the way easily enough, I need you and Rosalee to stay close and listen."

Then, without another word, the women stepped outside and hurried into the woods.

Sheriff Tate ordered dessert and dismissed the waiter, refilling Renzo's glass to the top. "I've never met anyone who's been to Italy, let alone speaks Italian."

Renzo took another sip, noting the restaurant's dwindling patrons and wishing he was tucked in his bed up on the second floor. "My mother wanted her sons to know her native language." He swirled the deep red liquid in his glass. "You know, this local wine *is* growing on me."

Tate grinned. "Do you like this one better than the first one?"

He thought about it and took another drink to make sure. "I think so."

"Good." The sheriff chuckled. "So, you can speak Italian and you're a crack shot?"

"Mmmhmm," he said, taking another sip.

"And you say you work in the shipping business your grandfather started?"

Renzo shook his head, regretted the motion and stopped. "My father and brother do. Not me. Not anymore."

"Is that so? Well, I admire a man who branches out. Here's to new directions." Tate raised his glass and Renzo joined him in the toast. "How long do you plan to stay in Rush Crossing?"

He'd originally thought only a couple days, but the food was good and he'd been given the best room in the house. "A week."

"Aw, you can't take a proper look around in only a week. And since Mabel is the cook here, she's going to want to make all her best dishes for you. That could take months."

Renzo patted his stomach, fighting to keep his eyes open. "I can't just sit around here getting fat."

"True. You need something to do." Sheriff Tate scooped up a spoonful of the blueberry cobbler the waiter set in front of him. "Did you see the help wanted sign in my window?"

Renzo picked up his glass again. "I'm no lawman."

"Says who?" Tate said around a mouthful. "You can handle a gun and seem smart enough to believe me when I say most times they aren't necessary."

Renzo yawned, wishing the sheriff would hurry up and finish eating and go home. "Our waiter knows more about Ohio law than I do. Hire him."

Tate's spoon paused in front of his mouth. "Come on. I just need someone who can ride out to check in with the farmers. I'd be here in town if you had any questions."

Renzo's lids were lead weights. "I appreciate dinner, Sheriff, but I've been riding for days-"

"I'm almost through. Just finish your drink. It'll help you sleep."

Renzo closed his eyes. Sleep. He could lay his head down on the table and be out.

"I'd only need you until my foot's better. Less

than a month…"

Chapter Four

Lucy placed another egg in her basket and glanced around the hazy interior of the henhouse. Wonder what it says about a person, when she avoids people but lingers over gathering eggs for the company of a flock of temperamental hens?

Shoving the question from her mind, she cooed to Mrs. Speckles, her best producer, and tickled the hen's head before reaching under her. As Lucy leaned forward, a knothole in the siding supplied a spyglass view of Agnes, her milk cow, munching on the tall grass caught in the fence. The sweet scent of fresh hay and the warmth filling the henhouse made her long to catch up on some sleep. But these eggs had to be made into breakfast for her secret guests. Lord only knew how much they'd had to eat along their journey.

Wink's barking signaled an unexpected arrival, and her stomach clenched. Thomas might have grown used to the tension of being involved with the railroad, but to her it was new and unwelcome sensation. Praying that Emily and Rosalee didn't make any accidental noises, she settled two more eggs in her basket and headed outside into the bright sunshine. The wood and wire door slapped in its frame behind her as if saying, "Hurry along". The Sheik, her contrary rooster, stood smack-dab in her way, so she scooted him lightly with her boot and went through the gate.

"Why, Lucy Neels, look at you." Mildred and Charles Hopper, her other nearest neighbors, bounced on the seat of their buckboard as it rolled to a stop. Mildred was the biggest worrywart in Ohio, so Lucy pasted on what she hoped was a carefree smile so as not to encourage a lecture.

As long as they don't get out of the wagon, everything will be fine. She silenced Wink with a pat to his head. Her companion might only have one eye, but he was the best protection she could ever hope to have.

"Lucy, are you ill? It's got to be eighty degrees already and you're wrapped up in that coat like it's October." Mildred gripped the rail of the wagon seat, her eyes wide. Since the Hoppers had never had children, she poured out motherly instinct on everyone she came into contact with.

Lucy considered removing her coat for all of one second, but Mildred would only find something else to fret about. "I'm just fine, Mizz Hopper." She forced herself to nod to Charles as he set the brake. "Mr. Hopper. What can I do for you?"

Charles glared at Wink, and a low growl rumbled from her pet.

"Have you got that dog under control? He's dangerous."

"Maybe to some," she agreed. "He's serious about protecting me." She rubbed Wink's head again, taking evil pleasure in remembering the time he'd prit-near torn a hole in Charles for raising his voice at her.

Mildred's hand settled over her heart. "Lord have mercy, child, you don't need protection from us. But if you don't mind me saying so..."

Lucy did, but nothing short of cannon fire would stop the woman now.

"...it simply isn't safe for you to be living out here all by your lonesome. Why, a young woman all by herself. It frightens me to death, thinking of all that could happen to you without your husband—God rest his soul—here to protect you."

Lucy stiffened her shoulders, certain to the depths of *her* soul that Emmett's hadn't passed anywhere near Saint Peter's gate. Still, it was one of Mildred's standard comments, and as such, it was getting easier for her not to get too worked up over it.

"Well, as you can see, Wink and I are getting along just fine. Now, what brings you by?" The sooner one of them got to the point, the sooner they'd skedaddle.

"I wondered if your colored man was here. One of my mares is lame and I want him to come take a look."

Anger bubbled inside Lucy, but she also had to choose her words carefully so Charles wouldn't go over to Thomas's cabin.

"Thomas Washington isn't anyone's colored man. He is a free man who, like you, farms for a living. You know very well he bought the land his cabin and barn sit on, and he leases two of my biggest fields."

"Oh, Lucy, Charles didn't mean to imply Thomas is your slave. Did you, Charles?" Mildred's pleading expression encouraged her husband to make amends. He grumbled something under his breath, then met Lucy's gaze.

"Oh, land sakes, I know he's nobody's slave. We're a free state. Now, is he hereabouts or not?" His cheeks had flushed and to keep him from riding over there, Lucy thought quickly.

"No, and I'm afraid he won't be able to doctor your horse. He fell and broke his leg. He'll be laid up for a month while it heals."

"Damnation." Charles screwed up his face. "A

month, you say?"

"That's right," she replied. "He'll be disappointed that he couldn't help you out." She couldn't resist adding the implication that Charles would have been in his debt.

"Now, if you'll excuse me, I have chores to attend to."

Mildred gestured to the basket in Lucy's hand.

"Since I know you trade with Anderson's and we're on our way into town, can we give you a ride or drop those eggs off for you?" Charles twisted toward his wife with a horrified expression. You'd think she'd suggested he kiss a hog's snout.

The tension on Lucy's shoulders eased, and she stifled a grin. Who'd have thought she and Charles Hopper would ever agree on anything? Speaking for herself, she would eagerly pucker up to a filthy porker before she would ride the short distance into town with Charles.

"No, thank you. I'll be going into town myself after I check on Thomas."

As soon as the Hoppers were on their way, she went inside to scramble the eggs. Then she took them out to the barn, along with milk and leftover cornbread. Although Wink trotted unconcerned at her side, the possibility of those slave catchers poking around made her glance over her shoulders. She shouldn't have to sneak around her own property, but it would be foolish not to take extra precautions.

Inside the barn she slowly climbed the ladder to the loft. Since she accepted hay as partial payment for Thomas' lease, it was piled high. Yesterday she'd dug out the far corner and spread some quilts to serve as a makeshift bed. She stepped around the edge to Emily and Rosalee's hollow. Emily was rubbing her round belly.

Lucy stiffened. "Are the pains starting up again?" She wasn't prepared to help bring that baby into the world.

Emily smiled and shook her head. "No, no. This baby's just letting me know that he's awake, is all. Seems like when I move around, he sleeps, but when I'm still he's running like a jackrabbit."

Good, not labor. Lucy's white-knuckled grip on the basket handle relaxed and she let out the breath she'd been holding. It had been so long since she'd prayed, but maybe it was time she asked for some heavenly support to make it through the delivery of Emily's child.

Rosalie shifted in the hay. "Mama said when I was in her belly, I was even worse." The girl's chin rested on her knees and her light brown eyes sparkled, brightening the dimness of the loft.

How could a child who had grown up in slavery seem so happy? *Happier than me?*

Lucy's throat burned and she backed toward the ladder. "I'm going to take some ham and beans over for Thomas and James. Then I have to deliver some things to town but I'll check on you when I get home." She left, knowing there was no need to tell them to stay hidden. The Tylers wouldn't have made it this far if they hadn't already followed that advice.

Renzo shot straight up in bed. With the shades drawn, he couldn't immediately recall where he was. He tried to sort out what was dream and what was real, but his head throbbed too much to manage. He gently rubbed his scalp, hoping to ease the pain. With a groan, he pushed off the mattress and stumbled naked to the window, inching aside the thick curtains. He squinted at the brightness of the morning and let go of the fabric.

Sonofabitch. Making it back to the bed, he slowly laid on his stomach and pillowed his cheek in soft linens. Too bad he couldn't fall back asleep and wake to find himself in his own bed. He turned his face in the opposite direction.

Recent memories floated through the haze but a memory just out of his reach made him open his eyes. As is vision slowly cleared, he spotted a star-shaped scrap of metal on the bedside table. Total recall suddenly had his heartbeat thumping in his ears. He moaned and rolled over onto his back, now wide awake.

Last night, he'd become Rush Crossing's new deputy.

Half an hour later he stepped out of the town's telegraph office, squinted and adjusted his hat against the glare of the sky. Soon enough the Hargroves would know he'd given up on the search, and his mother would know not to expect him anytime soon. His father would know why, and if William Ross wanted to share all the details of their argument with his wife—assuming she hadn't pried the information out of him already—so be it.

That task taken care of, he turned his mind to getting himself out of the pit he'd stumbled into last night. *Who'd believe it?* Deputized over a dish of blueberry cobbler.

He checked his pocket watch. No time like the present to go quit a job he'd never started. But as he walked to the sheriff's office, he reconsidered. Tate had said the deputy position was temporary, just until his foot was better. How long did it take for gout to go away? With Tate manning the office, the deputy's duties sounded straight forward. Ride around the county, meet the residents and keep the peace. And it wasn't as if he had pressing business anywhere else.

As he passed the barber shop his gaze snagged on a familiar piece of newsprint pressed inside the window. He stepped closer and scanned the text, confirming his suspicions.

One thousand dollars for three people's lives. The concept turned an already sour stomach. If the damned paper had been outside the glass, he would have ripped it down. Enforcing the Fugitive Slave Law was one sheriff's duty totally in conflict with his moral code. Then, even muddled from alcohol, his subconscious clicked like a tumbler falling into place.

Dragging his feet and *not* enforcing that law would

be one way of helping those escaping slavery. And what could the sheriff do if his lack of conviction became obvious, fire him? So what? The idea of seeing those slavers slink away without their prize made him smile.

He paused before stepping into the street to let a small cart drawn by a single horse roll past. Although the driver's face was shrouded by the biggest, ugliest bonnet he'd ever laid eyes on, he recognized that worn coat. A thick wheat-colored braid bisecting the plane of the woman's back confirmed his suspicion.

Lucy Neels. Mr. Anderson had kindly supplied her last name and marital status when he'd delivered Renzo's clothing the previous evening. Perhaps her arrival in town signaled yet another sign that keeping the deputy job was a good idea. Being able to stop by her farm on a regular basis certainly made it more appealing. Although she'd acted uninterested at their first encounter, he suspected she'd been trying too hard. If he kept the job he'd have some time to wear her down.

Chapter Five

Renzo watched Lucy's cart stop in front of the mercantile. By the time she'd climbed down, he was at her side.

"Good morning, Mrs. Neels." He tipped his hat. "Although we weren't formally introduced, we spoke inside yesterday." Her blue eyes rounded and she looked at him like a plump goose would a starving wolf. At home in society he was used to flirtatious or shy ladies, but he'd never made a woman so skittish he thought she might mindlessly run out in front of a rolling carriage.

"Are you all right?" he asked, taking hold of her elbow in support.

After a moment her eyes softened. "I-I'm fine. You startled me, is all."

"I apologize." He gave her one of his tried and true smiles. "Allow me to introduce myself. My name is Lorenzo Ross, but my friends call me Renzo."

Her brow straightened, but it was too late to hide the tenderness he'd seen in her gaze. His smile widened.

"How nice for them. Good day, *Mr. Ross.*" She raised her chin and circled around him, heading into the store.

He didn't bother to suppress his laughter. What do you know? The young Widow Neels had a backbone and a smart tongue. A very appealing combination. And, judging from her choice of bonnets—or any of her clothing—he was certain being appealing was just what she did *not* want to be.

He caught up with her before she shut the door and followed her inside, earning him a narrowed glare.

"Mr. Ross, I would prefer you not follow me." She whirled around and crossed to the counter. Of course he disregarded her wishes, tipping his hat to Mrs. Anderson.

"Ma'am. How are you today?" He pretended not to notice Lucy's corresponding huff.

"I'm just fine, thank you." The proprietress nodded. "I hope you're happy with all the items you purchased yesterday." Mrs. Anderson quickly winked her left eye.

Ah, a co-conspirator. The day is improving.

"Yes, indeed, but I found myself in need of a nightshirt last night." Would the widow Neels wonder what he had, or hadn't been, sleeping in?

He glanced over at her. He would probably be horrified to see what *she* wore to bed. He tried to mentally strip off all her God-awful garments. He imagined loosening the neck of her shift and sliding it off her shoulders. Kissing each inch of skin as he revealed it. Would it be soft? Freckled, like the bridge of her nose?

Mrs. Anderson cleared her throat. "Wilber orders our men's items. Let me go check with him to see if we have any." She took a few steps toward the back. "He's down in the cellar and it might take me a few minutes." The woman was as subtle as a chiming church bell. She held up a finger to Lucy. "I'll take care of your eggs as soon as I get back."

And then the two of them were left alone. He

turned and casually leaned an elbow on the counter, much as he had the previous day. "Mrs. Neels, would you care to have lunch with me at the hotel restaurant?"

Lucy studied the shelves behind the counter. "No, I would not."

He didn't bother to hide his smile. "Why not? Aren't you hungry?"

"No."

"Don't you eat?" Toying with her was proving to be the most fun he'd had with a woman, out of bed, in a long time.

She sighed. "What a ridiculous question. Of course I eat."

"What? Supper?"

"Yes, of course I eat supper." Exasperation was thick in her tone. "You really are trying, Mr. Ross."

"Harder than you realize." He paused, but hopefully not long enough for her to catch up with his thinking. "When?"

She started to turn her head, caught herself and looked behind the counter. "When *what*?" It was a good thing in this fine weather she wasn't carrying an umbrella, otherwise she might crack him over the skull in frustration.

"When do you eat dinner?"

Her pause made him think she was giving her answer a bit more thought. "At suppertime." Judging by the side view of her smirk, she thought she'd out-smarted him.

He straightened. "And what time is your suppertime?"

Surrendering to his barrage, she finally turned, rolling her eyes.

"Six o'clock, like most folks."

"Perfect. I'll pick you up at six." He started for the door.

She called after him. "I'm not going to dinner with you."

He paused with his hand on the doorknob. "Oh, you'd rather do the cooking? Very well. Never let it be said that Renzo Ross goes against a ladies wishes. Now I'm late for an appointment." He pulled the door shut as she sputtered behind him. "See you at six."

Chapter Six

Lucy felt as if her brain had been through the butter churn after that lightening-fire conversation. Even though the idea of Renzo Ross taking her to dinner at the hotel sounded like a lovely dream, she hadn't encouraged him one bit. Yet he'd twisted the conversation to sound as if *she'd* invited *him* for supper. Hurrying to the door, she scanned the walkway. She'd catch up with him and tell him in no uncertain terms to leave her alone.

But there was no sign of him, and she had no idea where the scoundrel lived. Lucy stomped her foot. The man was infuriating. And quick.

Then, as she closed the door, the full impact of their verbal exchange caught up with her.

Oh, Lord. Lorenzo Ross was coming to her farm tonight. The man was certainly clever enough to find out where she lived. If it weren't for Emily and Rosalee hiding in her barn, she would let him stand on the porch all night for his impertinence. But if she didn't invite him inside, he might go poking around the place and discover her secret.

She slowly walked back to the counter. *Do I dare slam the door in his face?* No, all she knew about him was that he was quick-witted and wickedly handsome. Her gut told her he wasn't the kind to make trouble out of spite, and part of her did enjoy being asked to share a meal with him, but perhaps her instincts couldn't be trusted. She'd been fooled by Emmett when he'd courted her.

"Did Mr. Ross leave?" Bess reappeared from the back of the store wearing a disappointed expression.

A retaliatory idea popped into Lucy's head. She might have lost when it came to Mr. Ross's slick talk, but she didn't have to play dead about it. "He had a pressing engagement and asked me to confirm his order."

"Oh." Bess said, having no reason to doubt her honesty. "Wilber says he has two different styles of, uh, that particular type of garment."

Land sakes, it's just a nightshirt. "He asked for two of whatever you had." That should set the scoundrel back a pretty penny. The fact that the Anderson's would financially benefit from the fib made her flick her concern away as if it was fluff from a cottonwood tree.

Bess took the few eggs she'd had left to sell, and Lucy set to work concocting a plan which would guarantee that, after tonight, Renzo Ross would stay away from the farm.

At just before six Renzo tied his horse to the fence post in front of Lucy's house. He bent to pet the dog that had romped out of the woods to meet him on the main road. The animal's rear end swayed back and forth and he panted loudly as Renzo scratched the brown fur on his jowl.

"Hey, boy. What happened to your eye?" He straightened, headed up onto the porch and knocked on the solid-plank door. After a moment Lucy answered, a bewildered quirk to her brow. When she spotted the dog at his feet, her eyes flared.

"He didn't bark."

Not sure if it was a question or statement, Renzo

shook his head. "Once, up to the road." He looked down at the dog sitting politely by his side. "But we're buddies now, right?" A single enthusiastic woof cut the air.

"Some watch dog you are." Lucy shooed the now forlorn-looking mutt away from the door, shaking her head. She backed into the house and gestured him inside. The pleasant aroma of fried chicken met him as Lucy took his hat and hung it on a peg near the door. His quick examination found her small home modest, but clean. Two doors opened off the large room where they now stood. One appeared to lead outside behind the house, while the other must be to a bedroom.

As he stepped further into the main room, the slow, stifling wave of a fire in the hearth rolled over him.

Cristo. It's July. With a cook stove burning, why would she need another fire? But just then he realized, this was the first time she wasn't shrouded inside that sorry excuse of a coat. Her serviceable blue day dress was faded, but the close fit to her waist and breasts made his mouth go dry. He'd known there would be more to discover about Lucy Neels, and her delectable figure was hopefully only the first of many pleasant surprises to come.

Burning in more ways than one, he pulled a handkerchief out of his vest pocket and patted his brow. "Aren't you a bit warm?" He tugged at his collar with his index finger.

"Oh, I'm sorry, Mr. Ross." She fluttered her lashes and his stomach did a boyish flip.

"Renzo, please."

"I can spread the logs out and let it burn down. I'll just put on my coat if I get chilled."

Hell, no. He didn't want her covering up her lovely curves. "No, no. I won't have you chilled in your own home. Please, leave it."

"Very well." She gestured toward a chair. "Why don't you have a seat? Dinner's all ready."

At least the warmth of the place had a positive

effect on *her*. Lucy's welcoming demeanor was a total reversal of the way she'd spoken to him at the mercantile. Maybe she hadn't had the attentions of a man since her husband died. Although he'd enjoyed flustering her earlier in the day, this was nice, too.

A drop of sweat ran down his temple and he looked around for an open window he could stand next to.

"Is there something I can do to help?" he offered. Like pour a couple cold drinks. His shirt clung to his back.

"Oh, no. You just sit down. I'll have everything on the table in a jiffy." Within moments, she set a plate before him loaded with fried chicken, steaming mashed potatoes, gravy and cooked greens.

Hell-fire. Although the food looked and smelled delicious, the prospect of filling his already roasting body with piping hot food made his shoulders sag. He watched her bring her own plate to the table along with an enameled coffee pot. She filled their cups with the scalding brew and set the pot so close it almost singed his knuckles.

Ugh. Now he knew what a pig on a spit felt like as another bead of sweat slid down his face. He mopped at it with his handkerchief.

"Aren't you hungry?" Her eyebrows rose and her blue eyes lost a bit of their sparkle.

What a cad. You trick her into cooking this fine meal and now you're acting ungrateful.

"I'm starving," he said, picking up a piece of chicken and pretending to take an enthusiastic bite.

Lucy watched Renzo dig into his chicken. The man deserved a prize for not spitting it out. She took a small bite of her mashed potatoes and suppressed a wince. Normally they were one of her favorite foods. Why, when she had been a little girl her mama used to say she could eat her way out of a room filled with potatoes, but tonight's side dish was purposely below standards. The entire meal, in fact, would make it seem as if Lucy had never heard of seasonings.

The chicken, which had to be as tough and dry as the table, had been rolled only in flour and overcooked. The gravy was mostly water and flour, added to what bland cracklings hadn't petrified to the skillet. Her greens and potatoes would be just as tasteless since she'd prepared them without a single spice or added flavoring. Hopefully, the combination of her horrid cooking—which for appearances sake looked like an earnest attempt to please her guest—and the sweltering heat would deter any future visits by Renzo Ross.

"Might I have some water?" He sounded like he'd just choked down a fistful of dust.

She turned her head to stifle a giggle. "Of course." She stood, not remembering she'd used the water for coffee until she looked down to see the pitcher empty. "I-I'll be right back. I need to go out to the spring house to fill this."

Renzo popped up out of his chair so abruptly the pitcher almost slipped from her grasp.

He grabbed the base and lifted it from her. "No, let me do that for you," he insisted.

No, she was trying to get rid of him for good, not give him more access to her place. Although Emily and Rosalee were quiet as church mice, the thought of him somehow stumbling on them made her wish she'd risked slamming the door in his face. "No, I'll get it."

But it was too late. He'd already opened the back door and was swallowing deep breaths. So her plan of overheating the man was driving him outdoors.

"No, this is the least I can do. Where?" He'd crossed the threshold and pointed right then left. At least the spring house was in the opposite direction of the barn. If she fought him anymore about fetching water he'd probably get suspicious.

She said quick prayer and gestured left. "The spring house is built into the side of the hill a ways up."

He nodded. "I'll be right back."

The door closed, and Lucy's hand flew to her forehead. Renzo was supposed to be making excuses to leave by now, not seeing the inside of her spring house. This whole plan had been a terrible mistake. When he came back she needed to get rid of him. She'd say she wasn't feeling well, which wasn't far from the truth. She crossed to the hearth and used the poker to collapse the pile of logs.

Just then urgent barking went up from Wink out front, and a second later she heard the pounding hoof beats of multiple horses. Oh, no. She'd orchestrated this evening to get rid of Renzo. She hadn't counted on having unexpected visitors to boot.

Setting the poker down, she hurried to the front door and out onto the porch. Wink joined her, still sounding his warning. The sinking sun behind the riders made it difficult to see who they were, but when they reined in their horses close to the house, she recognized the three slave catchers. Every muscle in her body tensed. She silenced Wink with a pat but, ever on alert and ready to jump to her defense, he remained by her side.

One of the men broke into a grin better fit for a snake.

"Well, hell-o there. If it ain't the little lady from the mercantile. You're lookin' mighty purdy tonight." His tongue circled his lips and he slurped.

She fought to keep down the few bites of supper she'd eaten.

Then the leader spoke up. "We were out this way having a look around." He scanned the house and surrounding area, pausing a bit too long in the direction of the barn. A sudden chill had her reaching to pull the plackets of her non-existent coat together. She crossed her arms instead.

His horse shifted and he tightened the reins. "You seen any sign of those runaways?"

She lifted her chin and raised her voice. "No, I haven't, and I don't like you and your men coming onto my property without an invitation."

The man leaned to the side, hacked and spit. "Touchy, touchy. You got somethin' to hide?" It was a good thing he wasn't any closer or he would see her quaking.

Keep your voice steady. "Of course, not. I'd like you all to leave and not come back."

If Emily and Rosalee could hear these men they must be frightened half to death.

One of the other men shifted in his saddle, the straining leather crackling. "I don't know, Carl. The little lady looks mighty nervous. Don't ya' think?"

Lucy's heart skipped a beat.

"Yeah, I'd say so. Maybe we should take a look around." Gil stood in his stirrups to dismount.

Do not let them see that you're afraid. She raised her chin. A bump against her thigh reminded her that Wink would protect her with his life. But if the men split up, her trusted friend couldn't keep them from doing a thorough search of the farm.

"I'm certain I heard the lady ask you all to leave."

She choked on a cry of relief and surprise. How could she have forgotten about Renzo? He came up behind her, resting his hands on her shoulders. But rather than wanting to shrink away from the man's touch she leaned back into his supportive hold.

"Sorry it took me so long, darling."

Darling? Had she hit her head and forgotten a whirlwind courtship?

"Well, well, well, if it ain't Rush Crossing's newest deputy," the one called Carl said. "Sheriff told us all about how you signed on until his foot's mended."

Lucy couldn't help but straighten away at that unexpected bit of news. She kept her sights fixed on the men in front of her, but danger now crowded her from all sides.

"That's right. And one aspect of my job is dealing with trespassers. So, unless you boys want to bunk down at the jail tonight, I suggest you move along." Renzo hadn't worn a gun so she hoped they respected his authority.

"No need to get yourself all worked up, Deputy." Carl switched his attention to her. "We lost those runaways in this area. And with one of 'em ready to whelp, I bet they haven't made it very far. We'll be close by. You can count on that."

He swung his horse around. "And Deputy, law says you're obligated to arrest anybody caught hiding them niggers."

Lucy fought a wave of nausea.

"I'm aware of the law," Renzo said. "But, since your runaways are probably half way across the state by now, I don't think that's going to be something I have to worry about." He slid his hands down her shoulders to rub her upper arms. "Good evening, gentlemen."

Carl tugged on the brim of his hat. "Ma'am. We'll be seeing you soon."

It was both a promise and threat.

Chapter Seven

With Renzo grasping her arms, there was no hiding her shaking. He led her back inside to a rocking chair and left her only long enough to grab her coffee from the table, placing the mug in her icy hands. Then he pulled over a straight back chair and positioned himself in front of her.

"Are you alright?" His amber eyes studied her with what appeared to be genuine concern.

What can I say? It was obvious the men's presence had frightened her. But now she knew, although Renzo had been playing suitor, he was also a sheriff's deputy. His job was to turn Emily and Rosalee over to those terrible men.

"I don't suppose you have any brandy or whiskey in the house?" Numbly, she shook her head. Alcohol only served to make bad things a thousand times worse.

"Damn." He leaned forward, leaving her nowhere else to look but at him. "I missed what they said that has you quaking in your boots."

Lucy racked her brain. Whatever she said needed a measure of truth to stand up to Renzo's clever persistence.

She couldn't mask the quiver in her voice. "It wasn't *what* he said. It was *him*. His manner. The way he spoke to me." She took a slow sip of coffee, stalling for time to gather her courage. "He reminded me of my late husband. Although it's not widely known," she'd done her darnedest to keep folks from finding out, "My late husband was a cruel and violent man."

Renzo's nostrils flared and his jaw clenched. On her behalf? How strange that it brought her a small measure of comfort. Even though he needed to be kept at arm's length, Lucy wished she could rest a hand on Renzo's cheek and tell him how much she appreciated even those small reactions.

"Without dredging up things that I'd rather stay buried, I'll just say he hurt us." When Renzo's brows rose, she added, "Wink and I." The words had come so easily. Maybe the passing of time did heal more than physical wounds.

Renzo stood and took her mug, setting it back on the table. Then he pulled her up into his embrace. "I hope the bastard is roasting in hell."

He is.

Renzo's arms felt warm, strong and capable around her, and she closed her eyes, relaxing in his hold. She shouldn't. She should give this new lawman a wide berth, not grant him liberties.

But it feels so right. Could this all be a dream? She tucked her forehead under his chin, inhaling his clean, masculine scent. A scent so foreign to what she'd known it had to be imagined.

Content to make this moment last, she said nothing, no further explanations, no horrible memories. Just comfort. And when his hands moved to stroke her back, Lucy's arms curled around his waist of their own accord. How could her limbs be so traitorous as to spur her into embracing this man? A man she'd just met? She was so broken she hadn't even been comfortable hugging her dearest friend. But Renzo's hug had tingles spreading throughout her body. All reason evaporated.

At some point he must have freed her bun and now his hands alternately glided down her braid to the small of her back. His touch felt so heavenly she wanted to sigh aloud. But fear of bursting the blissful bubble around them—returning them to opposite sides of a high moral wall—kept her silent. When her fingers instinctively spread over his back, a tear slid down the side of her nose.

Lord, I've missed this. Not since her brief courtship, had she been embraced this lovingly. She wanted to freeze this moment.

"Lucy." His voice vibrated through his chest and into her good ear. "I give you my word. Those men won't hurt you."

She pulled back, and he cradled her jaws in his hands, brushing the tears away with his thumbs. And then before she could think of anything beyond the sensation of sinking into warm honey, his lips were on hers.

Gesu Cristo. This isn't supposed to happen. In his past experiences this *didn't* happen. This connection.

You've just denied yourself for too long. Renzo wrapped his arms around Lucy and lingered in tasting her lips. Her response warmed from timid to curious. And when her lips parted, inviting him in, he forgot about simply offering comfort.

Her braid tickled his hand, and he gently wound it around his fist, easing her head back. She surrendered, and his kisses drifted to her temple then down to her neck. He sampled soft love bites along her smooth flesh.

"Ohhhhhh." Her breathy moan fueled his passion, and desire quashed all sense of finesse as his lips returned to hers. Hungry, devouring kisses. Lust drove away reason. His hand cupped her breast, shaping the soft mound. He pushed her against his aching erection and kissed the rapid pulse at her neck. *Take her. Now.*

Her body arched against him, and his hand trembled as he fisted her skirt and slowly began dragging it up the back of her legs. *Cristo.* He hadn't been this far gone by simple foreplay since his earliest sexual encounters.

Years ago.

Many, not two. His hand stalled.

How long had it been for Lucy? Had she had any lovers since her husband's death?

His desire argued, yes. *She's not kissing as if she's been living a celibate life.*

But her eager kisses, her grappling fingertips against his back, offered debate. *She kisses like she's been starved of passion.*

She wants this as much as I do. But Renzo's conscience battled a lust grown strong by months of abstinence. Lucy's tongue swirled with his in an erotic dance, and as the warring inside his head continued, he tried to wedge his honor into some dark recess.

But what little he knew of this woman wouldn't let it be hampered. Lucy Neels wasn't some pampered, socialite flitting between lovers and spending a generous widow's inheritance. She was a modest widow, a farmer. Even as he mentally cursed his ingrained sense of chivalry, Renzo released her skirts and slowly set her away.

He'd hate himself later for not taking what was offered. But he hate himself more if he used her. He dropped his chin against his chest and rested his hands on his hips, hoping to calm his desire. When he looked up, her eyes had opened and the haze of yearning began to fade.

One of her hands flew to her mouth—those magnificent lips swollen from his kisses—and her eyes rounded in horror. He wanted to pummel something. Himself.

Hell and damnation. Stopping *was* the right thing to do. This woman deserved to be courted, cherished and wed, not used and abandoned when he was ready to go home. But that didn't make stopping any easier.

"I'm sorry. I shouldn't have carried that so far."

With her mouth still covered, she nodded in agreement.

"Perhaps it'd be best if I left."

Although she silently moved her hand to the inexpensive brooch at her neck, her wide eyes and sealed lips affirmed his suggestion. Leaving was the dead last thing he wanted to do, but he grabbed his hat and paused in the open doorway.

"I don't know how long I'll be in Rush Crossing but, until I leave, I'll make certain those men don't come back."

He, however, would be.

As soon as the door shut behind him, Lucy dropped into the chair and stared, unseeing, at the smoking logs in the hearth.

Shameless.

How could the man's touch fill her with such heart-stopping, mind-numbing urgency? Marital relations with Emmett had been a distasteful chore, but just one of Renzo's kisses had had the power to wipe every prudent thought from her head. And heaven help her, his hand on her breast had produced the most deliciously wicked sensation between her legs. She squeezed her thighs together at the vivid memory. If he hadn't been the one to come to his senses, she'd be skirts-up on the table like a common floozy this very minute. Lucy dropped her face into her hands.

Even now, there was a part of her that wished she was. That longed to explore these remarkable, unfamiliar urges, no matter the consequences. Who knew a loose woman was buried deep down inside her? And not only was the sheriff's deputy the worst person she could take as a lover, he'd just admitted he had no real plans to make

Rush Crossing his home. She knew enough about herself to know she couldn't grant a man favors without setting herself up for heartbreak. A man like him was looking for a distraction, not a commitment.

Outside the door Wink barked once, his signal that he was ready for mealtime. She dried her eyes with shaky fingertips and let him inside. Gathering the plates from their uneaten meal, she pulled chicken off bones and put it into the dog's chipped crockery bowl. He gobbled the meat without chewing. Obviously Wink saw no shortcomings in her cooking.

As she cleaned up the dishes, she set her mind to what should be more important matters; keeping Emily and Rosalee from being discovered. Not only from Carl and his men, but from Renzo. A man she longed to, but could never, trust.

While Wink licked his long-empty bowl, she pulled on her coat and lit a lantern. She needed to check on the Tylers, to let them know everything was all right. The path to the barn was so familiar that even in the growing darkness, she had never been afraid. But with this evening's visit from the slave catchers, that had changed. She and Wink headed out. As they walked, the slightest nighttime sound made her jump.

To be safe, she would move his old blanket out onto the porch for nighttime. Tonight had shown her that until Emily and her children were safely on their way north, the farm shouldn't be left unguarded.

The next day Lucy stopped at Thomas's cabin on her way into town. The wooden shutters on the cabin remained tightly closed against spying eyes.

She knocked and opened the door. "Morn-" Her shaking hand rattled the door latch as she spotted broken dishes all over the floor. Her gaze flew to the bed. Thankfully, Thomas appeared unharmed. She rushed to set her things on the table, gesturing to the mess.

"What in the world happened?" There was too much destruction for it to be accidental.

Thomas gestured to the door. "Throw the bar on that, will you?" As she did, he leaned over the side of the bed and spoke softly. "It's all right, son. You can come out now."

James slid out from under the far reaches of the bed and scrambled into the older man's embrace. As he stroked the back of the boy's head and rocked him from side to side, Thomas met her gaze.

"We had some company last night."

She swallowed her gasp and pressed one hand to her stomach, not wanting James to hear her distress. "Was it the men I told you about?"

Thomas's bloodshot eyes simmered. "Yes. They must've known I was laid up 'cuz they just strolled right on in. James is sleeping under the bed, so luckily he was out of sight. All they did in here was break some dishes, but I could hear them banging round in the barn after that."

"I can't believe they would be so brazen as to barge into your home." Lucy could feel the anger coiling her muscles. "You can bet I'll complain to Sheriff Tate about this."

"No, not yet. They had their look around. Maybe that'll satisfy them."

She stormed to the corner for the broom and began sweeping the pieces into piles, her actions punctuated with fury. "I doubt it. They were at my place last night, too. They didn't search it, probably because Renzo was there." As soon as the deputy's name crossed her lips she wanted to kick herself.

"Renzo?"

She fetched the dust pan.

"Who's Renzo?" Thomas's insistent tone told her he would push until he got an answer.

She crossed to one mound of broken crockery, pretending to concentrate on her task. "Renzo Ross is

Sheriff Tate's new deputy."

"The slavers *and* a deputy were at your place? Do you think the sheriff and his new man suspect you're hiding runaways?" He kept his voice low.

She stood and met his gaze. "No." But rather than explaining exactly why Renzo had been at her place, she hurried on. "And I think if he hadn't threatened to arrest those men for trespassing, they might have searched the place. I'm leaving Wink there to protect the place from now on." Memories of the men's visit still made her quiver.

"Miss Lucy?" James's looked up with a frightened expression no child should ever have to wear. "Are Mama and Rosalee alright?"

She was grateful Thomas offered the boy the physical comfort he so obviously needed.

Lucy smiled, blinking to keep her eyes dry. "Yes, they're fine. As a matter of fact, they asked me at breakfast to tell you how much they miss you."

"I miss them, too." His voice squeaked, and it almost broke her heart. They'd both been fighting tears but only she had succeeded.

"That's it." She abandoned the broom and dustpan against the wall and fisted her hands on her hips. "You're coming to my place today." With a sudden gap-toothed grin, James straightened.

"Now, Lucy-"

She cut off Thomas's argument with a swipe of her hand.

"I'm not going to argue about it. This mess will wait. I have to drop off the milk and butter at the hotel then I'm coming back to get you." She crossed to the bed and wiped a forgotten tear from the boy's cheek, strengthening her resolve.

"I'll get James at dusk, unless I can think of another way to get him earlier. We'll be stronger if we stick together, like a bundle of twigs. And that's the end of it."

Chapter Eight

Renzo left the sheriff's office and readjusted the gun belt on his hips. He wondered how long it would take to get used to wearing it. Although he'd had a gun on his journey, he'd never worn it strapped to his side. He hoped no one mistook him for a gunslinger. His aim was good, but not *that* good.

He studied the rough sketch of the area that Tate had drawn. Even after convincing himself this was an opportune distraction, he'd still been tempted to tell the sheriff he wasn't the man for the job. But no, he'd follow through on the commitment. He'd also promised Lucy that those slave catchers wouldn't bother her, and he meant it. He started walking, mulling over a job he'd never expected to have and a woman who kept invading his thoughts. He had a sneaking suspicion that she'd be difficult to forget when he went home.

He folded the paper and tucked it into his vest pocket, revisiting the question that had plagued him since the previous evening. Why had those slavers decided to harass her? Her place wasn't near the Ohio River, but those men seemed pretty intent on their search. But they didn't know Lucy wasn't the type to welcome strangers. Mr. Anderson had said she was practically a recluse. Someone who avoided folks at all costs wouldn't get involved with the business of runaway slaves. Close interactions under circumstances as intense as those would bind people together, and that didn't fit with what he'd learned about Lucy. The woman avoided eye contact, unless she was feeling feisty. He smiled to himself, thinking about how her blue eyes sparkled with life when she got riled. But he supposed those men didn't know that either. And he meant to keep it that way.

He continued down the street and turned past the bank, heading for Mabel Wilcox's house at the edge of town. She'd popped out of the kitchen at breakfast to say that Mark had been asking after him, so he planned a brief visit before he rode out. The afternoon would be filled with meeting farmers and checking up on Mays and the Greenley brothers.

The front door of the Wilcox house opened before he lifted a hand to knock. A teen-aged boy, who looked like a taller, slimmer version of Mark, waved him inside.

"You're Deputy Ross, aren't you?" The boy swung the door open wider and took a step back.

He nodded and stepped inside. "I've come by to see Mark." He spotted a mismatched table and chairs, a black iron stove and shelves filled with jarred fruits, but no Mark. "How's he doing?"

"He's been hurting, but he'll forget all about that the second he hears you've come. I'm Logan." The young man held out his hand in greeting and he shook it, impressed by the boy's friendly nature. He followed Logan up a dark, stairway and into a long, narrow bedroom. Three beds lined up at even intervals along the back wall. Logan hurried to Mark's bed and jostled his sleeping brother's foot. "Deputy Ross is here to see you."

Mark opened his eyes and a grin brightened his

face. "Hi." The boy's injured arm was propped up with pillows and when he tried to sit up, the effort made him look like a fish flopping in a net. Renzo helped him up then took a seat in the empty chair beside the bed.

He pointed to the white bandaging that went from Mark's hand to his shoulder. "How's the arm?"

"Good. I'm fine." Mark gestured with his chin to his arm. "I wouldn't even be in bed except for Ma's making me." Logan made a scoffing sound. It reminded Renzo of something Roberto would have done to him. He suppressed a chuckle and pretended to ignore the exchange.

"Mothers do know best, but I'm glad to hear you're feeling better." Raising three boys alone must be quite a struggle. "I expect your mother's already torn into you about what happened."

Mark's gaze dropped. "Yes, sir."

The first time he'd gotten caught smoking his father had given him the most long-winded lecture of his life. But that was preferable to the spanking his mother would have given him, had she been the one to catch him. He thought back, trying to come up with a brief summary of his father's speech that would still relay the same message.

"Well, then I'm just going to say one thing. You're too young to smoke. It doesn't make you a man. What makes you a man is protecting and supporting the ones you love, no matter how hard that might be." He swiveled to meet Logan's gaze. "That's all there is to it."

Logan puffed up his scrawny chest, as if Renzo had passed on the wisdom of the ages. "Yes, sir." The boy spoke as if on authority of both Wilcox brothers, and the innocent gesture had Renzo holding back a grin. Borrowed wisdom imparted, he wasn't sure what to do now. He'd never been the center of a child's attention for this long before.

Renzo tapped the thumbs of his clasped hands

together. "I'd better get going." He leaned forward to rise.

"Wait." Mark pleaded. "Would you read to me for a little while?" The boy pointed to a well-worn book, titled THE ADVENTURES OF THE GREEN MOUNTAIN BOYS, on the small table by the bed.

"Pa used to read this to us."

Renzo was humbled at the invitation to carry on such a personal tradition. Glancing at the book's faded cover he smiled, remembering how the books in the library of his parent's home had fueled much of his boyhood need for excitement. Even before he'd learned to read, his father had spent hours with him and Roberto perched on each knee, reading. Tales of pirates, soldiers, explorers; as long as there was an element of danger, they'd been enraptured. Those were such cherished times. Back then, in the eyes of his two sons, Renzo's father rivaled any one of those adventure heroes. He exhaled regret. Too bad he still didn't feel that way.

"Please, Deputy Ross?" Mark's plea pulled him back from bittersweet memories.

He looked into the boy's questioning, brown eyes. "I'd be pleased to." He picked up the volume and settled back in the chair. "I think we can squeeze in one adventure." If he could extend their father's tradition for these boys, why then, the sheriff wouldn't mind if it took a little longer to make his rounds.

Later, as he mounted his horse outside the livery, Renzo spotted Lucy's cart down the road. Wanting to guarantee she got back to her farm safely, he set off in her direction.

Would she be angry about last night? If she'd been half as affected as he, it would still be fresh in her mind. Would she avoid his gaze? He hoped not, for her ice blue eyes, so unlike his own, struck him like bright skies over a wide, calm sea. He urged his horse into a canter.

Today she'd left her braid to trail down from

under a wide-brimmed straw hat, a marginal improvement over yesterday's hideous bonnet. The hat was a wise choice in this blazing sun. But the same ugly coat? How could the woman always be so damned cold? He reined in alongside her wagon and fingered the front of his brim.

"Afternoon, Lucy." She focused momentarily on his new gun belt before meeting his gaze. Did the thing look as awkward as it felt?

"Deputy." She didn't seem angry, but just once he'd like her to use his given name.

"I hope you haven't had any further trouble with Carl Mays and the Greenley brothers."

Her brow creased and her lips thinned. Gone was the frightened hare. Even with the dowdy clothes and hat, the spark of spirit when she was riled made her beautiful.

"No, but my friend Thomas certainly did."

The sheriff had mentioned Thomas Washington. Tate seemed to respect the free black man, although he hadn't offered an explanation why.

"The man who owns the farm next to yours?" He'd planned on visiting him today.

"Yes. Those men barged right into his cabin without so much as a how-do-you-do. He has a broken leg and is totally helpless. They riffled through his house and barn, and broke all his dishes." Her words suggested anger, but her pallor was reminiscent of when she'd been confronted by the men the night before.

His fists tightened on the reins. *Defenseless widows and blacks.* "I'll make sure that it doesn't happen again. Their business may be lawful, but they can't harass everyone in the area." Only bullies tormented colored folks who didn't dare sound off to white men. He'd speak with the sheriff about running the bastards off. Nothing but trouble would come from their continued presence.

"I'd planned to stop by Mr. Washington's place this afternoon. I'll make certain you get home safely and then ride over to see him."

She opened her mouth to speak then paused, her eyes narrowing. "I wasn't going home. I'm on my way to his place right now to get him and take him home with me."

Take Washington to her house? She said the man had a broken leg. How did she think she could manage that without help? He caught her studying his face as if he was some kind of mystery. *Cristo*, the woman was a puzzle herself.

He shifted in his saddle. "Sounds as if you're going to need help." There's no way she could have gotten a man with a broken leg in and out of her tiny cart without inflicting further injury.

"I accept," she said, and her sudden smile brought one to his face.

Finally he'd done something right.

Lucy reined in her horse in front of Thomas's cabin. She'd decided the risk of Renzo spotting James was smaller than that of her hurting Thomas if she moved him without help. She also wanted Renzo to see the damage Mays and his men had done, and report it back to Sheriff Tate.

"You can tie your horse to the wagon, Deputy." She spoke loudly enough for the cabin's inhabitants to hear. He gave her a curious glance before dismounting.

"I'll tell Thomas I've mustered some help to get him to my place."

She hustled inside and crossed to the big bed, whispering. "Trust me," she said to Thomas then, "James, I will be back at dusk to get you. Just stay quiet 'til then. Everything will be fine."

Just then Renzo appeared at the doorway. She gestured with her hands. "Thomas, this is Deputy Ross. He's going to help me get you settled over at my place."

Thomas's gaze bounced between the two of them. He nodded. "Deputy."

Renzo stepped over odd piles of broken dishes and offered his hand in greeting. "Call me Renzo."

She hadn't expected the gesture, and Thomas's slack jaw said he hadn't either.

Renzo nodded toward the mess strewn on the floor. "Mrs. Neels tells me you had some trouble last evening."

"That's right." Thomas glared at Lucy. "But I didn't want to antagonize them by reporting it to Sheriff Tate." He switched his gaze back to Renzo. "Unless you can guarantee they won't be back, then it'd be best to forget about it."

She hated that Thomas was right, but she feared confronting them for the same reason. If he involved the sheriff, they would probably find some way to cause even more trouble.

Renzo shook his head. "But they shouldn't be permitted to destroy your property. Part of my job is to keep an eye on them while they're in the area and report back to the sheriff."

Lucy steeled herself from squirming in the silence that followed.

Finally Thomas gave a single nod. "Maybe you can convince Lucy that taking me to her place isn't a good idea."

No, he can't. "Deputy, Thomas is helpless with that broken leg. It would be so much easier for me to take care of him if he was staying at *my* house." That was honest truth.

Thomas grumbled. "But it isn't seemly, a white woman caring for me in her home, and you know it."

She decided to ignore her friend until he started to cooperate. "I don't give a hoot about what wicked-minded folks think. I have a farm to take care of, and if I'm coming over here twice a day, that makes it impossible to get my chores done."

"It will stir up all kinds of trouble," Thomas

warned.

Renzo held up a hand in her direction, forestalling the argument about to cross her lips. "I can understand your hesitancy to stay in Mrs. Neels' home, but what if she made up a place for you in the barn?"

The barn? She stiffened, having been intent on keeping everyone far away from the Tyler family's hiding place.

Renzo met her gaze. "Is there some place in the barn to set up a cot?" He was waiting for her response so there was no time to think more than one step ahead.

"Yes." Even as she answered, Lucy looked further ahead in the plan. There *were* empty stalls. It might just work if she could get Renzo in and out quickly.

Renzo spread his arms wide. "That should solve the problem. Thomas will be close enough to check on throughout the day, but far enough from the house so as not to set tongues wagging."

She stepped toward the bed and, with Renzo behind her, let her gaze flick down to James's hiding place. She wanted her friend to consider the boy in this scheme. He could be with his mother and sister if they came to her place. After a moment, Thomas's silent scowl told her she had won. *Halleluiah.*

"Very well. I'll stay in the barn until I can get around."

"Until you can walk *and* take care of your horses," she added. He couldn't care for them properly while he was hobbling on crutches. "And if we take your horses to my place, I won't have to come over here at all."

"Sounds like it's all settled," Renzo said. "Lucy, how about you get what things Mr. Washington needs while I get him settled in your cart."

It took longer than she expected to get Thomas and the horses to her farm. Anxious for Renzo to leave, she held demons at bay and retrieved an old cot from the rickety smokehouse. She even worked up a sweat making up the bed with linens. Renzo took care of all the horses and helped Thomas in to his new guest quarters. When he was settled they left him to rest.

"Thank you for your help." She shoved her hands into her coat pockets, avoiding his gaze. "I'm afraid I couldn't have gotten Thomas here by myself."

"*That* must have been hard for you to admit." She did look at him then, to judge whether or not he was scolding her. The twinkle in his honey eyes told her it was harmless teasing.

"I suppose I am used to doing for myself."

"You know, it's not a sign of weakness to ask for help when you need it. Just look at Thomas. You don't think less of him for agreeing to come here, do you?"

"Of course not."

"Well, then."

His smile set butterflies fluttering in her stomach. She was becoming much too fond of Renzo Ross. Self-preservation set her wits scrambling.

"Well, I best get to my other chores."

"And I have farmers to meet." She followed him to his horse, a small part of her wishing he would trick her into another invitation. But his leaving was for the best. He would go carry out whatever duties the sheriff had assigned, and she would go on breaking the law.

Chapter Nine

Lucy retrieved James without incident, aided by the boy's excellent hearing. When they arrived safely at the barn, Emily's tears at being reunited with her son had Lucy's emotions teetering dangerously close to the surface. She quickly bid them goodnight.

"I'm leaving Wink outside," she said to Thomas. "He'll hear any strange noises and raise a ruckus." She handed Thomas an old cow bell she'd unearthed from another stall. "If you need me, ring this as loud as you can."

"Lucy," he whispered, halting her escape, "You got to make sure that deputy stays away."

She rubbed a dull ache at her temple. "I didn't invite him back."

"I know. But I saw the way he looked at you. He'll be back."

She dropped her hand but looked away, not wanting Thomas to see the spark of hope his words had ignited. "He was just being helpful."

"Just be prepared to send him away."

Too tired to argue, she said goodnight. Back at the

house she spread Wink's blanket on the porch and sat in one of the rockers. Male crickets chirped their courting songs, calling out to the available females, "Choose me, choose me." But only in the insect world could love be so simplified. So wonderfully uncomplicated.

Was Thomas right? Would Renzo visit soon? Although she hadn't been able to forget the kisses they shared, last night he'd regretted that it had happened and couldn't leave fast enough. Her plan to chase him off had worked all too well. No, Thomas had to be wrong. Renzo's help today had just been an extension of his deputy's duties.

Days passed and with nothing to do but rest, Emily's pains ceased. Lucy held out hope that perhaps Thomas's leg would heal and he could move the family to their next stop before Emily went into real labor. He had taken to reading aloud from his Bible, which the entire family could listen to from their hiding place above. He seemed younger and happier when Emily and the children were close, so if Lucy worked in the garden where she could see the entire length of the drive, the Tylers slipped down to sit with Thomas. The runaways were as silent as morning dew settling on grass, and had it not been for the need to prepare extra food and smuggle it out to them, Lucy might not have known they were there at all.

Renzo made a habit of stopping daily, but since his manner was always businesslike and he rarely took the time to dismount, she decided he was just being conscientious about the slave catchers leaving her alone. The one time he'd asked to visit Thomas, her neighbor had been so surly that Renzo hadn't bothered to ask again.

She didn't do or say anything to encourage him and there wouldn't have been time to take extra pains with her appearance even if she wanted to. With all she had to do she should have sleep soundly, but her nightmares became more frequent.

"You look ready to drop. I wish I could do something besides lay around." Although silver dusted Thomas's short, black hair, he was well used to demanding physical labor.

She handed him his breakfast tray. "Emily and Rosalee did all my mending for me. That was a big help." She wrinkled up her nose. "You know what a poor seamstress I am." She settled her hands on her hips and leaned back, her spine crackling like bacon in a hot skillet. "I'm taking the milk and butter in to Mabel Wilcox at the hotel." There weren't enough surplus eggs today to justify another stop at Anderson's.

"Maybe you'll run into the deputy in town so he won't need to stop by." Thomas gave her a sideways glance, but she was too exhausted to rise to his bait.

She hooked her cart up to one of Thomas' horses. They needed more exercise than they were getting, and the steady plodding of her Gertie would have put Lucy to sleep behind the reins. She encouraged the bay into a trot, hoping her old cart wouldn't crumble into a pile of tinder along the dirt road. Not only did the rough ride revive her, but her straw hat kept bouncing off her head. After a while, she gave up and left it hanging down her back. She was almost relieved to finally pull to a stop by the kitchen door at the back of the hotel.

"Morning, Mizz Neels." Mabel's oldest son, Mitch, trotted outside to help tote her containers. It seemed that the young man had surpassed her height since her visit here only days ago. She returned his greeting and climbed down, lifting the crock of freshly made butter out from the straw-lined wooden box.

Mitch swung up into the cart. "If you ever need me to pick this up for you, you just let me know. I'd be happy to borrow a rig and drive out to your place to fetch things."

Inside, fresh cherry pies sat cooling on the wooden counter, and Lucy closed her eyes to better appreciate the scent.

Mabel sat at a large kitchen table sipping what was probably a well-earned cup of coffee. "Mizz Neels, set that down there and come sit for a minute. I've been on my feet for hours and I need to rest a bit before the lunch rush."

Lucy hesitated, never having been asked to sit and socialize with the woman before. But indulging in a leisurely cup of coffee did sound heavenly.

Mabel filled Lucy's mug from the enameled pot and whispered. "I think my boy, Mitch, has a case of puppy love over you." She smiled innocently at her eldest son as he carried Lucy's milk can past them and down the stairs to the kitchen's cold storage. The hotel could afford ice, but the price was so dear Lucy made due with the spring house with its cold water source from the hillside.

"Me? No, he's probably thinking about some pretty girl his own age." She took a sip of coffee and closed her eyes for a moment to enjoy the decadence of doing absolutely nothing.

"No, it's you all right." Mabel shook her head, making the ruffles along the edge of her white cap flap to and fro. "Ever since Deputy Ross saved Mark, my youngest, my boys have been acting different. More mature. And since Mitch overheard the deputy asking about you, well, that's made you stand out like you're something special."

Renzo saved Mark? And he'd also been asking questions about her? She wasn't sure what to say. "What happened to your son?"

"Lordie, you didn't hear?" Mabel stirred another spoon of sugar into her coffee. "Well, I reckon you never were one to stand around and cluck with the others. Mark caught his sleeve on fire sneaking a cigarette." Mabel set down the spoon and her hand went to her bosom. "If he hadn't been hurt enough already, I'd have tanned his hide. Anyway, the deputy smothered the flames with his shirt.

Saved Mark's arm and maybe his life, sure as I'm sitting here." Her ruffles bobbled again.

No wonder Sheriff Tate hired him as his deputy. Renzo's bravery didn't come as a surprise, but he hadn't once mentioned the incident. Then again, she knew almost nothing about him.

"Is Mark coming along all right?"

"Oh, yes. Doctor Morgan has him healing up just fine. My middle boy, Logan, keeps an eye on him whilst I'm at work."

"I'm glad he'd on the mend."

"But aren't you curious about what he's been asking about you?"

She opened then closed her mouth.

"Aw, it's okay. A woman would have to be crazy not to be curious about a handsome man who was sweet on her."

Sweet on me? Lucy hadn't dared to hope since his job made him the absolute worst man to become involved with. But he had kissed her and made her feel more feminine and desirable than she'd ever felt in her life. And to hear someone else say they thought his attentions toward her were special made her imaginings seem less fanciful.

She lowered her voice. "What did he ask?"

Mabel leaned forward. "He wanted to know how long you'd been widowed. I told him I thought your husband had been gone a couple years. That's right, isn't it?" Although Lucy didn't want to discuss Emmett, she did want to hear more. She nodded.

"He also asked if I knew whether you had any gentlemen friends. I let him know that although you ran a farm on your own, you were a real lady and your reputation was as spotless as my copper kettle." Since Lucy had never been more than distantly polite, Mabel's support seemed undeserved.

Her gaze dropped to the white mug in her hands.

"Thank you."

Mabel patted her arm. "No thanks necessary for telling the truth. Now, don't you want to know what I've found out about him?" The older woman's eyes twinkled with mischief. "Alfred, down at the telegraph office, says that Deputy Ross sent a telegraph to his folks in Philadelphia."

She started ticking off fingers. "He seems to have plenty of money for paying his bill and buying clothes and such. It's obvious he's had a lot of schooling. We know he's brave, and although I was in too much shock to notice at the time, I seem to recall his form being, well, rather *manly.*"

So *that's* why she'd seen him in Anderson's Mercantile, practically bare from the waist up. It had made her so uneasy and intimidated she'd put it from her mind. Until now. His muscular chest and the strip of dark hair running down...

Mabel chuckled. "Why Lucy Neels, you're cheeks are pink as a Valentine heart."

Lucy popped up out of her chair, her hands flying to her face. "Thank you very much for the coffee but I really need to get back." She bolted out the door, calling over her shoulder, "I hope your boy continues to mend."

Mabel rushed to follow her. "But I need to fetch your money from Mr. Chambers."

"He can pay me next time." Lucy kept her face averted, checking that Mitch had situated her empty containers so they wouldn't topple.

"Very well." The woman's chuckle told Lucy she wasn't fooling her one lick. "I had one more tidbit that I thought you might want to know."

Lucy tried to keep her curiosity contained, but in her current state, it was too much to expect. She climbed into the seat, grabbed the reins and huffed out her breath.

"All right. You've got me so befuddled I probably won't be able to find my way home unless I ask. What else?"

Mabel's wide smile and eagerness to share chipped away another level of the wall Lucy had built around herself.

"He asked me to pack up a big picnic supper for him today. I have a feeling you might not need to do any cooking tonight."

The prospect of a picnic with Renzo had Lucy smiling throughout the afternoon. She tried to think of picturesque dining spots as she toted buckets of water to the garden and cleaned the henhouse. After all, if they left the farm, there was no chance of him discovering Emily and the children. And she could really relax. Memories of his kisses and his touch had her practically floating as she finished what chores absolutely had to be done.

She bathed, braided her hair and changed into a yellow print day dress. It wasn't her best blue, but it was clean and Emily had mended the tear in the skirt, making it almost invisible. She didn't want to appear as if she'd been expecting an invitation even though she wrapped a blue shawl around her shoulders instead of wearing her coat.

At suppertime she carried a heaping platter of ham sandwiches out to the barn. The melon she'd picked earlier had been chilling inside the big trough in the spring house. She went to fetch it while her company ate. Wink trotted alongside her, starved for attention and ready for his own supper. She was just heading back to the barn when the dog stopped in his tracks and barked.

Charles Hopper rode up the lane. Lucy pulled the melon tight against her chest. Good thing he hadn't arrived a minute later, for she would probably have allowed Wink to accompany her inside.

Lucy silenced Wink. "Mr. Hopper, what can I do for you?" Hopefully her raised voice had Emily and the children already climbing back up to their hiding place. The poor woman had no business going up and down a ladder this close to giving birth, but Emily claimed it was good exercise. Lucy thought it had more to do with the fact that she and the children enjoyed spending time with Thomas.

"Mildred pestered me into coming by to see if I could talk some sense into you." Charles dismounted but kept a distance from Wink.

Lord, but Mildred was a worry-wart. Lucy had expected the Hopper's interference days ago and since they hadn't stopped, she'd hoped Thomas's stay would pass without regard.

"I'm afraid I don't know what you're talking about."

"We heard Thomas Washington is staying in your house. Mizz Neels, you know what folks'll be saying."

"And just what will people be saying?"

Charles sputtered a bit before he found his words. "A white woman with a colored man in her home?" He'd imply the worst but didn't have the guts to speak plainly. If it wasn't for the presence of Emily and the children, Lucy would make him spit out every vile insinuation. But hastening his departure was more important so she forced herself to be calm.

"First of all, Thomas is like a father to me. Secondly, he is not staying in my house. He is sleeping on a cot in my barn. And third, the poor man's leg is broken." She tapped her toe in the dust for good measure.

His gaze flicked from the house to the barn. Did he think she was lying? Tempted as she was to crack the heavy fruit over his head, she decided to put the no-good skunk's worries to rest and be rid of him once and for all.

"And since you're here, I'm sure you'll be wanting to wish him a speedy recovery." She balanced the melon in one arm and opened the latch on the door, feeling chills at the daringness of her actions. Had her temper left her too confident?

Charles sputtered yet again—the man really did

need to expand his vocabulary—and followed her inside.

She scanned the barn, relieved but not surprised that there was no sign of the Tylers.

"Thomas, look who came by to wish you well." She set the chilled fruit on the empty sandwich platter by the cot.

"That's right nice of you Mr. Hopper. Right nice." Thomas nodded but didn't bother setting down his sandwich.

Charles finished looking around the barn's interior, probably for evidence of hedonistic sin. He nodded to Thomas's splints.

"It's very generous of Mizz Neels to take care of you while you mend."

"Yes, indeed." Thomas smiled. He was a master at ignoring insult, veiled or no.

"My missus wants me to tell you, should you want to go back to your place, we'll make sure someone stops in to check on you."

Lucy knew darned well Charles wouldn't allow his wife to care for Thomas herself. Perhaps Mildred meant the offer, but from Charles it was empty as Lucy's savings jar.

"Oh, no. Thomas is perfectly happy right where he is." She gave her friend a warning glare. "Isn't that so?"

"Yes, ma'am. But it sure is nice of you to offer your help." He popped the last bite of sandwich in his mouth. She could almost read Thomas's less charitable thoughts as his jaw worked the bread and meat.

Her courage depleting at a rapid pace, she searched for a way to get her neighbor back on his horse. "Oh, dear. I forgot a carving knife." She gave both men a *silly me* expression. "I'm sure Mr. Hopper has to be getting home, so I'll see him to his horse and then go back to the house and get one."

A sudden rustling from the loft made all three of them look skyward.

"What was that?" Charles asked, scrutinizing both of them.

She pulled her shawl tighter around her. "Probably just one of those silly barn cats."

Thomas nodded and picked up his water glass. "They wake me up every time I try to take a nap."

Charles's gaze slid back to her. "I haven't seen any cats. Maybe I'd better check it out."

She fought a wave of nausea. Clearly he doubted her story, but she prayed he was more interested in testing her reaction than actually following through on the threat. It was an awful chance to take, but she couldn't think of any way to distract him without making him more suspicious.

"How kind of you," she said. It was a balancing act, being polite, but not too polite. "I hate climbing up that ladder."

He glared at her before heading over to the bottom of the ladder. She forced herself not to rub the gooseflesh on her arms.

Please be all bark and no bite.

"Do be careful on the seventh and eighth rungs. They're partly cracked, but they hold my weight well enough." The knot in her stomach loosened some as she watched Charles hesitate, trying to examine the rungs above his head.

Just then Percy, one of her barn cats, strolled around from the neighboring stall and sat down to wash his paws. His after dinner clean up couldn't have been more perfectly timed. She made a mental note to reward the indifferent feline later with some of Agnes's fresh milk.

Charles noticed the cat and hemmed and hawed. "Well, maybe you were right. That there cat looks like he's just finished off a mouse." If he was relieved, it couldn't come close matching to her own relief. The man had wanted her farm since Emmett's death, and if he discovered her crime he'd have the means to get it.

"Midred will have my supper ready, so I'd better head on home." He hitched his braces and walked away without even saying goodbye, let alone wishing Thomas well.

She followed him, imagining hurrying him along with a firm kick in the seat.

"Be sure to give my best to Mildred."

Did I really say that? Lucy never bothered to send regards to his wife. All this anxiousness was doing the darnedest things to her brain.

Charles mumbled goodbye and trotted his horse down the lane, while Lucy fought total collapse. Would he forget about the incident or come to suspect after giving it more thought? She continued to watch him for any hesitation or sign of return. Just before he rounded the bend, Renzo appeared, driving a carriage. With Charles's unexpected arrival she'd forgotten about him. The men had a brief exchange and then each continued on his way. She caught herself fisting the front of her shawl and reshaped the knitting.

Act normally. Lucy forced a smile as she stood there, frozen to the ground.

Renzo halted the carriage and tried to find his voice. Although Lucy's eyes were shadowed with what he suspected was exhaustion—every time he stopped she toiled at one chore or another—she looked more beautiful than ever. A pale blue shawl clung to her shoulders and the yellow dress hugged her to perfection. Had she taken extra pains with her appearance because of him? The idea triggered an unfamiliar sensation deep inside his chest, one his gut warned him to sidestep.

"Good day, Lucy." He hopped down, determined to continue using her first name even though she'd yet to reciprocate.

"Hello, Deputy. Has something happened to your horse?"

"No, Terra's fine." He tucked his thumbs under his gun belt to keep himself from pulling her into his arms. "I borrowed something appropriate for transporting a lady on a picnic."

Her smile warmed but she didn't reply.

He tipped his hat back with a thumb and took a step closer. "That is if the lady likes picnics."

She let out a breath and it was as if he could see the cares of the day evaporating into the air. "I can't remember the last time I went on a picnic. Surely, when I was a little girl."

Had that louse of a husband never treated her to any fun? "Well then, Lucy Neels, I'd be honored if you would accompany me on a picnic."

"That sounds lovely, but I..." She hesitated, glancing toward the barn.

He reached behind the seat for the smaller of two baskets. "If you're worried about Thomas, don't be. I have a picnic for him as well." He held the basket up, but the tears gathering in her eyes hit him like a fist. He set the basket down and reached for her shoulders, careful to keep his touch gentle.

"What's the matter?"

"You brought Thomas a picnic."

"That's a problem?"

She loosened the grip on her shawl to swipe a tear from her cheek. "No. I'm just being silly."

Renzo wrapped his arms around her. Too bad his embrace couldn't make her burdens disappear forever.

"You're not being silly. You're just exhausted. Between running this farm all by yourself and taking care of Thomas." It felt like the most natural thing in the world to kiss the top of her head. Her hair smelled like honeysuckle, and he memorized the scent. He patted her back, offering comfort. Funny thing, he would have sworn he received it as well.

She made no effort to move, and holding her felt

mighty fine, but he knew each minute of daylight was precious. He was determined to get her away from the farm, at least for a while, so he forced himself to set her back to arm's length and leaned over to catch her eye.

"I'm going to take Thomas his supper, and then you and I can drive out to this beautiful spot I've discovered for our picnic."

"I can take it in to him." She dashed the last of the tear tracks from her face with the edge of her shawl. "It will just take me a second." The woman had a serious aversion to accepting assistance.

"Nonsense. I want to say hello anyway. We'll both go." He grabbed the basket and gestured for a strangely hesitant Lucy to lead him into the barn.

Chapter Ten

"I can't eat another bite." Lucy waved away the flapjack-sized molasses cookie, feeling as if the seams of her dress might burst. Renzo shrugged and bit into the cookie with a grin that was half devil, half scamp. Laughing, her gaze rolled past him and down the green hillside to the Ohio River. The idea of Thomas rowing his little boat to the opposite side to retrieve runaways threatened to trample her pleasure, but she squashed it. Renzo had worked too hard for her to spoil their picnic with pointless worrying.

"I'm going to have to get back soon." she said.

"Don't worry, I'll get you back before dark." He leaned back and propped himself up on one elbow, absently toying with a blade of grass. When she caught herself staring at the dark hair peeking through the open collar of his shirt, she shifted on the blanket, suddenly intent on packing up the remains of their supper.

He caught her hand. "Walk with me."

He stood, pulled her to her feet then hooked her hand into the crook of his arm. As they strolled toward the steep riverbank her skirt swished against his leg, and his closeness made her pulse quicken. She needed some kind of distraction before she did something foolish, like beg him to kiss her again.

"Tell me about your family." Although she'd dread the same inquiry, she couldn't keep the words from passing her lips.

He stopped and looked out over the water.

"Well, there's Mother."

He misses her.

"Isabella. Ross, now, but Costa was her name before she married my father. They met in Italy while my father was there on business." Renzo patted her hand, and in the quiet Lucy wondered if Isabella Ross would approve of her son spending time with a widow who tended a farm.

"My father's father came from Italy as well. The family name was Rossi, but my grandfather changed it to Ross, thinking it would make starting a business in America easier. The things people do for the sake of fitting in." Renzo shook his head and chuckled, a humorless laugh.

Sorry she'd caused his melancholy, she forced a gay tone. "Italian. That explains why you say 'Cristo' when you curse."

His eyes widened for a moment before he grinned. "A bad habit."

Lucy laughed. "Your heritage also explains those dark curls." She fisted her hand against the urge to reach up and finger his hair. If she did that she might pull his face down to hers. His kisses had been impossible to forget.

She covered up a sigh with a clearing of her throat. "Do you have any brothers or sisters?"

He nodded. "An older brother by three years. Roberto. He and his wife, Danielle, have two boys, Wil and Robbie."

Nephews? How could he not be anxious to return to his family? Didn't he like children?

"Robbie must be named after his father. Is William a family name?"

Renzo's voice hardened. "My father's."

Change the subject, Lucy. "So, have you ever been to Italy?"

He looked down at her and after a moment that his mind seemed somewhere else, he smiled. "Yes, my parents took us a couple of times as children to visit my mother's parents."

His tone had returned to normal and she relaxed. "Are your father's parents there?"

The distant blast of a steamboat whistle echoed along the river valley, making her wait for his reply. Lucy wondered if she would ever travel further than Rush Crossing. But such imaginings were foolish. She had animals and land to tend to. They depended on her as much as she needed them.

Renzo finally answered. "No. I was told they passed a few years before Roberto was born." He bent to pull a burr from the edge of her skirt.

The innocent gesture filled her with longing. For what? A friend? A lover?

No, more than that. A helpmate.

"How about you?" His turn in the conversation made her blink away her dreaming.

She hoped to avoid lying more than she already had. "Thomas is the closest thing I have to family."

"I don't mean to offend, but was he born a free man?"

Lucy shook her head and pointed across the river that divided slavery and freedom. "No, he bought his freedom and came north about ten years ago."

Renzo studied her. "Isn't that unusual?"

Thomas had never kept his history a secret, so she felt free to continue. "Yes. A kindly neighbor negotiated the sale, pretending she wanted to buy him. If his owner had known Thomas was buying his own freedom, he would have set the price much higher."

"A slave had money?"

"Oh, he'd earned it. Thomas is very skilled about caring for livestock. That's what he did for the owner of the plantation. But sometimes neighbors would pay him for his help. He'd saved for years."

She faced the setting sun, inhaling the faint scent of oncoming rain. "I need to get back. It's past time for Agnes's milking." As they strolled back up the hill and gathered their things, she paused to lift a Daddy Longlegs clinging off her sleeve, setting it carefully in the grass.

Renzo chuckled as she straightened. "I can't believe you just handled that bug." He shook his head, smiling. "I swear, every other woman I know, save one, would have screamed for me to kill it rather than worrying about that its safety."

She smoothed an errant strand of hair back behind one ear. A woman running a farm on her own didn't have time to worry about bugs. It was probably one of the hundreds of ways she was less feminine than society ladies. "They're harmless."

"I know." He took her hand in his and gave it a slight squeeze. Enough to set her pulse skipping. "I'm just not used to being around women who *aren't* afraid of bugs."

Hands clasped the rest of the way to the carriage, neither one of them acknowledged the connection, but it had to power to temporarily shove her insecurities aside. "Who was the other one?" Getting situated in the wagon, she flicked grass off her skirt.

"Other one?"

He might have forgotten his casual reference, but she hadn't. "The only other woman you know who wouldn't have been afraid of that Daddy Longlegs?"

"Oh, that. I was talking about Nanny." His wide smile faded. "She helped my parents raise Roberto and I."

"You speak of her in the past. Did she pass

away?" Lucy's fingers trembled, so strong was the urge to caress his arm.

He squinted in the face of the setting sun. "A few months ago."

"I can tell you were very fond of her."

"Yes, as was Roberto. She was family." The carriage hit a chuckhole in the road, and Lucy was careful to grab hold of the seat—rather than him as she longed to—for support.

"When we were young, we would show her all the creepy-crawlies we'd find." His eyes crinkled, and Lucy could hear the nostalgia lightening his voice. "We could talk to Nanny about anything."

"It's that way it is with Thomas and I." The only topic she avoided discussing with her friend was Deputy Ross. She wouldn't deny that Renzo's job presented a precarious dilemma, but no one had ever made her feel so special and truly feminine. When he was near he lifted her spirits and made her feel like a woman.

Lucy's thoughts flittered back to the delightful feeling of her hand engulfed inside his warm grasp. Her imagination soared to a place where there were no risks and secrets between them.

When he finally pulled to a halt in front of the house and encircled her waist to lift her down, she caught her breath. She wanted this man in a way that wasn't at all proper or wise, given her current status as a lawbreaker. It was as if his touch had the power to destroy every sense of self-preservation to her heart.

"I hope you enjoyed the picnic." He studied her as he absently petted Wink's head.

How long had she been lost in thought? "I did. I'm sorry, I guess I'm more tired than I realized." Perhaps that would explain why her head swirled with fairy tale dreams.

"If I knew how to milk a cow, I'd offer to do it for you so you could get some sleep."

She smiled, knowing Agnes would never permit such a thing. "And if you knew how, believe me, I'd let you." She turned to the barn. "Let me fetch Thomas's basket for you."

Renzo caught her hand and lifted it to his lips. He kissed it, whispering something she couldn't understand soft and low against her work-worn skin. His breath on her hand sizzled her skin clear down to her toes. He had probably kissed the hands of beautiful, sophisticated women all across the east coast and yet here he was, treating her like one of them, rather than a scruffy Ohio farmer. With his head still bent, she moved her free hand to touch his hair. But too quickly he straightened, and she dropped it to her side. *That was close.*

"Don't bother him. I'll get the basket when I check on you tomorrow."

How she wished she could invite him back for a meal. One that she didn't purposely sabotage. But encouraging visits to the farm was something she shouldn't do. Wouldn't do. "You really don't need—"

"Yes, I do. Mays and his men are still poking around. And until they leave, I have a promise to keep."

Lord have mercy. His amber eyes and protective nature made her knees wobbly as a newborn foal's. The memory of their passionate kisses flooded her. His strong arms wrapped around her, his warm breath on her cheek, her lips.

Wink barked, and she jumped away from where she'd leaned closer to Renzo. She spotted her dog just as he disappeared into the woods.

"Wink!" He didn't return at her call. She took a step toward the woods, scanning the section of trees where he'd entered. "That's strange."

"He probably heard a deer or a rabbit." Renzo grasped her shoulders behind her and squeezed reassuringly. "He'll be back."

"I'm sure you're right." She masked her concern.

If she appeared frightened, Renzo might stay to investigate. She folded her hands in front of her skirt and moved up the porch steps. "Thank you again for the picnic."

"My pleasure." He climbed into the carriage and waved, obviously not as reticent for the evening to end as she. "I'll see you tomorrow." He drove away, and she tried to convince herself it was for the best, that she really hadn't wanted to be swept up into his arms for a passionate kiss.

She went inside. As she changed clothes and tossed her dress onto the bed, she wondered for probably the hundredth time what it would be like to make love to Renzo. His kisses had opened her eyes to desire, and she longed to experience it again. But Emmett had taught her she could live without love, and Renzo wasn't offering his heart, so she'd go on surviving without its physical counterpart.

Distant thunder rumbled as she walked to the barn and milked an irritated Agnes. With the wind picking up, the scent of much-needed rain saturated the air.

Wink reappeared as she put the milk in the spring house. "You had me scared silly." The first raindrops dotted her face as they set off to bid Thomas goodnight. Emily and the children would certainly be asleep by this time. But when she reached the barn, creaking boards sounded from above.

"It's not like them to make noise." Thomas's worried expression probably mirrored her own.

"I'll see if something's wrong." The quickening sound of raindrops clattered on the shake roof as she climbed the ladder. At the top she was surprised to see Emily in full view, pacing back and forth. The woman's hands were pressed to the underside of her rounded belly.

Lucy rushed to her side. "What's wrong?"

"The pains started again." Emily winced. "They's worse than before." She'd barely finished speaking before she doubled over. The soft keening sound she made was quickly drowned out by the rumble of thunder. After a few seconds she straightened, her hands massaging her lower back. "I do believe this baby's decided it's time."

No!

But having given birth twice before, Emily must know.

"Should we wake the children and send them down to be with Thomas?" Emily asked.

"No, let them sleep. I'm not going to have you giving birth up here. Let's get you to my bed."

Emily's eyes widened. "Oh, no. I can't take your bed, Mizz Neels."

"You can, and you will. There may not have been room at the inn for the Baby Jesus's birth, but there's certainly room enough in my house for you and this child." Lucy wrapped her arm around Emily's back and started her toward the ladder, not giving her any time to argue. "Do you think you can make it down the ladder?"

Emily gripped the underside of her belly, but nodded.

"Good. I'll go first and you follow me down." Lucy went only a few rungs in front of her. Descending at a careful pace, they made it down safely.

She hurried to Thomas's cot. "The baby's coming. I'm taking Emily up to the house. I'll be back as soon as I can." She left, wishing she could forget the way he clutched his Bible to his chest. She felt jumpy enough on her own without that image in her head.

His reply barely made it through the sound of the rain. "I'll be praying for you both."

Moving as quickly as possible, they made their way to the back door. She was glad for the deteriorating weather for it would discourage spies. Had Wink run off earlier because he'd heard the slave catchers? The thought knotted her stomach. She wouldn't put it past them to have been spying from the trees. She slipped inside the house behind Emily, shielding her body as best she could. Thunder boomed closer and lightening flashed, illuminating the room. She threw the bolt on the door just as another pain doubled poor Emily over.

"Oh, Lord," Emily muttered.

Helplessness smacked Lucy between the shoulders, and all she could think to do was pat the woman's back.

"My water just broke." The liquid at Emily's feet mixed with the rain from their dripping clothes and shoes. "I'm sorry."

Lucy wrapped her arms around Emily and helped her to the bedroom. "Don't be silly. I'm not worried about this old floor. Here, let me fix the bed a second." She whipped her best Ohio Star quilt off the bed, threw it across a ladder-back chair and took an old one out of the blanket chest. Folding it in half, she laid it across the middle of the bed.

"There. Now let's get you out of these wet clothes and into one of my nightgowns." She lit an oil lamp and opened a drawer, pulling out a gown.

"I can't soil your bed linens. Maybe I should just—

"Emily, I will not argue with you about this. All these things can be washed. Now, let's get you changed into something clean and comfortable." She smiled to soften the effect of issuing orders and helped Emily change, pausing twice during the ordeal for the woman's contractions to pass. Once Emily was settled in the bed, Lucy made certain the front door was bolted and the shutters were closed tight.

"I'm going to get water. Just try and relax." She fled the room, hoping her inexperience in childbirth didn't show, let alone complicate matters. She ran past the springhouse to the well and filled a bucket. Carrying it inside, she locked the door behind her. The combination of nervousness and cool rain had her soaked to the bone and shivering. She lit a fire in the hearth, washed up as best she could and changed into dry clothes.

She carried a cloth and small bowl of cool water back into the bedroom, and the pain on Emily's face almost had her running to the barn for Thomas' advice. Instead, she dug deep for courage and crossed the room, setting her things on the bedside table.

"Emily, can you hear me?"

Emily's eyes were closed, her teeth clenched and sweat beaded all over her face, but she nodded.

"I'm afraid I've never helped deliver a baby. Since you've been through this before, I'm going to need your help." Lucy dipped a cloth in the water, rung it out and dabbed Emily's face and neck. Once the worst of the contraction passed, she exhaled and opened her eyes.

"The pains are coming fast and I's got the urge to push." Emily gasped for breath and squeezed her eyes shut. "Can you see the baby's head?"

Lucy said a quick prayer for strength as she rushed to the foot of the bed and pushed the nightgown to the top of Emily's bent legs. Lucy had many times witnessed the births of cows, horses and pigs, but those mothers hadn't needed her assistance.

I should have found a way to help Thomas inside. At least he could have talked me through this. This situation, with the lives of two people at stake, had her shaking in her soggy boots. She took a deep breath.

"I think I can see it. Lord Almighty, I'm not sure." She swiped at the tears blurring her vision and turned up the wick on the lamp. She could cry a whole river tomorrow, but not right now. She released a held breath. "I see it. Emily, your baby's got a thick head of hair." *Thank you, Lord. It's not breach.*

Emily began to groan as another contraction hit.

"Shhh. I know it hurts," she said, "But you can't scream." Even though a steady rain pelted the metal roof and occasional cracks of thunder shook the ground, if someone was watching outside they might hear her screams. Emily quieted with a nod, but her features contorted in a way that had Lucy gritting her own teeth. She refocused on her task.

"Emily, the baby's head is right there. Surely it's safe for you to push now." Lucy flexed her hands, hoping Emily couldn't see how much they were trembling. "Push."

Emily gripped the sheets and bore down, her chin pressed to her chest. Slowly, the top of the baby's head pushed out into the world.

Lord, God, this is really happening. Lucy cupped her hands and the barest tips of her fingers touched the child's curls.

Emily exhaled with a muffled groan and took another deep breath, bearing down again. Lucy supported more of the baby's head as it slid out and one shoulder emerged.

Then time froze.

The color's wrong. Although the infant would have darker skin than a white child, the color seemed wrong. Almost bluish.

And then she saw why.

The cord. It was tangled. And tightening.

Around the baby's shoulder and neck.

Chapter Eleven

No! Not again. "Push. Push hard!" Lucy supported the child's head with one hand and pulled gently on its exposed shoulder, trying to avoid crushing the straining cord. As the baby emerged, face down, fluid drained from its mouth and nose. Then, bless the Lord in heaven, she felt the child move.

It wasn't dead. This time wasn't like the last. She *would* beat death.

"Keep pushing, Emily! Push like you've never pushed before!" Emily bore down, and the baby's upper torso slipped out. Encouraged by the child's small movements and sputtering, Lucy concentrated her efforts on loosening the cord that stretched down around its shoulder. She remembered a girl from her childhood who had a withered arm. Folks had said it was because of her birthing. Well, by God, this child would be perfect in every way. If she had to promise her soul to the devil to serve alongside Emmett, she wouldn't allow this baby to lose the use of its arm.

"You're almost there, Emily. One more good push." Lucy had never felt so focused. So strong. She might have been unable to save her own child, but, this baby would thrive.

And with that thought, along with a final push from Emily, the rest of the infant's weight slid into her grasp.

"It's a girl!" She laid the newborn on its side on the bed and quickly freed her upper arm and neck from the cord. Then grabbing supplies from her sewing basket, she cut and tied off the cord.

Thunder shook the house as a drenched and elated Emily reached for her now squalling daughter. Lucy handed her the baby, watching mother and child become acquainted through a steady stream of tears. She said nothing, praying the storm would disguise the healthy newborn's cries.

I did it. For once, she allowed the tears to flow, but only because they were tears of joy. As she dealt with the afterbirth and began the wearisome process of cleaning up, her movements slowed. But before anyone stopped by, she had to destroy any evidence of tonight's events.

By the time the thunder had passed to the east the room was quiet, save for the rain still pattering on the roof. The baby, whose coloring had already turned to that of coffee with fresh cream, suckled at her mother's breast.

Lucy tidied up, proud each time she looked up and to see the child's tiny fist waving in the air. Her arm seemed fine.

Emily patted her newborn daughter's bottom through the scrap of cloth. "Thank you for bringing my little girl safe into the world."

Lucy smiled, pleased and yet filled with envy. "You did the hard part."

"All the same, I know this is painful for you." Emily glanced down at her nursing daughter and then back at Lucy.

"Thomas told me that you lost your child."

Sorrow sunk in Lucy's stomach like river rocks.

She shouldn't be surprised he had mentioned it. What with the way Emily's pregnancy would have been a constant reminder of her loss. But they never discussed the subject. Ever.

"That's right." She quietly left the room, put on her coat and went to the well to start filling the laundry tubs with cold water since quite a few things needed a good soaking. She would have a long day of washing ahead. That task completed, she shared the good news with Thomas then collapsed onto a makeshift bed of blankets by the fireplace. And for the first night in weeks, exhaustion was a kind bedfellow, whisking her away into a deep and dreamless sleep.

Renzo had long since given up on sleep. Sexually on edge, and his head a jumble of conflicting emotions, he sat up and lit the lamp. His father's telegram taunted him like a mean drunk wielding a broken bottle. He picked up the paper and smoothed the crumpled sheet, even though he'd read it so many times the words were emblazoned on his brain.

EXTREMELY DISAPPOINTED IN YOU STOP YOUR MOTHER IS TERRIBLY WORRIED STOP THINK OF NANNY STOP

Think of Nanny. Hell, that's exactly why he'd reacted the way he had. Someone had to stand up for her. Renzo wadded the limp paper into a tiny ball and sent it soaring across the room. He needed time and space to sort out his anger, this feeling of betrayal by the one man he'd grown up trusting. His father had added the part about his mother to make him feel guilty. Well, to hell with that.

He threw on his clothes and, borrowing an umbrella from a stand in the hotel lobby, stormed down Main Street's boardwalk with no particular destination in mind. But the change of scenery only refocused his thoughts on his other, more constant obsession.

Lucy. Every minute he spent with her only made

him want her more. She was strong, capable and stubborn in her independence. That woman would probably give as good as she got in the bedroom. And yet there were times, like when he'd pulled out Thomas's dinner basket, that her tough exterior cracked allowing him a glimpse of the tender woman inside. *This* woman he would make to love tenderly, long and sweet. On their picnic it had taken a monumental effort not to draw her down on the grass and slake his craving. But once wouldn't be enough, and she wasn't the type for a short-term affair. Keeping his hands to himself left him in a damned uncomfortable state and avoiding her was both impossible and impractical.

Impossible because he had tried. Tried to go just one day without riding out to her farm. But by mid-afternoon he'd ridden across what seemed like half the county just to get there before suppertime. And impractical, for how could he know if Mays and the Greenelys left her alone if he didn't check on her?

He trudged across the street, uncaring about the mud oozing over his boots. He reasoned all this uneasiness was because it had been many weeks since he'd had a woman. Right before his engagement, to be precise. But searching for a female willing to satisfy his urges by spreading her thighs—a pastime which had previously served him well—the idea, it-

Damn. He'd be a liar to pretend that Lucy wasn't the only woman he wanted in his bed. But his cursed conscience prevented him from seducing her. She deserved more. She deserved someone who intended to stay with her and provide for her. Someone who wanted to run a goddamn farm. And that wasn't his dream. So, until Mays and his black-hearted friends left, he was doomed to spending every minute in a state of semi-arousal.

A light flickered inside the sheriff's office and Renzo headed in that direction. Tate had mentioned that his foot pain often destroyed any chances of a good night's sleep. Seems they were in the same boat tonight. Maybe talking about his duties would help him get his mind off Lucy.

The sheriff looked up from a newspaper as Renzo swung open the door. "You're up mighty late." The man folded his paper and slid his spectacles further down his bulbous nose.

"I'm afraid so." Renzo closed the door, propped the dripping umbrella in the corner and pulled a chair away from the wall. "Does your wife know where you're spending your nights?" He managed a weak smile as Tate reached inside a drawer for another glass.

The sheriff topped off his whiskey and poured one for Renzo. "She's the one who kicked me out of bed. Says my moans and groans are driving her insane." Tate chuckled and took a sip of his drink. "It's a good thing I live close by. Since I can't get any sympathy at home, at least I can come here for a drink without getting nagged."

So much for giving up drinking. Renzo held up his glass. "Here's to sleepless nights." He closed his eyes as the unfamiliar brand burned its way down his throat.

Tate tipped his glass once more and then rested it on the shelf of his belly. "I'd ask what's got you losing sleep, but at your age it can only be one thing. A woman."

Renzo nodded. Lucy Neels didn't fit into his long-range plan of heading back to Philadelphia once Tate's foot had healed.

"What can you tell me about Lucy Neels?" he asked.

The sheriff's eyebrows rose. "The Widow Neels? Well, son, you've got mighty fine taste, but she's going to be one tough nut to crack."

Glass in hand, Renzo waved the comment away. "I'm not interested in her that way." Maybe saying the words out loud would help him convince himself.

"Too bad," Tate said, raising his brows as if genuinely disappointed. "That woman needs a good man. Lord knows, her husband was a good-for-nothing." The older man gazed into his drink.

Renzo flexed his jaw and took a calming breath. "How so?"

After a moment the sheriff set his glass on the desk and hooked his thumbs under his braces. "Emmett Neels was a half-assed farmer and a mean sonofabitch."

Renzo's pulse quickened.

"He bought that place and moved here from somewhere in eastern Kentucky about six years ago."

Renzo pictured a cruel-faced bastard slumped on a porch chair, watching Lucy toil away with a hoe.

"They pretty much kept to themselves," Tate continued. "She started selling eggs and such to the restaurant and Andersons. Oh, he planted a little corn and raised a few hogs, but it seemed to me Mrs. Neels did most of the work. 'Course, she sold off the hogs after he died."

Renzo had spent more time than he wanted to admit wondering about Emmett Neels.

"How did he die?"

Tate sneered. "He'd been making moonshine." The sheriff drained his whiskey and waved his empty glass. "He must have been drunk on his own hootch. All I could figure was the dumb-ass lit a cigarette in the wrong place and blew up his still. And himself."

Renzo's gut tensed. "Did Lucy find his body?"

Sheriff Tate studied him for long seconds.

Tell me the truth.

Tate took a deep breath. "I haven't told this to a living soul, including my missus, but you're a progressive thinker. You swear to keep this to yourself?"

He shifted to the edge of his chair. "Of, course."

The sheriff lowered his bad foot to the floor and faced him dead on. "Thomas Washington found the body. Said he heard the explosion from his place and went poking around in the woods between their farms to find out what it was." Tate poured himself another two fingers and offered the bottle to Renzo, who waved it away. The older man emptied his glass in one gulp.

Was what happened so horrible that he needed to be half drunk to repeat it?

"Thomas had gone to Lucy's place before he came here to fetch me." Tate's glassy stare made Renzo's muscles tense. "Seems that before he went and blew himself to kingdom come, Emmett Neels beat the ever-lovin' shit out of his wife and dog."

For the first time in his life, Renzo understood how it felt to hate someone enough to murder them. Luckily for Emmett, the man was already dead.

"I'd wondered if someone else might have done it, but when she regained consciousness, Lucy confirmed it'd been her husband who'd almost killed her. I guess the dog had tried to protect her, but paid dearly for it."

Renzo's hand shook, the whiskey sloshing in his glass. The sonofabitch must be burning in Hell.

"She begged me not to fetch the doctor or tell anyone else about the beating." Tate removed his spectacles and slid them into his vest pocket. "A matter of pride, I guess. Anyway, Thomas was able to patch up Wink. We buried what was left of Emmett, told folks he'd succumbed to a fever, and that Lucy had gone back to Kentucky for a visit with family. It took a couple months for her bones to mend. Plus, it was best to keep it all secret since the idea of a Thomas tending to her wouldn't sit well with some folks. No matter how bad off she was."

This explained the tiny scar at her left temple. Renzo stared at the dark puddle of water beneath the umbrella, battling mental images that tried to form of Lucy beaten and bloody.

After a moment Sheriff Tate reached for his crutches. "I assume Lucy hasn't had any trouble about Thomas staying in her barn since you haven't mentioned it."

Renzo helped him stand. "No. I ride by each day

to check since those slave catchers bullied them both." He followed the hobbling sheriff around the desk, extinguishing the oil lamp and locking the door behind them. "It doesn't seem right that we can't haul those fellows in for what they did to Mr. Washington's place."

The sheriff didn't meet his gaze. "You know a black man can't testify against a white man. Besides, Thomas is smart enough to know that some broken dishes aren't worth the other trouble those fellows could stir up."

The rain had slowed to a drizzle, so Renzo didn't bother opening the umbrella.

Tate maneuvered his way down the steps to the muddy road. "Have you heard anything about when they might be clearing out?" Although the three men hadn't broken any other laws their inquiries and sudden appearances were making plenty of folks nervous.

"No, but maybe it's time I gave them some encouragement."

Sheriff Tate stopped and lifted his chin to meet Renzo's gaze. "No. I've dealt with their kind before. Mean to the bone. Leave them be. They'll grow tired of waiting and move on."

Feeling like a wave butting up against a sea wall, Renzo ground his jaw in frustration.

The sheriff set his glare. "I'll have your word, Renzo. You'll not start anything with them."

Even though he wanted to do just that, he respected the sheriff's experience. "Alright. But I'd bet my last dollar that they'll start trouble soon enough."

The Sheik's cock-a-doodle-doo followed the rain and preceded the sunrise. Eyes only half open, Lucy fed Wink and milked Agnes by lantern light.

"Lucy," Thomas called in a loud whisper. She carried her bucket around to his make-shift room.

She spoke softly as well, not wanting to wake the children. "I'm going to take this to the spring house and then I'll bring out some breakfast."

"Is everything all right?" He studied her face.

This time, rather than avoid his gaze, she smiled. "Everything's fine. I'm just tired and have a lot to do. I'll bring your breakfast as soon as I can."

She prepared a tray for Emily and then delivered breakfast for the Thomas and the children. Rosalee and James had taken to crossing the hayloft and whispering to Thomas through the slits in the floor. That's how they'd learned they had a new sister. Lucy stood underneath their perch and called low.

"Come on down to eat with Thomas you two." Less than a minute later, the excited siblings were crouched on the ground next to the cot, shoving biscuits into their mouths.

"Who does she look more like, me or Rosalee?"

"Did Mama tell you her name yet?"

"Does she cry a lot?"

"When do we get to see her?"

"All in good time," Thomas whispered. "Mrs. Neels has lots to do. Besides, no one is going anywhere so you all can wait for some of your answers."

Lucy couldn't help but chuckle at their long faces, still puffy-cheeked with biscuit. "No, she hasn't cried too much, and no, your mama hasn't mentioned a name yet. Now you finish up your breakfast and mind Thomas when he says to head back up in the loft." No telling when someone could stop by, and with people hidden in both the house and the barn, Lucy was going to have to be diligent about sending visitors on their way. Even Renzo.

Renzo spotted Lucy hanging laundry as he came up the drive. Bed linens and drying cloths spanned the bowed line, dripping their excess water into the patchy grass and mud. With the storm that had passed through, she should have hung them dirty last night and saved herself some labor. Hard labor. The fact that she didn't have on her customary coat or shawl proved how hard she toiled. Part of him wanted to throw her over his shoulder and carry her back to Philadelphia, where she would never have to lift a finger again. Although the notion had come out of nowhere, it was absurd. The Lucy he knew wouldn't be content with the idle life of a society lady.

Nearing but still unnoticed, he took the opportunity to admire her. She had pinned her braid up into a bun but loose tendrils corkscrewed down around her face and nape in a way that made his position on the saddle damned uncomfortable. He shifted, already concocting excuses to draw out his visit.

Wink followed Terra past the house. Lucy's gaze flicked over her dog and fixed on Renzo, but she made no effort to pause in her task.

He reined in and dismounted. "You work too hard." For a moment he considered looping the reins over the clothes line. But this amount of washing must have taken hours, and if Terra managed to topple the line, Lucy would be after both of them with the axe she had lodged in that tree stump. Renzo held on to the reins and admired Lucy's backside as she bent to yank another wet item from her basket.

"That's the only way the work gets done." She pulled wooden pins from a large pocket of the apron covering the front of her skirt. Wash water had dampened the front of her blouse and shift, and her lack of a corset provided him with an enticing view of her breasts and pebbled nipples. Maybe a gentleman would look the other direction, but damned if he could look away from the plump mound as it jiggled with her movements. To disguise his growing arousal, he picked up her basket. Man and beast followed her to the next bare spot on the line.

"Is there something I could do to help you?" he asked.

She reached into the basket. "Doesn't the sheriff have things you should be tending to?"

Extra prickly today. She'd seemed fine when he'd left last evening. Was her sleep as disturbed as his? He smiled to himself at the possibility of being the reason she might have had a restless night.

Lucy shook out a nearly transparent shift and pinned it to the line. It was probably best she not see him grinning behind her back.

"Things are generally pretty quiet. Most of the time I'm just riding around checking in with folks." He and his horse shifted positions to follow her. "As I'm doing right now." He leaned in close enough to let his breath stir the hairs at her nape. "You seem a bit out of sorts. Did something disturb your sleep?"

She ducked around a frumpy cotton nightdress she'd hung—which was the unfortunate answer to what she wore to bed—and straightened it from the opposite side of the line. "Enough lightning and thunder to wake the dead."

She seemed to be working awfully hard to *not* look at him, which made him all the more determined to crack her veneer.

He tied Terra to the nearest tree and resumed his position. "Is that all?"

Her spine stiffened. "Humph." She wasn't giving him much verbal ammunition to work with.

"What can I do to help?"

She sighed aloud, an audible rolling of the eyes if he'd ever heard one. "I don't have time to teach you how to do all the chores that need doing." She finished pinning the last sheet to the line, met his gaze and reached for the basket. "I really have a lot to do, so if you don't mind-"

"I don't mind at all." He kept hold on the basket handles and shifted his fingers to cover hers.

Her eyes rounded and she dropped her hands. He followed her to the laundry tubs, grinning at her back.

"Go away, Deputy. I'm busy." She struggled to tip a tub off its metal stand, and he had to jump to dodge the flood of wash water.

"Busy doing what?" He knew he was irritating her, but damn it, he wasn't totally helpless when it came to manual labor. He and Roberto had both started out working on the docks of Philadelphia for their father.

She planted her hands on her hips let out a huff of air. "Let's see." She lifted one hand and began ticking off fingers. "I need more firewood chopped. Thomas wanted me to find some long branches for him to carve some crutches, his chamber pot needs to be emptied..." She smirked at him, daring him to offer his services on that jolly task.

Great. He swallowed a groan. "I'll take care of all those things." And ignoring her complaints about being in the way, he turned and headed to the trees. "First I'll find Thomas those sticks."

No! Renzo disappeared into the woods, followed closely by her ex-best friend, the traitorous Wink. Leave it to the infuriating man to pick today to get off his horse and insist on helping. She'd tried to be so unpleasant that he'd leave, but he seemed to interpret her foul mood as some kind of challenge.

She high-tailed it into the house and to the bedroom, careful not to make too much noise. Emily was sitting up in the bed, nursing the baby.

Lucy hesitated, swallowing her envy. "Renzo is here and he insists on helping me with some of the chores. Do you think you can keep the baby quiet?"

Emily glanced anxiously down at her daughter then in the direction of the barn. "I reckin' she'll be asleep here in a few minutes." Her brown eyes glistened. "I'd like to go back to the barn come dark. It was right generous of you to give up your bed, but fact is, we'll be safer if we go back. You won't have to worry 'bout keeping folks away from the house and my family will be together."

Renzo and Wink—who had trotted alongside him as if they were boyhood chums—emerged from the woods, loaded down with branches.

Lucy was nowhere to be seen. *Must have gone to check on her patient.* With Terra content to munch tufts of grass under the tree, Renzo carried the pieces of wood to the barn. He propped them against the plank siding to swing open the large door, but they clattered to the ground. Wink disappeared inside as Renzo gathered them and maneuvered through the open doorway. Bits of hay sprinkled down from the loft as he laid the pieces on the ground near Thomas's cot.

He pulled off his hat and wiped his forehead with his sleeve. "Is Lucy in the loft?"

Thomas suddenly grimaced and grabbed his thigh, rubbing his leg above the splint. "No. That's just barn cats. Wake me up every night with their mousing. Last I knew, Lucy was doing laundry." Thomas pointed to the pile of sticks. "She tell you I was wanting to make some crutches?" The poor fellow was probably desperate for some way to get around.

Renzo knew he would be, in similar circumstances. "Yes, I offered to find some branches for you." He kneeled and held up two pieces for Thomas's inspection. "Do you have a knife?"

"I do, indeed." Thomas pulled a wicked-looking Barlow knife out from under his pillow. After Mays and his men's invasion, Renzo could understand wanting to have a weapon close at hand.

Thomas gestured to one of the sticks in Renzo's hand and a second on the ground. "Would you mind holding those two up next to each other?" Thomas swung his bad leg off the bed, supporting his thigh with both hands, and lowered his bare foot to the ground. Renzo switched the branches to one hand and helped him stand on his good foot. They tried sizing a few different branches against him until he settled on a pair.

"I believe I'll start to work on them right now." A distinct dismissal.

Unsure what he'd done to earn Thomas's obvious disinterest, Renzo looked around for the chamber pot. Job number two awaited his very reluctant attention.

As Lucy came out the back door, Renzo was already carrying Thomas's chamber pot toward the outhouse. Her pulse tripped, and her gaze flew to the barn then back to him. He'd returned quicker than she'd anticipated, but nothing seemed amiss. The children must have stayed hidden. She blew out a breath, slipped her arms into her coat and headed to the garden.

On his return trip Renzo pinched his nose, started walking on tip-toe and held the pot out in her direction. He looked ridiculous.

"I finally got you to smile," he called, grinning.

But her amusement died as he disappeared into the barn. His being here was too dangerous. She closed her eyes, trying to think of *some* way to get him to leave, but came up with nothing. Lord, she was never going hear the end of it from Thomas.

She picked beans, her gaze continually flicking from the tall, staked plants to the barn door. Soon Renzo emerged and crossed the clearing to the axe and wedge. Obviously Thomas hadn't been able to discourage him. Large chunks of toppled trees that Thomas and his horses had gathered over the past few months lay haphazard on the ground.

Lucy blew a strand of hair out of her eyes. What a luxury to have help with the chopping. The task took so much of her energy, she put it off until there was barely enough wood to heat a kettle. She could tell Renzo had never chopped wood a day in his life, but it didn't take long for him to develop an efficient swing of the axe. By the time her basket was brimming with beans, he'd accumulated the beginnings of a nice pile of wood. She did a bit of weeding, harvested some carrots and went to the barn to check in.

"Any problems?"

Thomas paused in his carving. "Thankfully no. Is that the deputy out there chopping wood?" The distinct V between his brows spelled out his disapproval.

"I tried to get rid of him, but he wouldn't leave." She set her basket on the ground and tucked the same rebellious strand of hair behind her ear. "I don't dare stay in here long, but I wanted to tell you that Emily's coming back out to the barn tonight." A soft rustling above told her the children were listening. "You all have to lie still," she whispered to the rafters.

Thomas set down his knife and ran his fingers over the smooth surface of the wood. "Well, at least if Deputy Ross insists on hanging around then you'll have someplace to keep him occupied."

Lucy's thoughts whirled back to the evening Renzo had kissed her. Did she dare invite him inside again?

Thomas studied her. "You don't have tender feelings for this man, do you?"

She wanted to shout her denial, that no, she didn't have any feelings for Renzo other than gratitude, but couldn't.

"I know he's been good to you, child, keeping an eye on our farms and making sure those slavers aren't causing us trouble. And he's treated me with nothing but respect. But child, he's the law. And *this* time, Sheriff Tate and the law *aren't* on our side."

She blinked against the burning sensation behind her lids. Damn it, she knew Renzo was the law. For many days, she'd felt split down the middle. In the beginning she'd done everything she could think of not to encourage his attentions, but now that she'd had them, known what it was like to feel desired and cared for, she didn't want to go back to the way things had been.

"I know he's the law, Thomas." She blinked repeatedly. "I've done what I could to discourage him." Why couldn't Thomas see that? "Now, I've got to get back out there and *keep him occupied.*" She couldn't keep the bitterness from her voice. "I'll bring supper when I'm able."

Head held high, she left the barn, only to be brought up short by the sight of Renzo. He'd stripped off his vest, rolled up his sleeves and was chopping wood in his perspiration-soaked shirt. With each swing of the axe, the muscles in his back and arms flexed and rolled. One of his hands was large enough to grasp and stack chunks of wood that would take both of hers. And the recollection of them on her body heated her so that she set the beans on the ground and slipped off her coat.

Lord in heaven, he was beautiful. Thomas's warning taunted her and she shoved it back into a distant corner of her mind. Renzo was merely being helpful.

"Lucy?"

How long have I been standing here looking like a lack-wit?

Renzo pulled on his vest. "I've got a good start on the wood, but I need to go. I saw Mrs. Hopper in town and promised that I'd swing by their place. She said their dog has been acting strangely around dusk and she wants me to take a look around the woods."

This bit of news brought gooseflesh to her arms. Wink had come back from the woods no worse for the wear, but her worry about the slave catchers felt more justified.

"Has Charles taken a look?" But then she remembered how just the threat of a weakened ladder had put Charles off climbing it. If he thought there was even a slim chance of danger, he'd be happy to let someone else do the dirty work. Renzo buttoned his vest and she had to look away from his large, capable hands.

"Yes, but Mr. Hopper claims it's my job to do a

more thorough search."

Ha. Charles had probably spent all of two seconds looking from the safety of his porch.

It's the slave catchers. They're snooping around.

Renzo tugged down the front of his vest. "Have you started supper yet?"

"What?"

He waved his hand in front of her face. "Cooking. Have you started?"

She blinked. "I haven't had time." Although their picnic had been the most romantic supper of her life, surely he hadn't asked Mabel to prepare another.

"Good. How about I take you to the hotel restaurant for dinner?"

She smoothed her flyaway hair. "I can't. I'm a mess." But wouldn't it be heavenly?

"You've got time to wash and change. Like I said, I have to ride over to the Hoppers. That'll give you time to fix something easy for Thomas and then get ready. I'll come back here for you on my way back into town."

Thomas wouldn't approve, but at this moment his censure didn't rank above this chance to live like someone other than the poor farmer she was. Besides, Thomas wasn't her keeper. And as long as he took her to town, their being together didn't pose any danger to the Tylers. Wink would be here, and she'd take a rifle out to the barn to leave with Thomas, just in case. Renzo wouldn't question the precaution.

She smiled up him. "I accept."

Charles Hopper joined his wife and Renzo on the front porch of their large clapboard farmhouse. A fat, yellow dog lay panting in the shade, its tongue lolling out the side of its mouth, dripping slobber on the floorboards. The friendly canine had worn itself out running out to greet company.

Renzo lifted his glass of lemonade and took a

drink. "Just exactly how has your dog been acting strangely?"

Mildred handed Charles a glass as he sat, then returned to her chair. "It's not like Butterbean to take off."

Renzo coughed, covering his mouth with a fist. Butterbean? How was a farm dog supposed to garner any respect with a name like that?

Mildred's forehead wrinkled. "She's taken off into the woods on more than one occasion and although she doesn't raise too much of a fuss, I have the oddest feeling someone's out there." Mildred glanced at her husband, who drained his glass and held it out. She popped up to take it and set it on the small table at her side.

Charles pulled off his hat and fanned his face with the brim. "It's not like the animal to go missing for hours at a time. I think she's caught the scent of something, or someone out there and starts tracking." He scowled at Butterbean. "She ain't never been much of a tracker. Probably loses the scent and then wanders home."

Renzo didn't know much about dogs, never having had one, but Butterbean didn't look too valuable as far as hunting skills were concerned. She didn't look as if she strayed all that far from her supper dish.

"Well, I'll take a look around in the woods if you'll be so kind as to point me in the right direction." He followed Charles off the porch and they walked past the Hopper's sizable barn and corral to the tree line.

Hopper hesitated once they crossed into the shadows and pointed. "Mizz Neels' place is about half a mile as the crow flies."

Renzo's shoulders tensed. That meant if someone *was* sneaking around in these woods, they could just as easily be spying on Lucy. And would that someone be content to keep their distance?

"I'll take a look around." He entered the trees, much as he had at Lucy's earlier, only this time he wasn't certain what he should be searching for. Last night's rain thickened the air under the canopy and as he walked further into the woods, the earthy scent of wet vegetation overpowered the odor of the manure pile behind Hopper's barn. A rustling off to his right drew his attention in time to see a frightened deer—white tail pointing skyward—as it leapt away.

After a couple hundred yards, he turned and began walking a zigzag pattern back toward the clearing. About twenty-five yards from the tree line, he came upon a patch of flattened undergrowth. Had some small pack of animals bedded down? He circled the area, looking for clues. No fur tufts or droppings that he could see.

Something white poked out from under the crushed vegetation. He squatted to see what it was and happened to glance up. There was a clear view of the back of the house and two sides of the barn from this vantage point. A perfect position for someone interested in watching the movements of the inhabitants.

Remembering the reason he had crouched down, he reached toward a scrap of white paper. And then he knew.

There may be coyotes and wildcats native to the area, but neither species had flattened this undergrowth. The beast that had trampled this particular spot had been rolling cigarettes.

Chapter Twelve

Less than an hour later, Renzo reined in Terra in front of Lucy's house. Wink danced as if he hadn't seen him in weeks, and Renzo couldn't help but smile. Maybe he would get a dog when he went home. Since he'd also be buying his own house there'd be no one to object, and the unconditional love these animals doled out lifted his spirits. He gave Wink's jowls a quick scratch and then knocked on the door.

Lucy slipped out onto the porch, apparently ready to go. She had changed into her blue dress and shawl and the braided bun in her hair was still damp.

He, on the other hand, probably smelled like one of the Greenley brothers. "I hope you won't mind me leaving you in the hotel lobby for a few minutes so I can clean up."

"Not a bit."

"Would you mind driving your cart into town? I can hook it up in no time." He didn't even want to get too close until he'd bathed.

"I can do it." She started toward the edge of the porch, but he stopped her.

"No, you're all dressed up. Just have a seat here. I'll get it and be right back." He wanted a minute alone with Thomas anyway. Her furrowed brow reminded him she was used to doing things on her own, but he hopped off the porch and hustled toward the barn before she could object.

A moment later her shout had him pausing outside the door. "Why don't you hitch up one of Thomas's horses instead of Gertie?"

He waved and went inside to Thomas's temporary quarters. "Did Lucy tell you that we're going into town for supper?"

Thomas folded his knife. One crutch appeared to be completed. He leaned the second against the wall.

"That she did, Deputy."

"Call me Renzo." When there was more time to question the older man about it, he'd ask why he seemed so disapproving of him. "Listen, I was just over at the Hopper's farm. Someone's been watching their place from the woods."

Thomas's eyes widened and he leaned forward on the cot. "Do you think the same people might be watching Lucy?"

Renzo needed to take a look in the woods surrounding Lucy's place with a different eye than when he'd been out looking for branches. "I don't know. I'll be back tomorrow to check it out. Meanwhile, does she know how to use a gun?" He never again wanted to see her as upset as she had been the evening the slavers had interrupted their dinner. Telling her he suspected they might be hiding in the woods would probably scare her half to death.

Thomas grabbed the branch he had been working on and opened his knife back up. "Yes, and she's a decent shot, too." The knife froze on the wood. "Do you think it's because of me being here?" Thomas's dark brown gaze demanded honesty.

"I doubt it. That wouldn't explain why someone's watching the Hopper's place. If I had to bet, I'd say it was those slavers. They're probably switching off watching different farms." Renzo started backing away. "Lucy's going to wonder what's keeping me. I'll be back tomorrow. Tonight when she checks in with you, see if you can't encourage her to keep her gun at the ready."

If Renzo suggested it she would demand an explanation. At least Thomas had a few hours to think about how *he* could do it without raising her suspicions.

Lucy fiddled with the tin brooch at her throat as she studied the intricate pattern of the hotel lobby's large carpet. Not only was it the most beautiful floor covering she'd ever stepped on, but looking down helped her avoid the stares of folks as they walked past on their way into the dining room. Judging from the fine fabrics and lace-trims of the female guests, their dresses were much finer that her best attire. She drew her shawl tighter around her shoulders.

Think about something else. Emily and the baby were never far from her thoughts. Lucy had promised to try and keep Renzo away from the house until after dusk. Agnes would no doubt make her sorry for a late milking, but it would give Emily time to sneak back under cover of darkness. Wink was guarding the place, and there'd been no sign of the slave catchers since she'd seen them at a distance a week ago. But now, sitting here alone with plenty of time to fret, she wasn't feeling so confident.

"I hope I didn't keep you waiting too long." Renzo stood before her offering his arm, and every thought in her head evaporated. Save one. He was the most handsome man she'd ever seen. He had washed and changed into a crisp white shirt, tan vest, black trousers and shiny black boots. His wavy hair had been slicked down with water but was already beginning to curl charmingly away from his scalp. Then her gaze fell on his star-shaped badge, an ever present reminder of why their relationship could never deepen. She linked her hand in the crook of his arm the warmth of their contact robbed her of speech.

What's he doing with me?

As he escorted her into the hotel dining room, the finery of both the room and its patrons gave her so much to look at. Since this was probably the only time she'd dine here, she wanted to memorize every detail. Starched white tablecloths made a striking contrast to the elegant, pink and green floral wallpaper. The sound of flatware clinking against plates mingled with diners' conversations. Lucy had half-expected the room to fall silent as they entered, but they passed between the tables relatively unnoticed. They were shown to a small table in the corner and Renzo held her chair for her as she sat. She covertly studied the people around them, hoping to mirror their fine manners.

"Would you like some wine?" Renzo glanced at her over the menu.

"No, thank you." She smiled politely, but thanks to Emmett's drunkenness, she abhorred alcohol. Her shoulders relaxed a few minutes later when Renzo sent the waiter away with only their food order.

He unfolded his napkin. "It looks like Thomas will be finished with his crutches this evening." Renzo toyed absently with the handle of his fork. "He was already working on the second one when I went into the barn."

"Yes, I noticed that when I took his supper. I just hope he doesn't hurt himself trying to get around on them too soon." She anticipated an argument about him taking the Tylers back to his farm before his leg was completely healed. That would mean going back and forth to check on them. "I forgot to ask you, did you find anything at the Hopper's place?"

Renzo's fork clinked against the bottom of his water glass and he set it back in the place setting, clearing his throat. "Not much, but I don't have a lot of experience."

So he hadn't found anything. That was good news to her way of thinking. "Don't be too hard on yourself. There's probably nothing to find. You don't know Mildred the way I do. That woman's not content if she doesn't have something to worry about. Between her carrying on about me being attacked in my home and Charles frothing at the mouth to buy my place-"

Renzo leaned forward. "Charles Hopper wants to buy your farm?"

"Yes. He's made a couple offers since-" She smoothed the napkin in her lap. "Since I took over. I'll give the Hoppers credit, though. They're good farmers and work from sun-up until sunset. And there's really nothing wrong with wanting to expand." She lowered her voice and held a hand up to shield her mouth from anyone who might be good at reading lips. "But he's as cheap as they come. The two offers he's made were an insult." She rolled her eyes and straightened to take a sip of water.

Renzo chuckled. "I believe it. So, do you have family back in Kentucky?"

Her glass shook slightly as she set it down. *Who told him where I'm from? Sheriff Tate?* Just how much had Renzo found out about her past? She dabbed her mouth with her napkin and wondered if she really needed to be so secretive about everything.

"No, no family left." The waiter placed a glass of fresh lemonade before her. She took a sip and held it in her mouth as the tangy sweetness burst over her tongue.

Renzo paused in lifting his own glass. "Good?"

She swallowed and licked her lips. "Like a sugary sunrise." What a treat to enjoy foods that she couldn't afford or hadn't had to first grow and then prepare.

Their meals arrived soon afterwards, and neither one was shy about starting to eat. It had been a long time since she'd had beefsteak. After eating enough chicken, ham and eggs to fill a barn, she had forgotten how rich and satisfying beef could be.

She cut another bite-sized piece. "Why didn't you ever mention that you saved Mabel's son?"

Renzo shrugged. "It happened before we met. I don't know. I suppose it never seemed pertinent to our conversations."

Lucy admired both his bravery and the fact that he wasn't a braggart. She smiled. "I wouldn't have pegged you as a modest man."

He leaned forward and wiggled his eyebrows. "Do you mean if I'd told you what a hero I was, you'd have asked me to dinner willingly?"

"No." Her tone scolded, but it was impossible to suppress her grin. "And shame on you for tricking me that day."

He straightened and refocused on his plate. "But you have to admit, I did ask you to dinner politely first."

"True." And if she hadn't just gotten involved with hiding the Tylers, she might have been more amenable to the invitation.

He wiped his mouth. "Why were you so opposed then?"

Lucy popped a bite into her mouth to give herself time to answer. She didn't want to lie to Renzo any more than she had to. "I didn't know you at all. A woman in my situation has to be very careful who she's even seen talking to."

He lowered his voice. "So our having dinner together, is this considered scandalous?" He winked at her.

Lucy knew her cheeks had to be turning pink. Not because the two of them might be the focus of town gossip, but because his wink made her want to walk around the table, sit in his lap and kiss him until they were both panting for breath. Thankfully he dropped the subject of their "scandalous relationship".

She always had another question for him, since he'd seen so much more of the world. As they ate, he described the ocean and the voyages he taken on his father's ships. She told him how she'd had to leave school at the age of nine when her mother died, and that her father had still encouraged her to read, buying her the occasional book when he could.

By the time the waiter offered dessert, she looked down at her empty plate. She placed a hand on her stomach. "No, thank you. Everything was delicious." It wasn't until the man returned her smile with one of his own that she realized how outgoing she'd been tonight.

Renzo settled the bill and escorted her outside, helping her up onto the cart. His hand on her back burned clear through her dress and undergarments. He tied Terra to the back and climbed onto the seat next to her. When his thigh came into contact with hers, even with the many layers of cloth between them, her heart raced.

The cart rocked and jostled along the road, occasionally bumping them together until they began to sway from side to side as one. Her body heated and she let her shawl drop to her elbows. What a rarity, to be comfortably warm without being bundled.

But it was more than that. Thomas had been right. She *had* formed tender feelings for Renzo. Why did this man have to be the one to awaken her heart as well as her body? There could be no future for them.

"What time is it?" she asked.

He pulled out an expensive-looking pocket watch and flipped open the cover. "Just after eight-thirty. Is there a problem?"

Would Emily have taken the baby back to the barn yet? Although the days were getting shorter, it still wasn't full-on dark.

"Agnes will need milking when I get back." If Lucy stalled their return, poor Agnes would suffer again.

A bump in the road made her grab his arm for support.

"Would you teach me how to do it?"

What? She dropped her hand into her lap, unable to remember what they were talking about with his hard thigh pressing against hers. "Do what?"

"You were talking about milking Agnes, remember? Would you teach me how to do it?"

She chuckled. "With those big hands, you'd bruise the poor dear."

"I've never had a lady complain yet."

Lucy's felt her cheeks flame. A real lady would be outraged, but ever since he had come into her life, her thoughts had been far from ladylike. He'd probably had many lovers, but instead of being jealous, she wanted him to make love to her, too.

"I apologize." He glanced her way, and she hoped the dusk hid her high color. "That was rude." He snapped the reins and Thomas's horse trotted faster.

She wasn't certain how to respond. *I'm not insulted, I'm aroused. The thought of your hands has me jealous of my cow?* Heavens, how depraved.

"Last night's rain is keeping the dust down." It was sorry conversation, but pretending his erotic suggestion hadn't been said seemed safest.

Renzo flicked the reins again, wanting to kick himself. The sexual innuendo would have been charmingly scandalous with many a female acquaintance back in Philadelphia, but Lucy had been forced to retreat, resorting to niceties about the condition of the road.

Damnation. He couldn't seem to keep his thoughts from veering down the path of physical intimacy, and this time he'd given them voice. Every minute he spent with her served to increase his attraction. She was no pampered, perfumed socialite, but damned if she wasn't the most desirable woman he'd ever met. Her energy and purpose were contagious. Intoxicating. Addicting. But his addiction could only be satisfied by a single person. Someone who deserved more than a few delightful tumbles.

He turned the cart down the drive to the farm and neither one spoke until he set his hands at her waist to help her down.

She looked around. "Wink."

Renzo's nerves buzzed. With his earlier discovery at the Hopper's, the dog's absence was too much of a coincidence. They both called and whistled, but Wink didn't return.

Renzo took hold of the horse and started toward the barn. "I'm sure he'll be back. I'll put the horse and cart away."

She looked torn but then nodded and hurried to the barn to milk Agnes.

The combination of darkness and trying not to wake Thomas made Renzo slow at his tasks. Lucy had already left to carry the milk to the spring house, and the thought of her going so close to the woods—with its possible dangers—had him rushing after her. Lantern light sliced through the night as she opened the spring house door and met him outside. He took the lantern from her and held it aloft.

The light cast a soft glow in her face. "Thomas hobbled over to Agnes's stall on his new crutches and milked her before we arrived. All I had to do was put it away." She headed toward the trees. "Wink?" she called. The question in her tone sounded an awful lot like fear.

He stopped her from stepping into the trees by taking her hand. "I'll go look for him." He'd feel better if the dog was here to stand watch before her left. During the day Lucy had a decent chance of seeing trouble approaching, but at night she and Thomas depended on Wink's heightened senses.

"No, you need to be heading back. The other night I worried for nothing. He's probably just got some opossum holed up somewhere and is determined to wait the poor creature out." But the calmer she acted, the edgier Renzo became. He really didn't want to go without knowing Wink was on guard.

Hand in hand, they walked toward the house. "Why don't I see you back inside then I can take the lantern." *If Wink had stumbled upon Mays or one his men he might be hurt.*

Her brow furrowed and she slowed. "Is there something you're not telling me?"

Cristo, the woman is as good at sensing as any bloodhound. He considered lying, but in the end, arming her with information was more important than any weapon. Perhaps it would insure she take extra precautions.

"We'll talk inside." He tugged her hand until she fell into step.

As soon as the door closed behind them, she spun to face him. "What are you hiding? Do you think there's someone out there?" Her raised brows and wide eyes were at odds with her hands-on-hips stance.

"I'm not certain." He took gentle hold of her shoulders. "I found a spot in the woods behind the Hoppers' house that looked as if someone had been hunkered down, watching them."

She fisted his shirtfront. "Do you think it was those men?"

His gut told him yes, but many people rolled their own cigarettes. "I don't know." The crease between her brows compelled him to continue. "They're the first that come to mind, but not the only ones."

She let go of his shirt and pulled that damned shawl tighter around her shoulders. "Who else could it be?"

"I had to throw a vagabond in jail a few days ago. He'd stolen a chicken from Matthew Infordson's henhouse. Matthew and his son followed the fellow back to his camp, and when they found some tools he had taken from their barn, they trussed him up like a Christmas goose.

"And he isn't still in jail?"

"No, since Matthew recovered all his property, including the chicken, he decided not to press charges. He hoped a night behind bars might teach the fellow a lesson." Although Renzo wouldn't tell Lucy, he knew the man couldn't have been responsible for any mischief since then because Renzo himself had helped the man hire on to one of the riverboats early yesterday. "Maybe he'd been watching the Hopper's place before Matthew caught him."

She stared at his shirtfront, silent.

"And there's always the possibility that someone's taken exception to Thomas being here." A few mumblings *had* made it to his ears, but nothing that had raised any alarms. If he was wrong about that, then he had more than Mays and his men to worry about.

"But that wouldn't explain why someone would be watching the Hoppers," she said.

Damn, the woman was too astute. "You're right. But we don't *know* anyone's watching *your* place." Even though this entire conversation was speculation, the dinner in his belly had turned to lead. There was no way he was leaving until he could set his mind at ease. And if that meant sleeping on the porch, so be it.

"I-"

Two gunshots erupted from the woods. Lucy reached for the door but he pulled her down to the floor, shielding her with his body.

"Stay down!"

She fought to get loose but only managed to kick over a chair. "But they're out there without protection!"

"They? What do you mean?" He pushed up on an elbow and she froze.

"T-Thomas and Wink," she stammered. Her fingers dug into his biceps and she pushed against him once more. "I need to make sure they're okay."

"There's no way in hell I'm letting you go out there. I'll check on Thomas and look for Wink, but only if you promise to stay inside where it's safe." His glower warred with hers.

"No, I won't. They're my responsibility. I'm going with you." She shoved his shoulders. "I'll follow you, no matter what you say, so you might as well let me up."

The shooting had stopped after the two rounds, and unless he tied her down she'd do exactly what she threatened. Reluctantly, he got to his feet and helped her stand. "Do you have another gun besides the one you gave Thomas?"

She ran to the bedroom and returned with another shotgun.

"Is it loaded?"

She rolled her eyes. "Of course it's loaded."

"Would you *please* stay here while I check things out?"

"No, I'm going."

Why can't she ever cooperate? "*Cristo.* Alright, but stay behind me." He held her in place until she nodded her grudging ascension. Then he turned down the wick of the oil lamp and opened the back door. They slipped outside and thankfully she stayed close at his back. Halfway to the barn, the big door slid open. A backlit Thomas filled the opening, propped on his crutches.

"I'm okay. The shots came from the woods. Towards the Hoppers' place."

Renzo took hold of Lucy's upper arms. "You stay here with Thomas. I'll look around and be back." He half-expected an argument.

"Be careful."

Renzo pointed to the open doorway. "You and Thomas get inside and keep down."

He made his way up the rise and into the woods. Between the darkness and his unfamiliarity with his surroundings, he didn't intend to venture too far. Leaves rustled and twigs snapped under his feet as he passed through the brush. The chorus of crickets and cicadas that normally performed their summer songs had fallen silent. In the eerie stillness he thought he heard a baby's cry. His ears must be playing tricks on him. A wounded animal?

Wink? Please, God, no! Could the dog have discovered someone spying on the Hoppers and they shot him? A crashing in the underbrush had him swinging toward the sound and pointing his revolver.

"Show yourself." Suddenly Wink raced into view and Renzo lowered his gun, pushing out his breath. The dog jumped in circles and began barking, then headed deeper into the trees.

"Wink."

The dog retraced a few steps to bark at Renzo once more.

"What is it?"

Wink took a few agitated steps, and paused to look back at Renzo.

"Wait for me, boy." Renzo followed as quickly as the darkness and terrain allowed. He wasn't certain of which direction the dog was taking him. Towards Hopper's or Thomas's place? Then he smelled smoke.

Renzo picked up his pace, his pulse pounding like his uncertain steps. Just past the trees, he could see past the far end of a cornfield. Flames curled through the roof and out the windows of Thomas's small cabin. Smoke rose into the sky, blocking the starlight.

"Wink, stay." Renzo took off across the field, hoping that once he got closer, he might find the barn undisturbed. The cabin was lost, but he prayed that the fire hadn't spread to the barn. The stillness of the night would play in his favor, that and the fact that last evening's storm had dampened the ground and surrounding vegetation. It was obvious that even fifty men armed with brimming buckets couldn't save the cabin now.

Heat baked his skin, and he turned his head to shield his eyes. He sprinted in an arc around the front of the cabin and through a cloud of smoke. Struck by a sudden coughing fit, he stumbled to a stop, doubling over, trying to fill his lungs with something other than smoke.

That was when he spotted the hay. Trails of it stretching haphazardly from the barn toward the cabin as if someone had carried armfuls, dropping some along the way. Someone had fueled the cabin fire.

Still coughing, he dropped to his knees and began clearing the trail. Loud cracks sounded from the cabin and a sudden searing on the back of his shoulder had him dropping to his chest and rolling in the dirt. Then he scrambled back to his task. Once he had cleared a wide gap in the hay, he ran to the barn in search of a rake. If he could get it all, perhaps he could keep the fire from creeping along the trail.

The roar of the blaze echoed throughout the clearing as he threw open the double doors, located a rake just inside and sprinted back. For an instant he thought he heard a horse's whinny, but knowing Thomas's horses were safely corralled at Lucy's, he chalked it up as yet another trick of his hearing.

"Deputy!" He looked over his shoulder to see Charles Hopper running toward him. "I smelled the smoke. Is there any livestock in the barn?"

"No," he answered. "We just need to try and contain the fire." The flames seemed to be shrinking. Occasionally sparks from the cabin lurched through the air and gave one last burst before fading in the dirt.

"Some of the corn along the edge of the field will be lost from the heat. But since there's no wind, it looks like it might burn itself out."

"I've got some buckets in my rig," Charles said.

"Good. Let's start filling them from the well and wetting things down."

By the time they'd retrieved all the buckets, two more men had appeared. They began the exhausting work of filling buckets and soaking any surface or plant within fifty yards of the cabin. Finally, with the fire subsided, they slowed their pace.

When Renzo headed back to the well one last time, Lucy was there with Wink at her feet. One of her arms hugged her middle, while the other held the shotgun, muzzle down. Wink whined softly from his place at her feet.

Smoke and sorrow thickened the smoldering air, and Renzo's chest ached at the unshed tears glistening in her eyes. He wanted to take her in his arms, and would have if not for the others' presence. Town gossips were probably already spinning tales since he'd taken her to dinner.

"I'm sorry," he said. "By the time I got here, the cabin was lost." He didn't think now was the time to mention that the fire was no accident.

She nodded. "Mr. Smith says you saved Thomas's barn." Bud Smith, one of the men who'd come to help, stood close by.

Charles approached and set his empty buckets on the now muddy ground. He scowled at Lucy as he straightened and gestured to the rubble. "Come to admire your handiwork?"

Chapter Thirteen

"See what good's come out of your taking a colored man into your home?"

Lucy's hand froze on Wink's head and her jaw dropped.

But before she could speak, Renzo stepped toward Charles. "See here, Hopper. You owe Mrs. Neels an apology, and fast."

Bud, who could easily have been flattened by either man, raised his hands between the two. "Now let's calm down. What with the fire, Charles just got himself worked up, isn't that right?" He nodded at Charles.

But her neighbor was more stubborn than smart. "All's I'm saying is, this fire was set. You know it as well as I do. That cabin went up like a tinderbox."

"That doesn't give you reason to blame Mrs. Neels. If Thomas wasn't staying in her *barn* he could have been trapped inside his cabin and killed."

Safely tucked behind Bud, Charles piped up again. "Why would someone burn him out? He's never had trouble before. I'll *tell* you why. Because up until now, he's known his place."

That's it. She was sorely tempted to lift the shotgun to the snake's face. "Charles Hopper, you're a-"

Renzo covered her hand with his. "If anyone's crossed a line, it's you Hopper." She could tell he spoke through gritted teeth.

Bud pushed two buckets at a wide-eyed Charles and then picked up two more, nodding to the third fellow who'd hung back from the dispute. "I think it'd be best if we all went home. You'll let the sheriff know about this, Deputy?"

Renzo nodded, and the farmers left without another word. Lucy and Renzo stood silently by and watched the bones of Thomas's cabin smolder. Wink leaned against her leg.

"Poor Thomas." By now tears rolled down her cheeks.

Renzo pulled her into his arms and she nestled under his chin. The stench of smoke saturated his clothing.

"How do I tell my best friend that someone burned his home to the ground?" She swiped at her eyes and rested her fist against his chest.

"I'll do it." He stroked her back, and the temptation to let him perform the task enticed like Eve's apple.

"No," she finally said. "But, thank you. Thomas is a very proud man. I think I'd best speak with him. Alone." She pushed away from Renzo, fearing she might lose her nerve if she didn't get it over with quickly.

"Alright, let's go." He lifted the shotgun from her hand and looked down the drive. "Did you bring the wagon?"

"No. I came through the woods." She sensed more than saw his body stiffen. "When you didn't come back, I was worried." She wasn't about to tell him how frightened she'd been of going into the woods. "You don't know these woods. I thought you might have gotten lost. Then I smelled smoke and saw the glow of the flames through the trees."

He put his hand to the small of her back and started toward the field. "I'm too damned tired to scold you about going out in those woods alone."

"I had a gun." She'd have next to no idea where to aim the blasted thing, but now wasn't a good time to admit that.

He didn't belabor the point and, hand-in-hand, they walked through the cornfield. Wink lead the way once they crossed the tree line, and she was blessedly unafraid with Renzo along. Her earlier fear had been two-fold, what with the possibility of being watched, or worse, shot at, and worrying about why he hadn't returned. But now, without those concerns, she tried to decide how to deliver the devastating news to Thomas.

Halfway home, Renzo broke the silence. "Are you certain you don't want me to go in with you?"

"I'm sure." She'd been very lucky earlier. The baby had begun crying scant minutes after he'd left. The close call made it clear that from now on Lucy needed to send him away. "You're exhausted and need some sleep."

"I could say the same for you." He squeezed her hand. Lord, she loved it when he did that.

Enjoy it now, because you need to end this. Tonight. They crossed into the clearing at her homestead and fetched a lantern from the back stoop. Renzo followed her to the small corral by the barn.

Lucy fought to rebuild her defenses. It was time to say goodnight. And goodbye.

He passed in front of her to open the gate.

She gasped. "My God, you're hurt!" He had a hole burned clean through his vest and shirt.

He glanced over his shoulder. "It's not that bad. Just a spark that hit me." The man had a gaping wound which could easily get infected.

She pursed her lips at his lack of concern for his health. "You can't even see it, let alone tend to it. Go into the house and I'll take care of it."

"No, you go speak with Thomas. I'll see the doctor in town tomorrow." He pulled his saddle off the fence.

"Tomorrow's not good enough." She lifted a hand to his sleeve. "Please," she added. "If you put that saddle back and go into the house, I'll speak with Thomas and then tend to your back. It won't take me long."

Looking as exhausted as she felt, Renzo nodded once and flopped the saddle back on the fence rail. "I'm too tired to argue."

She handed him the lantern and headed into the barn. Thomas's oil lamp still burned atop the wooden crate he used as a side table. He sat with his leg stretched out on the ground and his crutches at his side, looking older than he had two hours ago.

"I smelled the smoke." His sorrowful gaze met hers and her stomach plummeted. He knew. Guilt climbed up onto her shoulders and weighed on her like the yoke of an ox.

"Thomas, I'm so sorry. This is my fault. If I hadn't insisted you stay here, this might not have happened." Now that she didn't feel the need to defend herself to the likes of Charles Hopper, she could admit the other man was right.

"The blame isn't yours, child." Thomas shook his head, his gaze falling to his injured leg. "Is everything lost?"

"No," she hurried to say. "The barn is fine. And so are your crops. You won't lose too much of the corn. Just what was scorched along the edge of the field." But for the moment, the devastation of losing his home made those things inconsequential.

Thomas summoned a weak smile. "Well, that's good. If it'd been the other way around, if all's I'd been left with was that old cabin, then things would've been in a sorry state."

She knelt next to him, taking his calloused hands in hers. "I'm so sorry.

"There's no need." He gave her hands a squeeze, then his gaze hardened. "Has the deputy left?"

"No." She understood and shared his concern, but it also hurt that he always disparaged the one person she longed to be with.

"He's in the house." Thomas's warning glare would normally raise her hackles, but tonight her guilt and fatigue far outweighed her pride. "He was burned. I need to bandage the wound before he heads back into town." She stood. "Is there anything I can get you?"

"No. You go on and get the deputy patched up so he can leave."

Renzo leaned his good shoulder against the fence and tried to ignore the pain biting his back. Although he'd offered to break the news to Thomas, he didn't envy Lucy her task. Was she crying right now? Just the thought of it turned his stomach.

The creaking door signaled her return and met her as she rounded the corner. Her cheeks were dry, but her shadowed eyes made her look ready to drop.

"I didn't want you walking to the house in the dark." With the lantern in one hand and the shotgun in the other, he couldn't hold hers. Strange how just holding her hand had become the most natural thing in the world. He planned to do it whenever possible.

Inside the house, she lit an oil lamp on the table and gestured for him to sit. She carried over a pitcher of water and bowl then gathered some things from her bedroom. The throbbing on his upper back hurt like hell now that the excitement was over.

"You'll need to take your shirt and vest off." Lucy was all business, tearing strips of white cloth and avoiding his gaze. Was she embarrassed about him disrobing or did she just want to finish the task and get to sleep?

Too tired to figure it out, he unhooked his gun belt and set it on the table. He pulled off his vest and started on his shirt, grinding his teeth as the cloth stuck to the wound.

"Let me help." The cool touch of her fingers soothed his skin. He tried to focus on that, as she slowly worked the cotton from his charred flesh.

She hissed. "I'm glad we didn't wait to clean this out. It's not huge but it's filthy."

"I rolled on the ground to smother the flames."

She dipped a cloth in the water. "I'm afraid this will hurt, but it has to be done."

Shit. He ground his teeth. Now he knew what Mark went through, and it was his whole arm. Renzo's respect for the lad grew tenfold. When Lucy finally applied salve and wrapped the bandage around his shoulder and back, he let out a long breath. Then she took another damp rag and positioned herself between his spread knees. Lightly brushing his hair out of the way, she wiped his forehead with the cool water. But his temperature spiked.

So much for leaving quickly. Having her so close, with her breasts right in front of his face. He couldn't fight it. His hands settled on her waist and his gaze fixed on a tiny white button between her breasts.

"I want you so damned much that it's killing me."

Her hand froze, and he felt her muscles tense under his fingers. Her silence, her stillness drew out the torture. But he couldn't move.

After endless moments, she set her rag back in the bowl. His heart thudded, as she lifted his hands away and twisted one of hers into his grasp.

"Come."

Chapter Fourteen

Stunned by his confession, Lucy could only utter the single word. Her heart raced as Renzo stood, his big hand encasing hers, and she led him to the bedroom. She wasn't certain what she would do once they got there since her experience when it came to marital relations was unremarkable. But this was Renzo. A man who'd brought out feelings in her she wouldn't have thought herself capable of. Surely she could count on him to take over, guiding her through the motions of *real* lovemaking. For as surely as she knew this could be their only night together, this would be the only time her heart would ever be involved.

At the bed she turned to face him. The room seemed to have shrunk since she'd fetched the first aid supplies only minutes ago. With Renzo's broad shoulders blocking the door and the only lamp burning in the other room, his face fell in shadow.

Should I close the door? Maybe her awkwardness wouldn't be as obvious that way. But not only did she want to *feel* his body against hers, skin to skin as God made them, she wanted to *see* him. The memory of this night would have to comfort her the rest of her days.

"Are you sure?" His deep voice echoed throughout the room.

"Yes."

He lifted her hand to his lips and kissed it so tenderly she wondered if she'd imagined the contact. When he stroked the same spot with his thumb, gooseflesh rippled up her arm. Then he laced their fingers and pulled her close, her breasts pressing against his chest.

"Mio angelo." His whisper stirred the hair at her temple.

She shivered. Whatever the words meant, they sounded divine. Raising her chin with one finger, he brought his mouth down onto hers.

She dared not move, for fear of waking. His kiss was both tender and dizzying, leaving her feeling as if she teetered on the edge of cliff. And when his tongue slid along the seam of her lips, she opened to him. This kind of kissing was intoxicating. Bewitching. Nothing like what she'd known before. She wanted to go on kissing him until the world ended.

She moaned and slid her arms around his neck, desperate to hold him and never let go. Would he know she'd fallen in love with him? For that's what this was. Love. And the thought of sending him away after tonight was ripping her in two.

I can't let him know. She locked her hands behind his head, kissing him as if their connection could pause time. *Not yet. Don't leave me yet.* She'd been starving for this, and her kisses turned greedy, hungry.

Suddenly Renzo was caressing her face. "Shhh. Don't cry, amore." His breath stroked her cheek, his lips catching the tears she hadn't realized were falling. For long moments he gentled her with soft murmurings and delicate kisses. And eventually the madness passed, leaving behind a woman, a man and their desires.

Renzo did his best to calm Lucy, while his body struggled with its own urgency. He wanted their lovemaking to go slowly. Her frenzy had him thinking she'd never been cherished, in or out of the bedroom. Her brute of a husband had probably—no, he wouldn't think about him anymore tonight. He needed to focus on drawing out what was left of this night, and her pleasure.

"*Angelo. Amore*," he whispered in between feather light kisses. The tension in her limbs faded and his stroking moved from her face and shoulders lower, to her breasts. He pulled back to see her eyes close and her lips part.

"That's it, just feel." He bent and tasted her lips again as he massaged her softness. "I've imagined touching you this way so many times. Have you dreamed about it, too?" With her eyes still closed, she nodded. He loved her honesty and lack of guile.

"Open your eyes."

She did.

"I'm going to take all of your clothes off."

Lucy blinked, wide-eyed, but didn't protest. Thank God. He reached for the brooch the base of her neck.

"Shall I return the favor?" Her voice quavered.

What spirit. He suspected taking a lover wasn't something she'd done often, but he also knew she was determined enough to reach out and grab what she wanted.

"I'm counting on it." He set her pin on the top of the tall dresser, already thinking about replacing it with a sapphire brooch to compliment her eyes.

Feeling her pulse flutter against the back of his fingers, he released the small top button on her bodice. Her eyes glistened as he slowly unfastened the next, and the next. She held her shoulders straight and tall as he pushed the bodice of her shirtwaist off her shoulders and down her arms. God, she was beautiful, and her trust humbled him. He'd do everything he could to guarantee she didn't regret their time together.

He tossed the cloth, still warm from her body, on a chair and reached around to unhook her skirt. Seconds later, it sank to the floor. She continued to stand before him, not shyly but tall in her unadorned, cotton undergarments. They did have one redeeming quality. They were blessedly thin. The shadow of her nipples taunted him through gossamer cotton.

His hand cupped her cheek. "You are so damned beautiful." He kissed her, at the same time loosening hair and cradling the back of her head. His lips nibbled all the way down to her neck with gentle love bites. While he nipped along her jaw line and back up to her mouth, her corset was tossed blindly away. Oh, her sweet mouth. Those soft, eager lips. This woman was made to be kissed. Often, and most thoroughly. Moments later her petticoat lay on the floor.

"I need you," she sighed against the corner of his mouth. "Make love to me."

"My pleasure." He pressed his arousal against the softness of her belly, and she pushed right back. *God, that feels good.* Their tongues tangled, and his hands slid under the hem of her shift and squeezed her smooth bottom.

She moaned into his mouth and drove her fingers into his hair. *Cristo,* her excitement had him too close.

Renzo broke the kiss. "Let's get rid of this. I want to see all of you." He lifted the hem and she helped send the paper-thin cloth flying somewhere into the darkness.

Finally, she was naked. And all his. This night was ending far better than he could have hoped.

He sunk onto the edge of the bed, taking hold of her waist and pulling her between his splayed thighs. "I've thought about doing this a thousand times."

She trembled, but the fingertips stroking his nape made him suspect her shivers were in anticipation, rather than fear. He pulled her closer and took one budded nipple into his mouth, determined to force everything from her mind but pleasure. Her startled inhalation melted into a long sigh as he suckled her sweetness. He would never tire of this.

Her fingers threaded through his short hair, and she arched her back in offering. Renzo smiled around her nipple then pulled even more of her soft flesh into his mouth. The scent of roses nestled in the warmth between her breasts, making him want to burrow deeper. She rocked into him, an instinctual motion he'd soon mimic when his body joined with hers.

Soon. But not yet. There was more of her to explore first. He released her breast and licked the straining nipple. Then he drew its twin into his mouth. Her legs buckled, and he caught her easily, laying her on the bed. Her long, wavy tresses fanned out behind her head, and her hands reached out.

She plumped her full bottom lip. "But I was supposed to undress you."

"I'll have you help next time," he promised, standing. Seconds later, he had stripped out of everything but his bandage. Looking down on her, naked and yielding with her arms lifted as in invitation, he counted himself as the luckiest man alive. He joined her on the bed and bent to her breast wanting to feast on her softness for hours.

Her legs shifted, and her fingertips dug into his back. "I need you."

God he needed her, too. So much. But if he sunk into her now, he'd be spent in a heartbeat. He slid his hand down her belly, searching for the place where she longed for him. And as he savored her nipple, his fingers reached between her moist folds to the center of her sex.

Lucy gasped. "Ohhhh."

Oh, indeed. She was *so* ready for him, but he fought it. The first time would be hers if it killed him. He moved to her other breast, still stroking. She writhed in cadence to his caress and levered her body flush against his.

"I need…"

He lifted his head, intending to obey her if she asked, but her request died on her lips as she stiffened, tumbling over the precipice of pleasure. He took her mouth, swallowing her cries of passion. Glorying in them. Fueled by them. Her hips rocked rhythmically against his hand, and she returned his kisses with a hunger as ravenous as his own.

I can't wait. Moving quickly between her thighs, he positioned himself at her entrance and thrust inside. "Santo-"

No feeling could ever surpass this. But when he moved and plunged into her again, he knew he'd been wrong. This was better.

Lucy's hands scraped down his back to squeeze his backside. "Don't stop. Don't ever stop."

"Not a chance." He was too damned close. That sense of urgency drove him and he pumped faster.

Her body gripped, tugged and massaged. Again and again, until-

Bam. He hit that summit full force and went flying over the ledge into oblivion.

After long moments Renzo came back to earth and rolled to her side. Lucy's eyes were closed and her soft breasts rose and fell with her breathing. She was so damned beautiful. Inside and out. So why had she kept herself hidden beneath sack-cloth coats and a prickly temperament?

"Oh, my." She sounded half asleep already.

He fingered a section of silken hair. It wouldn't take long to recover, and he was determined to take her again, but he'd prefer her rested and anxious.

"Shh. Sleep, *mio angelo.*" He stoked her hair, continuing to whisper in Italian. She curled into him tucking her head under his chin. And within moments, she slept.

But he stayed awake, his mind too busy

formulating plans. He'd come to care for Lucy, more than any other woman he'd ever known. No, he hadn't intended to become her lover, but now that he had, leaving her here when he left was out of the question. Should they marry here? Yes, it would be easiest to take her to Philadelphia as his new bride.

He heard an odd, clicking noise and suddenly Lucy began to shiver in his arms. Her teeth chattered.

What the hell? Sure, they hadn't bothered to pull down the quilt so they were naked on top of the bed coverings, but it was August. He eased off the bed and was attempting to cover her when she sat straight up in bed.

Her widened eyes were filled with panic, and she wrapped her arms around her shoulders as if for warmth. "Please, Emmett. Let me out. It's so cold."

Renzo's gut knotted. She was having a nightmare, and judging from the way her teeth rattled like a telegraph machine, it was realistic as hell.

"Lucy." He climbed onto the bed and took hold of her upper arms. "Lucy, wake up." Pulling her closer, he used his body to ease her nightmarish chills.

"Wha-" She woke with a start and sagged into his embrace. "Oh, God."

"You were having a nightmare." He rubbed her back and arms. "You don't feel cold, but you're teeth were chattering." She'd also been begging her sonofabitch, late husband to let her out. Of where? What the hell had the man done to her?

She sniffed. "I'm sorry I woke you."

Renzo concentrated on disguising his rage at Emmett Neels. "Don't be sorry." He kissed her forehead. "But I would like to know where you were locked up."

She stiffened in his hold. "It—it was a long time ago." Although she didn't physically pull away, her reluctance to discuss the nightmare was tangible.

"That may be true, but you were living through it all over again. If you're still having nightmares after all this time, then maybe you should try talking about it." Bottling up all her fear hadn't helped.

"You think I should face my demons."

He wouldn't blame her if she refused but he also didn't see how talking about it could make things any worse. He kept her tucked snug under his chin, hoping his closeness helped.

After a few moments, she took a deep breath. "What exactly did I say?"

"You were begging Emmett to let you out. Where did he lock you up?

After a moment of silence, she said, "In the smoke house."

I'll tear it down with my bare hands. He pulled the quilt up over her shoulders, giving her time to sift through her thoughts.

"It was January and I only had on what I'd worn out to the henhouse to gather eggs..." Her voice wavered, and she took another deep breath. "I'd forgotten to buy coffee the last time I'd been in town." That's where she left off her story.

He knew heartless men who worked on the docks, but to freeze your wife to death because there was no coffee? That kind of cruelty was inhuman.

"How long did he leave you in there?"

This time she was quiet for a long time.

"I'm sorry. Forget I asked."

She swiped at her eyes. "No, you're right. Maybe if I tell someone I can finally put it behind me." She paused, and he held his breath. "I was in there two days."

Two days! In January? *That God-damned bastard.*

She gently cupped his cheek, pulling him to face her. "But I survived." Her smile and reassuring tone pole-axed him. The woman had survived outright torture and she thought he was the one who needed comforting?

Protectiveness slammed into him with unexpected force. No one would ever hurt her again. "You are *the* bravest, strongest, most honest woman I have ever met."

She dropped her chin, but he wouldn't allow anything to come between them. Not even modesty. Tilting her face up, he pressed his lips to hers, cutting off what she was about to say. It could wait. She'd already shared her deepest secret with him, and he didn't have the words to tell her how much he appreciated her trust. So he'd show her.

Her arms twined around him, as his hand glided over her hip and palmed her bottom.

She coxed him in between her parted thighs and his eager sex prodded hers. "Make love to me . . . Renzo."

He froze. "Finally, you used my given name." She kissed the spot on his chest above his heart. Could she know it threatened to burst through the wall of his chest? He raised himself up with one hand and guided himself to her entrance, plunging inside.

Gesù Cristo. He held himself still, giving her time to adjust to his rough invasion.

"I'm fine." Her fingers trailed over his flanks and gripped his backside, setting off a tingling that rippled from the base of his spine to his nape. As he bent and kissed her, he began to move. His tongue mated with hers, swirling and mimicking the motion of his hips. She hooked her heels behind him, holding him a willing prisoner. Urgency grew and swelled within his chest like an endless rising tide, building, building. Every inch of his length throbbed with need. He broke the kiss and lifted his upper body, raising his face to the sky and speeding his thrusts. Faster, harder, driving, conquering.

She cried out in pleasure just as lightning flashed behind his closed lids, bursting white light again and again in the darkness of his mind. He drove into her and froze, his back arched in ecstasy as he spilled his seed into her warm depths. The spasms of pleasure radiating throughout his body went on and on, draining what little strength remained.

Early morning sun peeked around the edges of the shutters as Lucy slit her eyes open. From there, her sense of touch—for her bare back was pressed up against Renzo's bare front—brought her full awake. Last night hadn't been a decadent dream. They'd made love and fallen asleep in one another's arms.

The memory of their love-making still tumbled through her brain and hummed within her body. It had been glorious. Totally different than the marriage act she had known. The exquisite pleasure when he had touched her. And when he had pushed inside her body, oh, even now she longed for him to do it again.

But her longing accompanied a wave of despair, for the night had ended. The Tylers were in her barn. It was imperative that she drive Renzo away quickly, without falling apart in the process. An impossible task. She couldn't think about spurning him while she lay snuggled next to his warm, hard body. And she definitely couldn't talk to him naked.

She lifted his wrist, surprised at the dead weight of his arm, and tried to slide off the bed. He moaned sleepily and pulled her back flush with his body. A firm arousal pressed against her bottom, and she bit back a cry of frustration, knowing that what she wanted and what was best were on opposing sides of a very broad divide. The time to push him away had to be now, and if she didn't do it fast, she'd never be able to.

She hardened herself against the threat of tears and squirmed her way out of his hold. Grabbing her shift and drawers from the floor, she pulled them on. Hearing him stirring, she stepped into her petticoat and fastened the waistband.

Renzo pushed himself up on one elbow and scrubbed his hand through his hair. "If it wasn't for last night's tragedy, I'd ask where the fire was."

She forced herself to look away. Having him lying

naked in her bed, with the scent of their love-making still clinging to their bodies brought on another wave of despair. She didn't want to send him away. She wanted to tell him about the Tylers. She wanted him to hold her and say that he chose her over the law.

"Is there something wrong?"

"No," she said, almost choking on the word.

The bed-springs creaked. "Lucy, I know neither one of us planned on what happened last night, but we can't pretend it didn't."

"I have a farm to tend to. Poor Agnes is probably ready to burst." She pulled a blouse and her brown skirt off a hook, praying she could get them on and leave before he got out of bed. She wouldn't be able to play her role if he stood naked as a jay-bird in front of her.

She heard him flip the covers back and stand. He crossed to her and tried to take her in his arms.

"I keep forgetting about the animals. Can I help?"

"No!" She swatted his hands and stumbled away, her breathing suddenly ragged. "You shouldn't be here. Everyone in town will know what happened since you didn't go back to the hotel." She didn't really think people took much notice of her, but it was the best excuse she could think of. Her throat burned from holding back tears, and her conscience was in shreds for treating him as if he'd done something wrong.

His rounded eyes and raised brows tripled her guilt. He stood there, palms up and splendidly naked. "Lucy, what the hell's the matter?"

"I told you." Needing escape more than her next breath, she scanned the floor for her boots. "I want you to leave, Renzo. Last night was a mistake. One that I won't repeat." She pulled on one boot, not caring that she didn't have on stockings.

"Talk to me." He took a step forward then froze when her glare dared him to take another. Frustration spread across his features, creasing his brow and forming his lips into a straight line. He bent to gather his clothes.

She prayed he was angry enough to leave rather than follow her. "I'll saddle your horse," she offered, pulling on her other boot and hurrying from the room.

"The hell you will," he called after her.

Damnation. She could run outside, but Lucy had a feeling he wasn't going to leave without an argument. Best to keep it inside the house. Thomas and the Tylers don't need to hear all the details. She went to the kitchen to fill Wink's bowl and fix Thomas's breakfast tray.

Renzo followed, bare-chested save for his bandage, and still tugging on his trousers. "Tell me what I've done wrong." His unshaven jaw flexed in thinly controlled anger.

While she sliced bread, she tried to summon a bit of the strong-willed temperament she regularly showed Charles Hopper. "You didn't do anything wrong. Last night was a mistake, is all. Now the women in these parts will be worried that I'm after their husbands, and the men will want to find out if I'm as loose as they've heard." She set the bread plate next to a jar of apple butter and met his gaze. "I appreciate what you did for Thomas last night, saving his barn and crops. And I also thank you kindly for dinner in town, but I'd like for you to leave now and not come back." She bit the inside of her cheek.

He pushed his arm through his sleeve and waved a hand. "Now wait a minute. If you'd just listen." He shook his head. "This isn't the way I wanted to do this."

"That's right. Let's not argue. If you'd just leave we can forget-"

"Damn it, Lucy, you're going to marry me."

Chapter Fifteen

"What did you just say?" Her eyes narrowed.

Shit. That came out wrong. "I mean, I want you to marry me. I want to take you back to Philadelphia with me. I'll buy you a house. A house that would make this place seem like a..."

Her eyes suddenly widened and her lips pressed together.

Well, hell, it wasn't like he'd planned on this. But what's done is done. She could already be carrying his child and he wasn't about to shirk that kind of responsibility. He buttoned his shirt.

"It doesn't matter what folks around here say. As my wife you'll have everything you could ever want." What woman in her situation wouldn't give anything to have the kind of lifestyle he was offering?

"How very generous," she practically spit each syllable, "But no thank you." Tears pooled in her eyes. She spun and marched, stiff-spined, to the back door. "Now, if you're through insulting my home and the way I live, I'd like you to leave." She grabbed the knob. "See yourself out."

Wink pushed his way in the back door as she opened it, then seemed to be deciding whether he should follow his mistress or run to his breakfast dish. Food won out, and Lucy slammed the door behind her.

Renzo ground his teeth, whipping out a chair to sit and pull on his boots. He didn't know what had happened between last night and now, but it was like he'd awakened with a different woman in his arms. Maybe they both needed some time to think. After all, neither of them had planned on becoming lovers.

He stood and buckled his gun belt around his hips. Funny how quickly he'd grown accustomed to wearing the thing. Just as surprising, he'd come to think of these people as more than mere acquaintances. He'd miss Mabel and the boys, Sheriff Tate and the Andersons once he took Lucy back to Philadelphia. And, dammit, she *would* go with him. Ross Shipping had provided a generous living to his family. She'd never again have to do this backbreaking work. Didn't she understand that? He pounded both fists on the table, focusing absently at a stitched sampler propped on the mantle.

Did her reluctance come from the idea of leaving her home and moving to a strange place?

That's got to be it. A few hours alone to think back on how easy her life could be would have her seeing reason and packing her bags. But what was worth packing? The battered table? Certainly not her clothing. He'd buy her everything new, from garters to bonnets to cushioned chairs.

Convinced at how sensible his plan was, he headed out the back door and toward the paddock. He'd report back to Sheriff Tate, then clean himself up and return. Surely she'd be in a better frame of mind by that time.

He'd seen the direction she'd taken through the window, but she was still out of sight. So, she intended to hide in the privy? Fine. He'd be back soon enough and she wouldn't be able to avoid him then. He saddled his horse, encouraged by Lucy's inability to face him. Perhaps she knew he'd be able to convince her with a bit more persuasion. And after last night, he knew exactly what method of persuading he'd use.

By the time he'd mounted Terra there was still no sign of her. *Too stubborn by half.*

Renzo turned his horse toward the drive and was just about to give him heel when a noise inside the barn broke the morning quiet. His stomach twisted as it continued to sound.

A baby's cry. Suddenly bits and pieces of the past weeks snapped together, forming a cohesive canvas of deception.

He jumped off Terra's back, tied the reins off and strode into the barn. From the loft above, the infant's wailing went on and on.

So that's why she was in such a damned hurry for me to leave.

"Deputy, listen." Thomas hobbled toward him on one crutch, the man's other hand curled behind his back.

Renzo drew his revolver and pointed it at his chest.

Thomas halted, fighting for his balance.

"I don't want to shoot you, but if you take one more step toward me, I will." Renzo hoped they might avoid that tragedy. "Drop the knife."

Feet pounded outside and the door groaned. Wink bounded inside and spun round in excited circles.

Lucy followed right behind. "No! Don't shoot!"

Thomas dropped the knife at his feet as she ran between them.

Renzo lowered his gun, circled her to retrieve the knife and pitched it into the far recesses of the barn.

She tugged at his sleeve. "Renzo, please. You can't turn them over to those men. They just want their freedom."

The impact of her words robbed him of speech. The fact that she thought him the kind of man to turn in runaway slaves cut deeper than any blade could. He shrugged her off and climbed the ladder, determined to face all her secrets.

With each rung, the baby's muffled cries drowned out Lucy's tearful pleas. He stepped into the loft and rounded the mound of hay, freezing in his tracks.

A negro woman, flanked by two older children, pressed a tiny newborn to her chest. Three pair of wary eyes watched as if they expected him to start shooting. Their terrified expressions would haunt him for the rest of his life.

He held up a palm in a gesture of assurance. The other went to his aching chest. *What have I done to make everyone consider me such a monster?*

"There's no need to fear. I promise you, I won't tell anyone that you're here." He backed away and climbed down the ladder. Wink danced at his feet, but he ignored the dog and headed to the door. He needed to put some distance between himself and these people. From Lucy and her lies.

She rushed to him, stopping short of touching him. Her blue eyes glistened. "You won't hand them back to the slave catchers, will you?"

He fought the urge to rub his hand over his aching heart. "No." He went around her, determined to keep walking.

"How do we know we can trust you?" Thomas called.

Renzo stopped and turned just shy of the door, meeting the older man's gaze. "You don't." Then he looked at Lucy. "Neither of you really *know* me at all."

"Renzo." She stepped quickly to catch him by the sleeve. "Maybe you should stay so we can talk."

He shook her off and slipped out the door, unwilling to do or say anything more to slow his escape.

Ten minutes ago he would have sold his soul for her to ask him to stay.

But that was before he knew he'd been betrayed by someone he'd trusted.

Again.

Lucy watched the door close, biting back a cry. Tears ran rivers down her cheeks. He couldn't even bear to look at her. She had no right to expect an ounce of pity or forgiveness. After all, he'd done nothing to deserve the way she'd treated him. All the lies.

Nausea twisted in her belly and she grabbed the wall, steadying herself. Lord, it was all too much. Finding Renzo pointing a gun at Thomas—who'd had his own knife at the ready. Seeing the two men she loved most in this world inches away from killing one another. She pressed a hand to her stomach.

The danger they all faced now was her doing. If she hadn't encouraged Renzo's attentions, if she'd followed Thomas's advice and sent him away from the very beginning, none of this would have happened.

"Lucy," Thomas said. "You should check on Emily and the children. Then we need to decide what we're going to do." He gave her a nod.

By the time she reached the loft, the baby had quieted. Emily and the children had gathered their few belongings and sat together, ready to leave. Lucy had expected them to bombard her with questions about how they could get away during the daylight, so their quiet calm took her by surprise.

Lucy tried for a smile of reassurance. "Deputy Ross didn't arrest me or any of you. I believe he'll keep his word."

"How can you be sure?" Emily asked.

Lucy knelt in front of them, wishing Emily had witnessed the respect Renzo had always given Thomas, and the way he'd put himself in danger trying to save the cabin. "I can't look inside his heart and promise you. But I can tell you that he has never done anything to make me question his word."

Emily lightly bounced the drowsy baby in her arms, her gaze hard and serious. "After those three men come here, did you ever ask the deputy if he was looking for us, too?"

Lucy gasped. "No. I've never discussed you or the slave catchers business. I didn't want Renzo even considering where you might be."

"Do you think he'd forgotten about us just because you never talked about it?" Emily's voice held no censure, but her unwavering gaze scolded well enough.

Lucy squeezed her hands together, fighting the urge to defend herself. "No. I've been kidding myself. About a lot of things."

"Don't matter now. We're ready to leave."

"You can't go. Not in daylight. Mays and his men have been watching from the woods. I'll talk to Thomas about getting you somewhere safe tonight."

It took a few more minutes, but finally Emily agreed they should wait until dusk.

Lucy left, needing time to think. About Renzo, his vow not to reveal the Tylers. The way she'd hurt him with her lies of omission. Perhaps it had been the look of devastation on his face that made her think he'd keep his word. Although he despised *her*, what he'd said and the way he'd acted had her thinking they *could* trust him. Too bad she hadn't felt that certainty earlier, before her lies had become insurmountable. How ironic this situation was. She'd *finally* managed to drive him away, but not before he'd discovered everything.

"They seem alright." she told Thomas. "Come over to Agnes's stall so we can talk while I work." Streams of cow's milk rung against the bottom of the metal pail by the time Thomas hobbled in.

"I need to move them tonight."

She shook her head. "You aren't able to walk, let alone run. And neither is Emily." Lucy leaned her cheek against Agnes' warm side as she worked. It helped her relax. "Besides, I think we can trust Renzo."

Thomas leaned against the wall. "Your feelings for him have blinded you. He's the law."

That's where Thomas was wrong. She hadn't been blind. She'd seen the danger the entire time she'd been falling in love. Stupidly, she'd hoped that spending time with him away from the farm would be safe.

But now she considered the possibility she and Thomas had been wrong all along. "I don't think Renzo is a danger. You saw his face and heard what he said. He promised Emily that he'd keep their secret. Why would he do that if he didn't mean it?"

Thomas moved closer and lowered his voice. "Your blind faith in that man is putting all of us at risk."

She pressed her cheek more firmly against Agnes, trying to borrow from the cow's steady calmness. "What choice do we have? You're in no shape to take them anywhere. And it's not like I can start traipsing through the woods with them in broad daylight. I also don't know the first thing about that kind of journey. So unless you see those slave catchers riding up the drive, no one is going anywhere before nightfall."

Thomas straightened. "You're right about us not having much choice. Better start praying you're right about the deputy being a man of his word." He hobbled away, and she blew out her breath in a huff. How could she convince Thomas that Renzo wouldn't give them away when her argument was grounded in nothing more than intuition?

As difficult as it was relive what happened, she couldn't keep her mind from it. She'd seen Renzo furious at Charles last night, but today his blank expression and unwillingness to stop and listen was very different. Whatever was going through his head, he'd made one thing clear. He wanted to have nothing to do with her. If the price of his silence was leaving him be, she'd pay it. She'd known her memories of last night would have to comfort her from now on. Didn't make it hurt any less.

After breakfast and tending the animals, she returned to the loft. The Tylers had washed and rinsed the baby's spare nappies in a bucket and had stretched a line for them to hang dry.

Emily whispered to the older children. "If you promise to stay still, you can take the paper and pencils over to where there's more light." Rosalee and James carried their precious supplies to the edge of the loft. Neither one uttered a word, and Lucy hated that their feeling of safety had been destroyed because of her selfishness.

"That was mighty kind of you to get those," Emily whispered.

Lucy nodded. "I'm sorry they can't be running and playing and laughing."

Emily sat down next to her sleeping baby. "Can you sit a while?" She gestured to the hay. Perhaps the children weren't the only ones who were anxious and bored. If Emily was used to days as busy as Lucy's, then the woman was probably going stir crazy, too. Besides, even though Renzo had returned to town a few hours ago and nothing had happened, Emily was probably still worried about him coming back to haul them all into jail.

Lucy sat on the opposite side of the baby and couldn't resist caressing her tiny fist. Amazing, her thumbnail was smaller than a tiny kernel of corn.

She met Emily's gaze. "I'm sorry, I haven't spent much time with you all."

"With all you have to do?" Emily waved a hand. "Why, even back in Virginia, I had Rosalee to help me with my work. You got no one."

Lucy hoped their conversation would keep Emily's mind off Renzo. "That's why I sold off the hogs. I buy ham and bacon from one of the other farmers. Between tending the chickens, Agnes, the garden and trips to town, there's plenty to keep my busy." She crossed her ankles under her skirt. "So the children were allowed to stay with you in the kitchen?"

Emily's smile faded and she bent to stroke her baby's dark hair. "Yes, but Rosalee was 'bout to be trained for a house maid."

"I don't understand. I mean, wouldn't working as a maid be better than laboring in the fields?"

From his bunk below the children, Thomas started reading aloud from his bible.

Emily continued in a whisper. "Not better for Rosalee. See, she be blossoming soon." Emily met her gaze, and suddenly understanding twisted Lucy's stomach.

"Massa Barnaby already been taking too much notice of her. That's why we had to leave right quick."

"But she's just a child," Lucy said through gritted teeth. "What kind of lecher would prey on an innocent child?"

Emily blinked back tears, looking down at her newborn daughter. "That one would. He done it to me often enough." Then after a thoughtful pause, she met Lucy's gaze. "Started about thirteen years ago."

Lucy's hand flew to her mouth, stifling her gasp. Emily's owner had raped her thirteen years ago. Oh, Lord. She hadn't wanted to ask about the father of her children. That explained why the children had such light coloring. And that devil would have done the same thing to Rosalee. His own daughter!

She crawled around the baby's blanket and pulled a teary Emily into her arms. She rocked her, just as Thomas had done to James after the slavers had wrecked the cabin.

"I'm so, so sorry. We'll get you to freedom. You shouldn't have to worry about your children's safety that way." They were quiet for a long time, the only noise the occasional rustle of straw and the faint ruckus of chickens in the yard.

Finally Emily sat back, wiping her eyes on her thread bare sleeve. "I'm so grateful for all you done for us. It's cause of us you had to lie to your man."

Caught off guard, Lucy struggled for words. "He, he's not my man." No matter how much she wished it. Even though they'd shared their bodies, Renzo wasn't in love with her.

"I've seen the way you look after he's been here. And I've heard how he talks about you to Thomas when you're not around. That man's in love."

But Emily was wrong. Renzo had been helpful the past few weeks, and he felt sorry for her living in what must seem like squalor, but he'd said nothing of love. She couldn't let Emily go on thinking her family had separated two people desperately in love.

"No, I've lied to him time and time again." He hadn't even been able to look at her before he'd left. "I encouraged him when I knew it wasn't wise and look what's happened."

Emily stiffened. "But you said you trust him with our secret."

She patted Emily's hand. "I do. He may hate *me*, but he said he wouldn't give you away, and I believe him. Besides, if he planned to arrest us, he would have done it by now." She squeezed Emily's hand until the woman's grip relaxed.

The baby stirred and Emily reached over to rub her back. "Your soul's entwined with his."

Lucy's stomach fluttered. "What?"

"That's what my momma used to say about true love. Souls are wound around each other, like those pole bean vines out there in your garden."

"No, we may have—" She cut herself off, but it was too late.

Emily's gaze said she knew what Lucy'd been

about to admit. "If you love that man then you should be showing him every chance you get. Thomas said the deputy would be heading back east soon enough. I wouldn't be surprised if he don't ask you to go on along with him."

A lump swelled in Lucy's throat and she dropped her gaze. Renzo had brought up marriage short hours ago, even though it had been for pity's sake. Undoubtedly, he was thanking his lucky stars she hadn't accepted. She picked up a piece of hay and bent it in half.

"Why, with a big, strong man like that, you'd have your own crop of children soon enough."

Lucy's head shot up, and her heart skipped a beat before taking off like a weathervane in a windstorm. Children? If she'd been standing she would have toppled to the ground. As it was, she sunk a hand into the hay to steady herself.

Why hadn't the possibility occurred to her? When was her last cycle? She thought back through recent weeks. Over three. Although the chances were slim, the idea that she could be carrying Renzo's child sparked a bittersweet flame inside her breast. The Lord had blessed her once already, but she'd lost that child. She should have left Emmett as soon as she'd figured it out. Was it possible that she'd get a second chance at motherhood?

"Lucy?" Emily's fingers touched her wrist. "I'm sorry if I upset you." She met the woman's dark brown gaze. "Just because you lost one child don't mean you won't have more."

"No, I'm fine. Really." What better way to lift her spirits than to imagine that their union might have created a child. "But I'm afraid Renzo and I aren't meant to be together. My lies have been too great."

She stood, brushing the hay from her skirt. "I'd better get moving. Since I didn't make it into town yesterday, I'll be missed. I need to take the milk and eggs in before someone comes to look for me." And she'd dream about a baby with ebony curls and honey-hued eyes all the way there.

Renzo spurred his horse as if trying to outrun this nightmarish morning. He leaned forward, pressing his weight into the stirrups, and let his muscles stretch and flex along with Terra's movements. The wind filled his shirt like square sails on a blustery day, but did nothing to cool his temper. Any fool would have seen through to the real reason Lucy feared those thugs. How could he have been so blind?

"Ha-yah," he yelled, encouraging more speed from the horse. The trees blurred in his periphery and yet self-disgust remained doggedly on his tail. Even if Terra sprouted wings like the mythical Pegasus and rose above the clouds, he wouldn't be able to escape the shame of being duped.

Terra's nostrils flared and he snorted, drawing Renzo back to reality. His horse's heavy breathing brought him more shame.

He straightened. "Ea-sy, boy." They slowed and he guided Terra off the dirt road to a shady spot under the canopy of trees. The slave catcher's camp was only another mile down the road, and he wasn't sure he could follow through with the sheriff's instructions. As he dismounted, he thought back to his conversation with Tate.

"You're wearing your heart on your sleeve, son. Not that I like slave catchers either." But the sheriff didn't know the real reason for his anger. "But you're emotionally involved, what with getting to know Thomas and Mrs. Neels, and fighting the fire. All I need you to do is tell Mays I want to speak with him. Nothing more. Can you do that?"

Renzo had gritted his teeth and said yes, but now he wasn't so sure. They'd burned Thomas's house to the ground. Just because he was a negro. Evil bastards.

He ran his sleeve across his brow and continued

walking Terra under the cover of the trees. Not far away, the faint trickling of a stream invited them to search it out. He turned and led his horse through the trees and down a small incline to the water.

By now, Sheriff Tate would have driven a rig out to Thomas's farm to have a look around at the damage. As soon as Renzo delivered the sheriff's message to Mays, he was to contact the surrounding farmers to see if anyone had seen or heard anything that might be related to the fire. But he knew it had been intentionally set. Even that horse's ass, Charles Hopper, thought so.

Renzo led Terra back up the hill to the road and within minutes they trotted into the slaver's camp. Fred was sleeping by an unlit fire. Dead to the world, he cradled a half-empty, open whiskey bottle in his arm. With only one horse tied nearby, Renzo figured the other two men were out scouting.

The thought of one of those bilge rats knuckled down in the woods behind Lucy's place made his shoulders knot with tension. He clenched his fists, so powerful was the urge to pulverize the three and ship their remains back down south as a message to others of their ilk.

And as much as he didn't want to return to Lucy's place, his conscience wouldn't allow him to ignore the threat. Their safety, all of them, had to take priority over his shredded pride.

Deliver the message and get the hell out.

"Hey!" he yelled.

Terra shifted under him and blew out his own equine summons.

Fred woke with a start, dropping the bottle. "Fuck!" He fumbled for it as it rolled, emptying most of its contents. He scrambled onto his hands and knees and finally managed to right the bottle.

"You sonofabitch. Look what you done." He wiped off the top with his grimy shirttail, forcing dirt down inside the neck of the bottle. Further proof that Mays was the brains of this ragged crew.

"Where are your friends?"

Fred stood, glaring at Renzo with blood-shot eyes. "None of your fuckin' business. That's where."

Renzo squeezed the reins. "I have a message for your boss."

Fred's nostrils flared, but surprisingly, he listened.

"Sheriff Tate wants you all to stop in to his office today."

The man stumbled forward. "Has he heard something about our runaways?" The question took Renzo by surprise. Fred sounded like he didn't know they were suspected of setting last night's fire.

Renzo didn't think the man could be that good of an actor. "All I know is he wants to see all three of you. Today." Fred's unexpected reaction added to his mounting unease. He swung Terra's head about and galloped away, seeing past his anger long enough consider the possibility that Mays and Gil could indeed be watching Lucy's place. Right this minute.

Chapter Sixteen

Lucy bid a quiet goodbye to the children and climbed down the ladder to find Thomas hobbling along the wall without his crutches.

Her hands went to her hips. "What are you doing? It's too soon for you to be putting weight on that." She retrieved his crutches and pushed them into his hands.

"I'm just seeing how I get along without them. I know you think we can trust the deputy, but I don't have as much faith in him as you. I could move Emily and the children out tonight. Maybe get them over to Southington." The small community of free, colored families liked to help runaways but it was more than twenty miles away. At the rate Thomas and Emily would travel, it would take a lot more than one night.

"Last week Renzo mention the slave catchers were spotted over by Southington. Besides, look at you." Under normal circumstances he took the summer heat in stride, but now, leaning heavily on his crutches, perspiration trickled down his face and marked his shirt.

"Your leg isn't fully healed." She laid a hand on his arm. "Please lay down before you do some permanent damage."

He let her help him settle back on his cot, but gripped her arm, preventing her escape. "If you're wrong about the deputy-"

She yanked her arm free. "If he intended to arrest us, he would have done it before he left." Renzo had been gone for hours and no one had stormed the farm to capture Emily and the children. Each minute that passed proved he was a man of his word. "I have to get going. Bess and Mabel will both be looking for me today since I didn't make it yesterday."

Wink shadowed Lucy as she gathered her wares and hitched Gertie to the cart. "Sorry, Wink." She patted his big, furry head then climbed up onto the seat. "You've got to stay here and keep your eye on things." But as she picked up the reins, two men came into view down the drive. Slave catchers. She struggled to take slow, even breaths.

Wink growled and bared his teeth as Mays and one of his menacing companions approached and reined in alongside her cart. Their horses were streaked with sweat.

"Quiet, Wink." The dog silenced but stood alert. Lucy tightened her grip on the reins but pressed her hands in her lap to hide their shaking. Renzo wasn't here to intimidate them this time and she couldn't let them sense her fear.

She raised her voice. "I made it clear you weren't welcome. I haven't heard anything about any runaway slaves, now head on out."

Mays smirked at his friend. "Why, you got us all wrong. We was just hoping to water our horses. Then we'll be on our way." Both men dismounted before she could to stop them.

"Maybe you have a couple a buckets in your barn we can fill." Mays took hold of the other man's reins. "Gil's just gonna fetch them." Unlike Charles Hopper, these men weren't interested in watching her reaction.

They wanted to search her barn. They'd probably climb up onto the roof if they thought the trip might offer a clue as to where the Tyler family was hiding.

Lucy scrambled down and planted herself between Gil and the barn door. Wink came to stand next to her, growling low.

"There's a trough by the well. Use it and be on your way." Although she clenched her teeth to mask their rattling, she wouldn't cower.

Gil advanced two more steps, enough so the tips of his boots disappeared under the hem of her skirt. Wink snarled and bared his teeth, waiting for Lucy's permission to attack.

Gil stumbled back and drew his gun. "Call off your goddamn mutt or I swear I'm gonna put a bullet through his good eye."

The devil, he'd probably enjoy it, too.

"Wink, down." She held out her hand and Wink backed down, sitting against her leg with his head under her palm.

Mays—who'd tied their horses to the side of the wagon—stepped forward and motioned for Gil to lower his gun. He, too, stopped when Wink gave him a warning growl.

"You got something in that barn you afraid we're going to find?"

Lucy's chin went back up. "My neighbor. Remember, the man with the broken leg whose property your destroyed?"

Gil spit at her feet "Why you must have us mixed up with someone else."

She could feel the tension radiating through Wink. She needed to get rid of these men quickly, not only for the Tylers' sake, but for her dog's. If taunted, he could lunge at one of them in less than a heartbeat. He might maim one man, but the second would certainly shoot him.

"Go on. Water your horses and get off my

property."

Gil looked over at Mays. "Bossy little bitch, ain't she? That deputy must not be man enough to put his woman in her place." His gaze slid down her body, making her feel as if bog water had been poured over her head. "I got a hankerin' to show you what a real man is willing to take from a woman."

He grabbed his groin and her stomach roiled. Luckily anger topped the other emotions weighing on her. Never again would she fall victim to abuse, of any kind.

She stiffened her spine. "Are you prepared to kill me? Because, I promise you, that's what you'd have to do." She would defend herself until the second her heart stopped beating.

Her threat silenced him. Perhaps she'd finally found a line they wouldn't cross.

The sound of hoof beats interrupted their stalemate, and she looked past the men to see Renzo galloping down the drive.

Thank God. She hadn't expected him to return, maybe ever again. She knew he wasn't here to cause trouble. Did he mean to honor his promise about keeping the slave catchers away?

Gil grumbled under his breath.

Mays gestured with his head. "Take the horses over to the well behind the house and water them."

What? Her gaze snapped to the direction of the well. How did he know where it was? It wasn't visible from where they stood and she hadn't said. At some point he must have snooped around behind the house. She wiped her palms on her skirt as Gil led the horses away.

Seconds later Renzo reined in his horse and dismounted. His chiseled expression passed over her and settled on Mays. "Any trouble here?"

Lucy fought the urge to run to his side, but this was her problem to deal with. She wouldn't show the men any sign of intimidation.

Mays smirked. "No, the lady here's offered to let us water our horses."

"And then they're leaving." She'd been forced into the invitation and Gil was halfway there already, so she decided not to delay their departure by arguing the point.

Mays left, following in Gil's path around the back of the house.

She gazed at Renzo, feeling some of the tension in her shoulders ebb. She couldn't help but remember the first time he'd saved the day, when he had pretended to be her sweetheart. He certainly hadn't implied any such relationship this time. His continued silence spoke louder than The Sheik's morning call.

She reached for his arm. "Renzo, I'm sorry-"

He whipped his arm away from her touch. "Don't." His sharp tone shredded any hope of his letting her try to make amends. He looked into her cart.

"Headed into town?"

"I was, but I'd better not." There was no way she could leave knowing Mays and Gil were skulking around. She'd lead Gertie over to the springhouse and put everything away.

"Go ahead. I'll stick around so you can go take your goods into town. But wait until these two leave so they don't follow you."

After the way he'd snapped, his offer of assistance took her off guard. But she had to consider things practically. If she didn't take things in to sell, Mabel might worry and send Mitch out to check on her.

"Thank you." She wanted to add how much she appreciated his keeping their secret, but the tick of his hardened jaw sealed her lips.

He gave Terra's reins a tug and started toward the back of the house, not glancing back. "I have a message to deliver. As soon as they head out, you can leave. Take Wink with you and avoid the sheriff's office in town. That's where they'll be heading."

Renzo didn't like the way Mays and Gil spoke in hushed tones and appeared more interested in looking around behind Lucy's house than watering their horses. When they spotted him closing the distance between them, they moved on to the trough.

Gil spit into the water. "Your lady friend send you back here to keep a eye on us?"

Ignoring the man's jeers would mean they'd leave sooner. "Sheriff Tate wants to see you boys at his office. I just gave the same message to your friend back at camp."

The two men looked at each other. "Hot damn, maybe he's got some news for us," Gil said, rubbing his hands together.

"Appreciate you playing messenger boy." Mays mounted up. "You tell that lady friend of yours that we'll see her around."

Renzo's jaw twitched, but he held his tongue. He needed them gone now. Who knew when the baby might cry again?

The two didn't waste any time leaving, and Renzo realized as he watched them spur their horses that they'd been pleased about being summoned to the sheriff's office. They hadn't even bothered to ask what Tate wanted. Wouldn't they want to avoid the sheriff if they were guilty? Was it possible that they hadn't set the fire? No. They had to have done it. Or maybe just one of them. Mays. He was the brains of the clan. If he set the fire on his own, that would explain why the other two acted as if they had nothing to hide.

Renzo watered Terra and led him to the paddock, feeling Lucy's eyes on his back. She'd wisely decided not to force a discussion he wasn't ready for, instead climbing up onto the cart and urging Gertie down the road. Smart woman.

Now was as good a time as any to check out the woods.

"I'm so relieved to hear no one was hurt." Mabel rested her hands on the rail of the hotel's back stoop, while Mitch carried Lucy's milk can slowly up the steps.

She couldn't blame either of them for their questions. Bess Anderson had been equally curious. Luckily, with Renzo keeping watch, Lucy felt it safe to make her transactions without rushing. No sense raising eyebrows. Wink barked once, his way of asking permission to get down.

"Stay," she told him.

Mabel held open the door for her pokey son and shooed him inside. "So Mr. Washington's home is lost? Nothing salvageable?"

Lucy lifted the wooden lid off her box and pulled the straw away from the top of the butter crock. Her late night had caught up with her, so she decided to let Mitch carry it inside. "No. It's gone."

Mitch hustled back out the door. He must have flown down those cellar stairs. He lifted out the crock.

Lucy moved out of the way. "Once Thomas's leg is healed, he'll have to start from scratch."

Mitch looked at her as if she'd hung the stars. "I'd be glad to help Mr. Washington when he's ready to rebuild." Okay, so maybe Mabel was right about his case of puppy love.

"That's kind of you." She curled her fist. "I just wish we could make the men who burned it down build him a new one."

Mabel motioned Mitch to stop dawdling and get the butter down into the cold storage. "Men? So the sheriff knows who did it?"

What's the matter with me? She'd spoken more to Bess and Mabel in the last few weeks than the previous six years, and now she was spreading rumors. "No, I meant whoever did it.

Mitch reappeared with an empty milk can and

butter crock from the previous visit. He repacked the crock in the wooden box and swung the can over the side of the wagon. "Do you need any help at your place?" He petted Wink and then made a show of readjusting the can so it wouldn't tip over. "If you need anything at all, let me know."

Mabel rolled her eyes and handed Lucy her payment. "What *I* need is for you to stop lollygagging and haul that wood in like I asked you." She ruffled her son's hair as he tried to duck.

"Thank you, both." Lucy laughed as she urged Gertie forward. When she realized she'd been smiling she thought perhaps denying herself friends had been as punishing as Emmett's blows.

Renzo came back to the clearing, no wiser about possible spies than when he'd left. His gaze settled on the barn. It had to be sweltering hiding up in the hayloft. He wanted to help, but the fear he'd seen on the runaway's faces haunted him. They'd all thought him to be a heartless fiend. No better than Mays, and the comparison sickened him. He had to prove to them how wrong they were. All of them.

He got a pitcher from the house and carried it to the stone spring house, pausing inside to let his eyes adjust to the dimness. A pipe protruded from the far wall, directing a steady flow of cold spring water into a large stone trough, which in turn spilled over into a trencher. Spying a tin cup on a shelf, he dipped it in the water and drank. The icey cold shocked his parched throat and cooled him all the way to his stomach. This would cool them, along with getting them down to ground level for a while. He filled the pitcher and carried it to the barn, ignoring Thomas as he came in.

"Come on down," he called. He set the pitcher on the make-shift table. "It's safe. I'll make certain no one comes in." He turned to Thomas, who'd shifted to the edge of the cot. "It's too damned hot for them up there."

Hay sprinkled down from between the floorboards, and Renzo looked up. Barn cats, indeed. He'd been too damned trusting.

"Thank you, Deputy," Thomas said to his back as he left.

His pride wouldn't let him reply.

Alongside the road, a fat groundhog nibbled dandelions in the sunshine. Wink had abandoned Lucy's side to sprawl in the back of the cart and she fought the temptation to pull off under the shade of a tree and join him for a nap.

The last twenty-four hours had pushed the boundaries of her emotions, and she was ready to collapse. Making love with Renzo, his discovering the Tylers, standing up to Carl Mays and Gil, visiting like friends with Mabel and Bess, the thin chance of being pregnant, wondering whether they'd get through another day without someone finding the Tylers... Even if she broke into tears, they could be of joy, desperation, fear, heartache or half a dozen other sentiments.

As she rounded the bend, she spotted Renzo sitting on the front porch. She wondered if he had spoken to Thomas or Emily while she was away. He stood and headed toward the barn. His unwillingness to let her explain frustrated her to no end, but she prayed that in time his anger would subside. By the time she reined in Gertie and walked around to the paddock, he was already tightening Terra's cinch. Wink had run ahead and danced at his feet.

"No trouble in town?" he asked, not bothering to make eye contact.

"None. Here?"

He bent to pet Wink. At least his grudge was only with her.

You don't know me at all. The words still stabbed at

her conscience. And if his pain was half as deep as what he'd inflicted when he said them, then his suffering was acute.

"Fine," he said. Then he did meet her gaze, stepping closer and lowering his voice. "It's way too hot up in the hayloft. You need to find somewhere else for them."

Exhaustion and defensiveness sharpened her tongue. "Well, why didn't I think of that?" she whispered through gritted teeth. "The hotel was full up, otherwise I would have gotten them a room."

His brow straightened. "Damn it. You know what I mean."

"Yes, I do." She closed the distance between them and poked him in the chest. "Do you think I want them to suffer?" As her temper rose, she moved to pull off a coat she wasn't even wearing.

"So what are my options?" she continued. "I have the house, the spring house, the chicken coop and, Lord help me, the smoke house." She held up four fingers and ticked off two. "The henhouse is full of chickens and spring house isn't big enough." She ticked off a third finger.

"The smoke house," she swallowed a lump in her throat, "has been purposely neglected and is in such a sorry state of repair it's not safe." This left one finger.

"The house is the only other building large enough. Emily spent the night she had the baby in the house. By the next morning she was desperate to go back out to the barn with everyone else. And I have a feeling the children weren't the only ones she missed." Although Emily hadn't admitted it, Lucy'd seen the way the woman's face practically glowed when she was with Thomas.

"That leaves the barn." She swiped her hand over her forehead.

"I urge them to come down whenever possible. If anyone's cautious about them being down with Thomas,

it's Emily. She has three children to protect, damn you."
Hot tears mingled with the beads of perspiration on her
face. She spun, intending to retreat but he pulled her back
against his chest.

"I'm sorry." His breath was warm against her
good ear and he pulled her under his chin. She could feel
his heartbeat pounding at her back. "I know you've done
the best you could for them."

God, her frustration at the slave catchers, at
Renzo, at being forced into this situation by her own
conscience was so intense she wanted to scream over the
treetops. Part of her wanted to shove Renzo to the dirt
and run. And keep running. Leaving all this turmoil so far
behind it would cease to exist.

Her breath hitched. She fought against the part of
her that wanted to turn into his arms and bury herself in
his protection. What a relief it would be to let him take on
the responsibility for all her problems. While she slept. For
days, weeks, somewhere cool, where this heat couldn't
flame her vexation.

Her head jerked up. Heat? Since when did heat
bother her? But the evidence trickled down between her
breasts. She was never overheated. Chilled, yes, but hot?
Never.

Renzo turned her in his arms and examined her
from head to toe. "Are you okay?"

"No." She yanked out of his hold, tuning out his
questions while she tried to recall when she'd first noticed
the heat. He put a hand to her forehead but she pushed it
away as well. *Think.* She hadn't worn her coat into
Anderson's...the drive into town had been so warm...

"You're burning up. Damn it, Lucy, can you hear
me?"

She blinked. When Gil threatened her. Rage had
consumed her. By the time the two men had left, her
jacket lay on the seat of the wagon. Was this a fluke? Or
maybe she was falling ill. But whatever the reason, this

honest sweat was a thousand times more refreshing than nervous chills.

Renzo lightly shook her, staring into her eyes until she finally focused on him. "Lucy. Say something. You're scaring the hell out of me."

"I'm fine." She pulled his hands away, slowly this time, feeling a smile spread across her face.

"What? What happened?" Confusion softened his features.

"An awful lot has happened." She met and held his gaze.

Finally he exhaled a long breath. "Yes, it has." And with his grudging nod, hope took root.

"I'd like to explain."

Weariness dulled his eyes and creased his forehead. "But it'll have to be later. I was supposed to speak with the men who came to the cabin last night to see if anyone heard or saw anything else that might be helpful."

"I understand." Selfishness made her wish he'd brush aside his duty and put her first. But proving Mays and his men had burned Thomas's home shouldn't be put off long enough for them to cover their tracks.

Renzo mounted his horse. "I'll come by in the morning so you can take your wares to town. After you get back, we'll talk. No more secrets, Lucy."

Sheriff Tate put his foot on the chair, wincing. "Bartender at the saloon confirmed Fred and Gil's story. They were there drinking and playing cards from supper until about nine o'clock last night."

Renzo pulled off his hat, slung it on the desk and ran a hand back and forth over his scalp. "But Mays doesn't have anyone to back up his story."

"Well, no. Says he was at their camp alone until the boys came back."

Renzo pulled up another chair and sat. "He's got

to be lying. Thomas doesn't have a single enemy that we know of. Those three tore up his place and got away with it. Mays probably figures he'll get away with this too."

"But we have to have proof." Tate pulled his whiskey bottle out of the desk and gestured to him.

He waved away the offer. He needed his wits to find that proof.

"They seemed genuinely surprised when I told them about the fire. Not upset mind you, just surprised." The sheriff poured three fingers into his glass, taking a sip even before corking the bottle. "Of course they all denied involvement. Didn't even seem put out about being questioned, but I suppose they're used to being looked at sideways whenever they cross into the North."

Renzo stood and paced in front of the desk. "Well, no one I spoke with today had any information." He'd saved Charles Hopper for his last stop of the day, hoping that by then he still wouldn't want to rip the man's head off. It hadn't worked. He'd kept the visit short when it was apparent Charles had no real clue as to who the arsonist could be. But if the farmer suspected a friend, some other bigoted white man who disapproved of Lucy's friendship with Thomas, would he tell? Probably not.

Tate drained his glass. "I sure am glad to have your help. Just riding in the wagon out to Thomas's place and walking around has aggravated my foot in the worst way." He gestured for his crutches and Renzo passed them over.

Tate stood and steadied himself before meeting Renzo's gaze. "I heard a rumor over at the hotel that you didn't make it back to your bed last night."

Shit. Lucy had said this would happen. He held the man's gaze but said nothing.

"Although you don't plan to make Rush Crossing your home, I want to remind you that Mrs. Neels does have to live here. And now Charles Hopper is mouthing off about her putting Thomas up at her place."

Renzo squeezed his fists, replaying the accusation Charles had directed at Lucy. That sonofabitch was like a dog with a shank bone.

"Lucy's had an upstanding reputation up until now, but if he gets folks worked up, they might not be so eager to do business with her."

What the hell was he supposed to do? He'd asked her to marry him. Okay, so it had been more of an order, and yeah, he'd insulted her home in the process, but she'd been kicking him out at the time.

"Sheriff, we both know Lucy isn't a loose woman. And I'll have words with anyone who wants to spread those kinds of rumors."

"Afraid it's too late for that." The sheriff hobbled to the oil lamp and turned down the wick to extinguish the flame. "Just wanted you to know that there's a rumor. I'm confident you'll do right by her."

"I've tried, but next time I won't take no for an answer."

An hour later, Renzo stepped out of the copper tub, itching for a fight. With someone big enough to beat the crap out of him. He deserved it for spending the night at Lucy's. Privacy was next to impossible to keep in a small town.

Thank God she'd managed to keep the runaways under wraps thus far. If it killed him, he was going to make sure no one found out about her hiding the Tylers.

The hotel's neatly made bed called to him as he dressed to go out for the night. But if Mays and the Greenley brothers were out making trouble under the cover of darkness, he wouldn't catch them at it while he slept.

"I'm finished with the tub," he said to the desk clerk as he passed. But just as he was about to walk out the door, inspiration struck. "I'll be out on patrol again tonight." He held the clerk's gaze. "Still trying to track down whoever started that fire and make certain he doesn't set any more. Tell the maid I'll be working all night *again* and she won't need to worry about the bed in the morning." He headed out the door and along the boardwalk, satisfied that the story might make folks question the rumor. Once he convinced Lucy to marry him and move to Philadelphia, none of it would matter anyway.

As he went down the side steps a sniffling sound from the alleyway caught his attention. "Deputy, I need to talk to you." Mitch Wilcox, Mark's oldest brother, stepped out of the shadows between the hotel and Patsy's Bakery. He sounded as if he'd been crying.

"What's wrong?" Mark's injury couldn't be the problem since the lad had been running around town, albeit bandaged, for days.

Mitch swiped his nose with his sleeve. "I need to turn myself in, sir."

Renzo put his hand on Mitch's shoulder. Although the lad was tall as some men, his muscles were still those of a growing boy. He gestured to a pair of barrels by the building and they sat. "What are you talking about?"

Mitch lifted his chin. "Well, first off, I want to say, the only reason I did it is because I thought it'd help Mizz Neels."

Mention of Lucy made the hair stand up on his arms. "Mitch, what did you do?

"I set fire to Mr. Washington's cabin."

Chapter Seventeen

Mitch could have confessed to killing a man and Renzo couldn't have been more stunned. He scanned the area and leaned forward. "Why-the-hell would you do that?"

The boy held his gaze while nervously picking the palm of his hand. "I'd heard some men rumbling about how Mr. Washington had no business being at Mizz Neels' place. How he had a home and she should take food to him there if she wanted to be a good neighbor. One of them even said somebody ought to do something about it."

Renzo said nothing as Mitch paused.

"His cabin was barely standing. I figured if he didn't have a place then folks wouldn't mind so much about him being at Mizz Neels' house." Although Mitch helped his mother support the family, he obviously had no idea how a man who'd worked to buy is own freedom would feel about the destruction of his home. Dilapidated or no.

"But I have my pa's tools and, I swear, I'm going to help him build a new cabin. A better one." Then the boy slumped. "After I get out of jail, that is."

So, the person who'd started the fire was a hard-working, honest boy of sixteen. Renzo wasn't sure what to say. He'd already made the mistake of mentally trying and convicting Mays for the crime, so Mitch's confession had him speechless.

He took off his hat and ran a hand through his hair. Setting a fire was a serious offense, but he understood the lad's misguided intentions. Both of them wanted to protect Lucy. Mitch had known the cabin was unoccupied, so he assumed no one would be injured. Wasn't there some better way for justice to be served than to arrest him?

"Does anyone else know about this?"

"No, sir. I thought it'd be a secret I'd take to the grave since it would make everything better for everybody. But then, when I heard some men at the barber shop accusing Mizz Neels of being the cause of all the trouble. I don't reckon I could live with myself, knowing what I done hurt more than it helped." He swiped at his eyes. "Even though he'd probably tan my hide for what I done, I wish my pa was here. I won't ever be the man he was."

Renzo wrapped an arm around Mitch's shoulder. "You're owning up to your mistake, Mitch and that's an honorable thing. I'd say your father would be proud of you for it." His throat tightened. Had he shown his own father any honor? Renzo had refused to hear him out and he'd done the very same thing to Lucy. Damn if his pride didn't keep getting in the way.

"I won't do anything like this ever again. I swear."

What would happen if he arrested Mitch? Shit, the lad sported only the first traces of facial hair. He wasn't some hard-hearted criminal who needed to be locked away.

Renzo rocked his hat back onto his head. Even though the law was clear, damned if the justice system wasn't riddled by more shades of gray than Sheriff Tate's sideburns. In the long run, the only person adversely affected by the fire was Thomas. Renzo wasn't looking forward to speaking with the man who'd contemplated killing him that morning, but he'd get Thomas's opinion about whether he wanted to press charges.

Renzo stood. "Why don't you head on home and we'll keep this between us for the time being."

Faint lantern light from a window above reflected in Mitch's rounded eyes. "You mean you're not going to take me to jail?"

"Not tonight."

"So you're not going to tell anybody?"

"I didn't say that. I'm going to tell Mr. Washington about what happened."

Mitch nodded but pulled his shoulders back and held Renzo's gaze.

"I'll tell him about your offer to help him rebuild. That's quite an undertaking. He might prefer that be your punishment rather than lazing around in a jail cell. Mind you, I'm not making any promises."

"I understand." Mitch nodded. "My pa used to say a man takes whatever punishment he deserves."

"Your pa was a wise man." He watched Mitch head home and continued on toward the livery, wishing he could turn around and go back to the hotel. Now he knew Mays and his boys hadn't set the fire. Since there was no need to keep looking for proof of their involvement, he should get an undisturbed night's sleep. But that didn't mean the men weren't up to other trouble after dark. One or more of them could be lying in wait at some innocent farmer's place right now. Like Lucy's.

He saddled Terra himself, promising the horse extra oats for his late night efforts. But as they trotted out of town, he couldn't deny he had only one destination in mind. In one day he'd been dragged, heels first, through pleasure, frustration, hurt, betrayal, fear, anger...the list was as long as Lucy's braid. But in the end, none of that torment could make him walk away from her.

Insistent tapping at the bedroom window forced Lucy from sleep. Her heart rate doubled as she swung her feet to the floor, grabbing the shotgun from where she'd propped it in the corner. *Why isn't Wink barking?*

"Lucy. It's me." Renzo's husky whisper lured her to the window and she could hear Wink's toenails clicking on the plank flooring of the porch. Some watchdog.

She spoke through the latched shutters. "What's wrong?"

"Nothing. I told you we'd talk later."

Now? But thankful that he was willing to listen, she lit a lamp and hurried to the front door, throwing open the bolt. Renzo signaled for Wink to stay outside and closed the door behind him.

"I thought you said we'd talk tomorrow." She realized she'd forgotten to grab a shawl when his gaze slid down her thin nightgown. Her nipples beaded against the cotton, and her body hummed at his silent stare. But she shouldn't think about making love with him when he'd yet to say he'd forgiven her.

He lifted the hurricane lamp from her hand and set it on the nearest table. "And we will, but for tonight I couldn't stay away." He slid a hand behind the small of her back and pulled her flush with his body. Her stomach fluttered like butterfly wings as he cupped the back of her head, his mouth descending. Lips warm and satisfying as melted butter molded against hers.

She raised her hands to his chest, intending to push away so they could talk. But that fast, his kiss consumed her. Their physical connection was so new and strong, it overpowered her doubt and allowed hope to replace it. She fisted his vest and clung tight. They could talk everything through later. For now, they both needed this.

His lips trailed kisses across her jaw. "You're all I

think about." He lightly sucked a spot below her ear.

Her legs wobbled. "I was afraid you'd never forgive me."

"Shhh, not now." One of his hands moved up to stroke her breast, and his maleness ground into her belly. "You feel so good," he growled. His bold words should have shocked her, but instead they fed her newly discovered sexual hunger. She reached between their bodies, sliding her hand over the front of his trousers.

"*Gesu Cristo.* If we don't move into the bedroom, I'm going to take you right here on the table."

Memories of the night he'd come for dinner flashed in her brain, but this time the prospect of such an encounter aroused her. "I don't care."

He squeezed her bottom and winked. "But I do." Sweeping her up in his arms, he carried her to the bed and began unfastening the buttons of her nightgown.

She sat up and started at his shirtfront, equally as eager to be with him. He might not love her, but she was certain he cared for her. That was enough for now. She'd not waste this opportunity to love him, in every sense. Her fingers trembled as between them they twisted and tugged off clothing. Soon they lay facing each other, naked on the bed.

She'd known from that first day in the mercantile that his shoulders were broad and his belly flat, but now her gaze lowered to his powerful erection, jutting out toward her. His reaction when she'd touched him through his trousers made her want to please him once more. Lucy ran her fingertips over his length, and he inhaled with a soft hissing sound.

She looked up to find his eyes closed, and smiled to herself. She was in control of his pleasure. Power unlike any she'd ever known swelled within her, making her even bolder. She wrapped him in her fist.

"Easy." His eyes opened, and his face drew closer. "Like this." He showed her how to glide her hand over his flesh. "That's it. Yeah." He cupped the back of her head and pulled her to his hungry kiss. They tasted, licked, sucked then shifted for breath. Again and again. "Stop." He pulled her hand away.

Lucy tried to understand as she caught her breath. "Have I done something wrong?"

But instead of answering, he pulled her body higher and drew one of her nipples into his mouth.

Merciful heavens. She gasped, and her eyelids slid closed as she gave herself up to sensation. With each pull of his mouth, she felt a delicious tug between her legs as if some cord was strung through the center of her body. Lucy combed her fingers through his hair. "Don't stop." If he did she would shatter into a million pieces.

"Not a chance," he said, shifting to her other breast.

"Oh, yes." She arched her back and bit her bottom lip to keep from crying out. If she hadn't, she surely would have awakened everyone in the barn. "More." She wanted this and more. She wanted him. Inside her. Filling her body as fully as he'd filled her heart. She couldn't lie still, she had to move. Move closer. Higher. "Renzo, I need you." Lucy rolled onto her back, her fingers digging into his sides, slick with sweat.

He moved over her and filled her, nudging her womb with his thrust. Love, desire and the sweet pleasure pain of their joining, made her heart race. Surging, climbing higher, reaching toward the ultimate release that she'd only discovered with this man.

Their bodies rocked and swayed together, joined so fully that they moved as one. First smooth and slow, then faster, pounding. Rising up. Each sensation belonged to both of them, and when she finally went shooting skyward Renzo soared through the clouds alongside her.

Afterwards, he held her pressed against his chest, and she swore their hearts beat as one. What a way to turn the day's troubles around.

Lucy shifted her clasped hands under her cheek so her good ear wasn't totally buried in the pillow. Time to talk. "I'm sorry," she said. When he didn't immediately respond, she held her tongue. Forcing him to say something wasn't the answer.

After a moment he shifted a hand down to rest on her hip. "I won't say it didn't hurt like hell when I found out you'd been lying all this time." She held her breath. "But I understand why. The Tylers were depending on you for their safety. We'd never really talked about slavery so you didn't know what I would or wouldn't do."

As the air escaped her lungs, the boulder of guilt she'd been carrying rolled off her shoulders. "Thank you for understanding." She nestled closer. "If it makes you feel any better, I've been torn in half. I wanted to tell you so badly, but I was afraid. And I feel terrible about putting you in this situation with the sheriff."

"Huh?"

"I know that the law says you're supposed to help Carl Mays and his men track down fugitive slaves."

"Yes, but I can't ignore my own moral code. The Fugitive Slave Act only came into being as a damned compromise. Part of the Compromise of 1850. It pacified slave-state politicians so California could be admitted as a free state."

A tear slipped out of the corner of her eye and dropped on the pillow. How could she not love this strong, honorable man? If only Thomas could hear Renzo. The distain in his voice when he spoke of the law. By golly, she'd make sure to tell Thomas when she took his breakfast.

"A person's skin color shouldn't matter anymore than eye or hair color. Every human being is entitled to their freedom."

His passion surprised and pleased her. "I'm so glad you feel that way. There are too many people around here who still aren't willing to stand up for the rights of colored folks."

"I've met a lot of good people in Rush Crossing, but it'll be some time before this area is as enlightened as Philadelphia."

Another reason why he's anxious to return home.

Her eyes had grown heavy but she didn't want to fall asleep. Not yet. "May I ask you something personal?"

He chuckled behind her and patted her hip. "You're the most determined woman I've ever met. I doubt I could stop you if it's something you really want to know."

She stifled a yawn and restacked her hands under her cheek. "Do you and your father not get along?"

His hand stilled and his deep exhalation stirred the hairs on the top of her head. "We never had a problem, until recently."

At least there hadn't been a long-standing rift. If they had a strong basis of love and respect between them, perhaps they could work out their dispute.

"What happened?"

But instead he kissed the crown of her head and pulled her snuggly back against his arousal. Did he think to distract her?

But then he took another slow breath. "He lied to me."

Any interest in *being* distracted disappeared. The hurt in his voice reminded her how she'd hurt him doing the same thing.

"Although I didn't find out about it until recently, he should have told me years ago."

"Did you ask him why he didn't confide in you?" She'd had a good reason for deceiving Renzo, though she regretted hurting him. Was that was the case with his father, or was she simply trying to dilute her own guilt by comparing it to his lies?

Renzo paused. "I know why." He didn't explain further.

"I have a feeling your father is largely responsible for the fair-minded man you've become. Maybe his reason isn't what you think." She hoped he would consider the possibility. What she wouldn't give to still have her parents. If there was any chance for father and son to repair their damaged relationship, she wanted that for Renzo.

Finally he broke the silence. "I don't want to discuss my father right now. What I want to talk about is us.

The abrupt change in topic, combined with her physical exhaustion, confused her. "What about us?"

"About you coming back to Philadelphia with me, and us getting married."

No mention of love. Although her heart belonged to him, why would he want to marry her if he didn't love her?

"You do realize, you could be carrying my child."

Ah, a *child.* Not that having Renzo's children wasn't a wonderful dream, but she wanted more. For both of them. She didn't want a marriage based on obligation, and he deserved a woman he loved desperately who could give him a passel of children. Someone elegant and refined, from his world. Not some dirty farmer who probably wouldn't ever conceive again.

"I'm sure there won't be a baby so there's no need to feel obligated."

He lifted his head and looked down at her profile. "How can you be certain?"

"Because I was married for five years."

Renzo mentally winced. Lucy was barren? He ran a hand down her arm and laced his fingers with hers. It didn't matter. Yes, he'd always taken precautions against children with past lovers, but his liaisons with Lucy had been wholly different. Being with her had been more than sharing a pleasant pastime with a pretty girl. He wanted to spend the rest of his life with Lucy, in or out of bed. He loved her drive, her loyalty, her independence. And now that they'd become lovers, he knew he couldn't leave her behind.

She yawned, reminding him of how he'd awoken her from much needed sleep. Tomorrow would be soon enough to resume this discussion, after she was better rested. She hadn't argued or said no outright this time, so he wasn't fool enough to force a decision on her now. Whatever it was that kept her from accepting could be worked out. Even if it meant hauling Agnes, Gertie and all the rest of the animals back to Philadelphia with them.

"Will you at least think about marrying me?"

Lucy yawned again and snuggled into the pillow. "I do all the time," she said, sounding half asleep.

Well, that was encouraging. He freed his hand and stroked her hip. *Cristo.* He wanted her again and wouldn't be able to guarantee he wouldn't wake her a few more times before dawn to make love. But they both needed rest. Better head back to the hotel and come back after breakfast.

Renzo leaned over and kissed her on the temple. "I love you."

"Lucy Ross." Her sleepy voice trailed off.

He smiled, liking the sound of it, too.

Chapter Eighteen

The next morning Rosalee and James scrawled letters on the dirt floor of the barn, as Lucy stacked the last of the dirty breakfast plates into her basket. She'd been disappointed to wake up alone, but Renzo's note assuring her he'd be back for an answer to his proposal had made her eager for the hours to pass. Perhaps if she said yes and loved him enough, in time he might come to love her.

"I should be providing food for the table." Thomas sat sideways on his cot, his arms crossed. He'd been grumbling about his relative helplessness ever since they'd heard rifle fire from someone hunting in the distance.

"Oh, don't you worry." She winked at Emily and straightened. "After you're back on your feet for good, you owe me." She tapped her chin as if tallying a bill in her mind.

"At least a dozen quail." She knew it was a wildly exorbitant price to repay her for eggs and biscuits, but her good mood made it impossible not to tease him.

"How about a deer?" he offered. "That would last you longer."

"No. I can hit a deer myself. No, quail will do nicely." She ignored his half-hearted grumble. "Does anyone need anything before I get ready to head into town?"

Emily stepped toward her. "Thomas helped me make a list. Would you hold the baby while I fetch it?" She handed off her sleeping daughter before Lucy could reply.

Dumfounded, she could do nothing but accept the bundle. The tiny girl was plump and healthy, and settled into her cradled arms as if they were safe and familiar. Without thinking, Lucy slid a feather-soft touch along the skin of the child's arm.

"Have you chosen a name for her yet?" Lucy asked. "She's so beautiful. I can't just keep calling her *the baby*."

Emily perched on the end of the cot. She and Thomas weren't touching, but the crease in his brow had all but disappeared. "Thomas has been giving me lots of suggestions. He knows I was wanting another flower name, like Rosalee's."

"I'm partial to Phloxy," Thomas said with wink. "Although Emily doesn't like it."

Lucy shook her head and chuckled. "Good for Emily."

"Remember those orange lilies you brought into your bedroom the morning after she was born?" Emily asked. "I admired them all day long."

"Yes, I remember." The bright blooms lined one whole side of the house. She'd thought they might cheer Emily up if she was feeling lonely. "So you've chosen Lily?"

"Close. Lilyann." Emily pointed to her oldest daughter. "Rosalee thought of adding Ann."

The girl crawled over and leaned her elbow on her mother's knee. "Like you added Lee to my flower name."

A grinning Thomas pointed. "I hear James was almost named Pansybeth."

185

"I wasn't either." James crossed to the cot and tried to poke Thomas but got grabbed up in a hug instead.

Suddenly the barn door slid open. Charles Hopper stepped inside, followed by a basket-toting Mildred. Lucy instinctively gripped Lilyann tighter to her bosom, hoping her suddenly quaking heart wouldn't awaken the baby. Why hadn't Wink barked? She'd left him right outside the door when she brought breakfast.

Charles strode closer, outlined by the sunlight from the open doorway. "I *knew* it. I *knew* there was more going on here than you let on. You've been hiding these runaways all along, haven't you?"

Mildred came up alongside her husband, her eyes bulging. "Oh, my, goodness gracious."

"See Mildred?" Charles said, glaring at all of them. "I told you she was up to something."

Lucy looked to Thomas, praying he didn't reach under his pillow for his knife. He didn't. Probably because of the children. She handed Lilyann back to Emily.

She pressed her palms together. "Please don't tell anyone they're here." She focused her attention on Mildred, whose gaze seemed glued on Lilyann. *The baby.* Mildred, the mother hen of all mother hens, had never had a child of her own.

"Mildred, can't you see? Emily is a mother who just wants to protect her children. She wants them to grow up without fear of being mistreated." She stepped closer trying to draw the woman's eye.

"Don't you listen to her, Mildred. She's just playing to your kind heart. They're all breaking the law and it's our duty to inform the sheriff." Charles turned back to Lucy. "I bet that deputy knows all about this, doesn't he? That's why you're snuggling up to him."

Leave it to Charles to think the worst.

"Oh, please don't tell Renzo they're here and that I've been lying to him. He'll never forgive me." She desperately needed Charles to think Renzo was still in the dark about her secret. And somehow she had to convince the Hoppers not to turn in the Tylers.

Charles took Mildred's elbow, but Lucy grabbed his other arm. "Please, *please*. Think about this. These people are *human beings*."

Charles shrugged off her hand but looked past her at Thomas and the Tylers. Lucy only hoped he was seeing reason.

After a moment that felt like hours, he met her gaze. "Mrs. Neels. I'll have a private word." His eyes sparkled, which couldn't mean good news for her. Charles released Mildred's arm and walked toward the door.

Lucy followed, her chest tight and her legs wobbly. She stepped between him and the others, blocking their view.

He lowered his voice. "My silence comes with a price. You sell me your farm and I'll keep your dirty little secret. From everyone, including your deputy beau."

Her throat closed up as if a noose had been tightened around her neck. She'd known Charles wanted her farm, but she wouldn't have thought he'd stoop to blackmail to gain it.

"I-" The word ended on a croak. Her mouth was suddenly as dry as aged kindling.

"I'll even give you what I offered last time, provided you leave the livestock."

She'd underestimated Charles. The man wasn't just cheap, he was evil.

"I, I need some time to think about it." He stiffened, so she hurriedly added, "I don't know where I'd go or how I'd make a living." Which was true. Running this farm was all she knew. Tears loomed so close, but damned if she would give him the satisfaction of seeing them.

"I'll give you until tomorrow, but that's all. If you're not willing to sign over the farm to me by noon, then I'll go straight to the sheriff. And don't even think about letting them run off during the night. If you do that I'll sic those slave catchers on them in two shakes." He looked over her shoulder, probably confident that a woman who'd recently given birth and two children couldn't get far in one night.

Her heart sunk. Either way, she would lose the farm. To Charles in this devilish deal or in a public sale to pay the exorbitant fine for helping fugitive slaves.

I have no other choice. Lucy dug deep for any traces for fortitude she might have left. She needed at least one night to try and get the Tylers away.

"You can see they're in no position to travel. Emily's just had a baby. Please, won't you give me more time to think about it?"

"Why, so you can find them another hiding place? No, you've got until tomorrow noon to give me your answer." Charles pushed Lucy aside and went to gather his wife.

Lucy followed, her mind churning like water over rocks. The Tylers huddled close to Thomas with Mildred only two paces away, staring at the baby.

"Mildred." Charles had softened his voice, but his wife seemed so entranced by Lilyann that she didn't look his way.

"Is it a boy or a girl?" she asked.

Emily glanced at Charles and answered in a soft voice. "A girl. Her name is Lilyann."

"Mil-dred." Charles lost his scowl.

"Lilyann," Mildred repeated. "That's beautiful."

He touched her elbow. "Mildred, it's time to leave."

She moved as if sleepwalking when Charles led her away.

Lucy held up a finger toward Thomas, wordlessly saying, don't move. Then she followed the Hopper's outside. Their little one-horse gig was hitched up in front of the house rather than close to the barn. That's why no one had heard their arrival.

She looked around for the still absent Wink, gripping a hand to her nervous stomach and praying he'd return soon. She stood outside the barn door, not daring to move until the Hopper's were out of sight. Then she high-tailed it back inside.

Thomas was up, balanced on his crutches. "We've got to leave. Charles isn't about to keep quiet about this."

"He will until noon tomorrow." She couldn't help but pace in front of the group, trying to figure out how to explain her sudden disappearance.

"I know I misjudged the deputy," Thomas said, "But we *both* know that Charles Hopper is no friend to colored folks. He's probably on his way to the sheriff's office this very minute."

"No, I don't think so." She needed to get Emily and the children somewhere else for today. Anywhere else. Just in case.

"What are you saying? What did he say to you over there?" Thomas reached out to stop her from wearing a trench in the dirt floor.

She met his gaze. "He said if I sold him the farm, he wouldn't turn them in."

Her friend's nostrils flared and his dark eyes flickered. "No. If I get us out of here, he can't force you to do that."

He turned, but Lucy rounded him. "And just how far do you think you'd make it on foot," she argued. "With you on crutches and Emily still recovering from birthing? And you can't get in and out of a wagon seat. I've already decided. I'll take them to Canada."

He shook his head. "You don't know the first thing about the routes."

"No, but you do. Tell me what to do and draw me a map."

"And how are you going read that map in the dark of night? No, I'll take them."

She didn't have time for arguments. "How far is it to the closest station? Because if it's more than a thousand feet, you won't make it." And he knew it.

He glowered. "About fifteen miles as the crow flies, but they can't go there. Mays and his men have been scouring the county and the next stationmaster won't risk it when there's slave catchers that close."

"That brings us back to me. It's settled."

He was about to argue, but Emily's touch stopped him. "She's right, Thomas."

The look of anguish the couple exchanged ripped at Lucy's heart, but there wasn't time to consider anything but preparation.

"I have a plan. I'll tell Mabel and Bess that I have a sick relative, an aunt somewhere, and not to expect me for a while. You stay here and keep Agnes comfortable. The barn cats will be happy to drink whatever milk you don't. Dump the rest. I don't care."

Thomas opened his mouth to argue but closed it again as he looked at the family. Rosalee's eyes pooled with unshed tears, and James clung to his mother's skirt.

Thomas's shoulders slumped, then he met Lucy's gaze. "You can only travel after dark."

Lucy nodded. "I'll drive them in my cart. It'll be tight, but Emily and the baby can sit up front with me while Rosalee and James squeeze in the box with supplies."

"Don't wait until dawn to start looking for a good spot to hide yourselves and the cart. And no fires, no candles, no lights."

"We can do that. Meanwhile, I'd feel better if they hide in your barn until dusk. Just in case Charles decides to keep an eye on me. We'll go through the woods."

She thought of Wink. He should have returned by now. If she sent him into the trees, he could sniff out any watchers. In his absence, she'd have to play scout.

Lucy spoke to Emily. "I'm going to check out the

woods and then I'll be back for you and the children. Gather up what you need." Not that they had much more than the clothes on their backs, but the time it took her to look for watchers would give them a few moments to say goodbye to Thomas. She couldn't witness that heart-wrenching farewell.

"Once I get back from your place, I'll drive my wares into town and spread my story."

"What about Renzo?"

Thomas choosing now to use his given name didn't escape her notice.

"With Emily and the children at your place, he doesn't need to stand watch."

"I mean, are you going to tell him?"

"No!" Lucy winced and lowered her voice. "I don't want him involved with this. I've already caused him enough trouble." She didn't want him arrested, too.

Noticing the basket Mildred had set on the ground, she peeked inside. Charles must have been pretty suspicious and needing an excuse to stop by to allow his wife to provide such a feast for Thomas.

"Good. We'll take this with us now. That'll keep you all fed the rest of the day and into tomorrow." She handed the basket to Rosalee. "We'll need to leave as soon as I make sure it's safe."

She scurried out the door and got the shotgun from the house, hoping that having it would ensure she didn't need it. Although sunlight dappled through the canopy, entering the tree line on this sunny day made her edgier than the night of the fire. After a moment, her eyes adjusted to the partial shadows. She walked to the left for a few hundred yards, scanning the area.

A noise—was it a whimper or the chirp of a small animal?—sounded through the trees. With her hearing loss, she couldn't determine the direction from which it came. Damn. Mays could be doing the two-step on a tree stump and, as long as it wasn't in her sights, she wouldn't be sure where the sound came from.

Determined to make her vision work twice as hard, she turned right and went the other way, all the while looking for anything out of the ordinary. When her skirt caught on some thorny underbrush, she stopped.

Her head popped up when she heard the sound again. She scanned the forest floor in a circular pattern. Seeing nothing but trees and low growing vegetation, she bent to work the sturdy fabric free, absently setting the shotgun on the ground. Accomplishing her task, she reached for the weapon and the air whooshed from her lungs. Oh, Lord. Blood.

Chapter Nineteen

The blood trail, still wet, ran in opposite directions. As if something, or someone, had been on the move after being wounded. She turned toward her place and ran along the dark red path.

After going less than twenty yards, she froze. Wink lay sprawled in the brush, the fur on his side and hind leg bloodied and matted. The walls of her chest squeezed her lungs like a vice.

She ran to him. "Oh, God!" Her dog's side rose and fell in quick, shallow breaths. Tears flowed from her eyes. She stumbled to the ground, dropped the gun and burrowed her forehead in the thick, brown fur of her dog's neck.

"Oh, Wink. Oh my God, Wink." She sat up, examining the wound through the blur of tears and the ooze of blood. Could she save him? He'd lost so much blood. Thomas might be able to help. But as she realized the severity of the wound, sorrow hit her like an iron fist.

She stroked his brow. "I love you, boy. You're the best dog in the whole world."

Her pet tried to lift his head, but got his muzzle

off the ground only an inch before flopping back down. Thomas had told her how Wink had almost died from the beating Emmett had given him, but seeing him in this condition made her realize how lucky she'd been not to have seen his suffering back then.

Another deluge of tears poured from her eyes. She'd hunted enough game to know her dog was dying. She threaded her fingers in the fur at his neck and bent to nuzzle his head. He was past the point of whimpering. Breathing sucked every bit of energy from his straining body.

Who could have done this? But as soon as the thought came to mind, the answer followed. Mays or one of the Greenley brothers. That bastard Gil had threatened to shoot Wink just yesterday.

Wink tried to move, but it didn't amount to much more than a shudder.

"I love you." Her throat tightened. She kissed the side of his muzzle and rubbed her tears into his fur. Did he understand how much he meant to her?

"You've been my best friend." She nuzzled him again, grateful for the small favor that she'd found him before he died out here all alone. Hopefully he wouldn't suffer too much longer.

She shifted on her knees, not wanting to put undo weight on his body. When her toe kicked something hard, she turned to see her shotgun lying on the ground. Then her gaze swung back to Wink and her heart seized with understanding. Hadn't she already been tested enough for two lifetimes?

Lord, help me be strong. She leaned down and nuzzled her forehead in the thick fur below her friend's ear, then reached for the gun. Yielding no time for hesitation, she rose, aimed and pulled the trigger. The blast ricocheted through both the woods and her body, mocking the sudden emptiness ripping its way through her soul. Then, overcome by a wave of nausea, she swung away to retch in the brush.

The farm was eerily quiet as Renzo trotted up the drive. No Wink, no Lucy. Only the clucking of chickens and the occasional whinny from Thomas's horses in the paddock. Perhaps Lucy was in the house and hadn't heard Terra.

"Hello?" he called as he dismounted. He looped Terra's reins to the fence, expecting at least his one-eyed friend to come running. His stomach tightened until he heard the hinges of the barn door squeal. He relaxed and rounded the corner of the building, but quickened his steps when he saw Thomas's fearful expression.

Renzo grabbed the man's arm. "What's happened? Is Lucy alright?"

Thomas scanned the area. "Come with me."

Renzo released his arm and followed him inside. The door barely had time to close.

"Is she hurt?"

Thomas shook his head. "No." He hobbled back to his quarters, slammed his crutches against the wall and dropped onto the cot. "Lucy's not hurt. Not physically, anyway."

What the hell? "Did someone find out about the Tylers?" As an afterthought, he looked around. "Are they still here?"

"No." Thomas's cupped his forehead. "The Hoppers were here. Just as we finished breakfast. None of us heard them and they walked right in." He reached under his pillow and pulled out his knife, then grabbed up a chunk of wood.

"So what did Hopper say?" Renzo wanted the whole story, now.

"He gave Lucy an ultimatum. She either has to sell him her farm or he'll go straight to the sheriff and tell him how she's been hiding Emily and the children." Thomas's sharpened blade sliced through the wood as easily as if it was a hunk of bread.

Too bad he couldn't use it on Hopper.

"Where is she now? Is Wink with her?"

Thomas settled both items in his lap and clenched his fists into thick knots. "Wink is dead."

Cristo. "How?"

"Someone shot him. We heard a gunshot during breakfast, but it was a ways off. We just figured someone was out hunting."

Renzo's muscles ratcheted. Was Lucy out investigating? Wink's death would undoubtedly have her so devastated she wouldn't know up from down. She could she be walking into the path of a bullet even as he stood here talking. He needed to find her.

"Where is she?"

"She took the Tylers to hide in my barn. Just for today. She aims to drive them in that little cart of hers, all the way to Canada."

He slapped his hat against his leg. "Ah, hell. She'd never make it."

"I know. They'll be caught, sure as the sun sets in the west. And when Charles Hopper finds out she's taken off with them, he's going to go straight to the sheriff. Those slave catchers will hunt them down and-" Thomas covered his mouth.

"Don't worry, I won't let her do it." He fingered the small sapphire ring in his vest pocket. *I never should have taken the time to stop at the sheriff's office or shop for a ring.*

"How much time does she have?" His thoughts tumbled over each other like a pack of boys in a scuffle.

"Tomorrow, noon. Although I don't trust Hopper not to come calling before then to make sure she hasn't done exactly what she's planning to do." Thomas was right. Hopper must be frothing at the mouth to gain possession of her farm. There was no way he would just sit at home until tomorrow and wait patiently to collect.

"I agree. He'll need to be dealt with. And we've

got to come up with some way to keep Lucy safe." God, he wanted to sweep her into his arms and take her far away from all the heartache she must be going through. He tossed his hat onto the cot and raked a hand through his hair. "If only there was some way to appease Charles, let Lucy keep her farm and get the Tylers safely away." *Think of something, dammit.* "I should have done something about them yesterday."

Thomas stiffened and Renzo realized he hadn't been clear.

"I mean I should have offered to take them north myself. I should have looked past my pride and left with them last night."

"I wish my leg was healed. I truly would love to deliver them to freedom." The older man's dark eyes glistened. "I guess you could say I've formed a strong attachment to all of them."

As Thomas's words sunk in, an idea began to come together in Renzo's mind. "If your leg was healed and you could get them to Canada, would you have been able to leave them?"

After long seconds of contemplation, Thomas met his gaze. "No." The corners of Thomas's mouth turned up. "I've come to think of them as mine."

"Then let's make that happen." Renzo had a plan.

Thomas sat up straighter. "How?"

"If you're serious about staying in Canada, what would you do about your farm?"

Thomas's eyes widened. For a man, born a slave, to own property and then throw it away, was a monumental decision. "What's your idea?"

"I know it's a lot to ask, but we could offer it to Charles at a very good price. It may not have the acreage of Lucy's place, but it does have a newer, larger barn than either of their places. That's got to be enough to tempt him."

Thomas's face brightened. "It would tempt him

alright. Plus, he could have the harvest. And if Lucy's willing, first option to lease her fields for next planting season."

"Do you think she'd be willing to let Charles take over your lease?"

Thomas paused for a moment then nodded. "She'll probably curse the man 'til his dying day, but she'd do it."

Having witnessed plenty of her anger since they'd met, Renzo could picture her flushed cheeks. "Okay, so there's our carrot to dangle in front of Charles. Rest assured, I'm not going to accept no for an answer." He could always offer the man an additional financial bribe. "How long before Lucy gets back?"

"Half hour or so."

"Good. Let's talk about how I'm going to get you and the Tyler's to Canada." He looked at Thomas's splint. "None of you can make it on foot, that's for sure."

"Lucy's cart is too small," Thomas added.

Renzo rubbed the tension at the back of his neck. "But Charles has a couple large wagons, doesn't he?"

"He sure does."

"So one of his wagons will be part of the payment for your farm." Or Renzo would buy it outright if he couldn't negotiate for it. "We'll use your team. Besides, you'll need them once you get settled up north."

"Right." Thomas reached for his Bible, gripping it tightly. "They'll make good time for us at night."

"Oh, we won't be traveling just at night."

Thomas's mouth dropped open. "But we can't be seen."

"Why not?" Renzo reasoned. "You're a free man. You have papers, right?"

"Right here." He patted the Good Book. "But what about Emily and the children?"

"You mean my wife and daughters?"

Thomas's eyes rounded. "What?"

Renzo waved a hand. "At least for appearances sake. I'll explain later. Now, for Lucy's sake, we have to figure out how to keep her out of all this."

Thomas shook his head. "All I can think of is you hog-tying her to the post over there."

They were in firm agreement on her pig-headed determination. If it would solve all their problems, he'd do it.

"I don't think a rope exists that could hold her. Besides, we need to think of a way for her to remain above suspicion."

"The Hoppers are the only witnesses. If they agree to the deal, then there's no problem."

"But if no one knows that the Tylers have moved on, Mays and his men will still be snooping around here. No, I don't want Lucy here by herself unless they're gone."

Thomas stared off, tapping his index fingers against the worn leather of his Bible.

Renzo paced. He went over all the twists and turns, needing one last puzzle piece to snap in place. "So, we need the slave catchers to know the family's left, without them knowing they've been hiding here. And we also need to keep Lucy from being part of the escape."

"But how?"

"If there was only some way for Mays and the Greenleys to spot Emily and the children, but not be able to get to them." If some great divide stood between them.

"That would have to be some magic trick," Thomas said.

Renzo's mind raced, thinking of all the things he needed to do. "Not magic, but with the help of friends, maybe a grand illusion."

"What friends?"

"Do you know of any the Quakers that are sympathetic to the cause?"

"They won't harbor, but Caleb Yoder provides money sometimes. Why?"

"Because I need to borrow some clothing for my wife and daughters."

Thomas smiled and nodded.

Renzo rubbed his hands together. "With the large-brimmed bonnets and gloves some of the stricter Quaker females wear, we could be a family traveling north who decided to help an injured colored man along the way."

"But what about Lucy?" Thomas asked.

That's where the plan got trickier. Renzo puffed out his cheeks as he exhaled. "We're going to have Charles get her thrown in jail."

Chapter Twenty

"Jail? Have you lost your mind?" Thomas said.

Renzo hoped Lucy's fury at being detained would overcome any fear she might have of being locked up. If everything went off as planned, it wouldn't be for very long.

"If we can get Sheriff Tate to arrest her while she's in town, then there's no way for her to get caught up in all this."

"But why would he arrest her?"

"That's another place where Hopper will come in handy." Renzo might have to use some intimidation, but the fellow deserved it. "If he accuses Lucy of hiding the Tylers in front of Mays, then Mays will insist she be detained while they check it out. If there's no sign of them here, Sheriff Tate will have to release her. By that time our plan will already be in motion and she won't know where to find us."

Thomas shook his head. "I'm not certain I'm following all this, but I'm going to trust that you are." He extended his hand. "And I want to apologize for not trusting you before now. Thank you for your help." They shook but when Renzo tried to release his grip, Thomas held on. "I need to ask... Once I'm gone, who's going to be here to take care of Lucy?"

The stubborn woman didn't make taking care of her easy.

"I've proposed twice. I think she's softening to the idea, but it's got to be her decision. She's going to be pretty angry with me for not including her in the plan, so we'll just have to wait and see." Thomas released his hand. "Now I've got to get going. There's a hell of a lot to do before tonight."

Thomas reached for his crutches. "And I've got a long walk to my place after Lucy heads in to town. By the way, when you speak with Hopper, make certain he agrees to take care of the livestock until Lucy's freed."

"Right. I hadn't thought of that."

Thomas steadied himself on his crutches. "Are you certain Lucy won't be implicated?"

"Certain? No. But if everything goes according to plan, it'll look like the Tylers have been hiding up in your hayloft the whole time. You'll look guilty, but that won't matter. You'll be starting a new life with them in Canada."

He picked up his hat and put it on. "There's more that I'll explain later, but it'll have to wait until I see you at your place. I'll come back to get the horses. You can wait for me to get Hopper's wagon if you don't think you can make the walk."

"No, once Lucy heads out I'll go. I'd like some time alone with Emily and the children to, well, propose." The grin on Thomas's face made him look ten years younger.

At least one of them would end up with the woman he loved.

Renzo held out his hand again. "Congratulations. Now, if you want to make it north to your wedding, let's pray that everything goes according to plan."

Lucy took a detour on her way back from Thomas's farm to mound branches and brush overtop of Wink's body. That might slow down predators until Renzo could retrieve it. She'd have Thomas ask him to bury her dog near the front porch where they'd spent many a quiet evening over the past two years.

Back at the barn she cleared the hayloft of any evidence of the Tylers, loaded her goods into the wagon then hooked up Gertie.

"I'm headed into town now," she told Thomas.

She hoped to leave without him mentioning Wink again. To her surprise, he didn't draw her into conversation, but opened his Bible. Saying goodbye to Emily and the children had been difficult, for all of them.

"Don't worry about me. Go on, you got a lot to do." She turned to leave. "Lucy," he said, "Thank you for being my friend."

She went over to the cot, bent and kissed his cheek. "And thank you for being mine."

She headed to town, uneasy about how much their exchange had sounded like last goodbyes. Catching herself pushing Gertie too hard, she slowed. She had to act normally. Don't rush but don't dawdle.

At the mercantile, Bess was busy with a customer so Mr. Anderson recorded her credit for eggs and assembled her supplies. He didn't seem at all vexed when she told him about the pause in her supply due to her upcoming visit to her a sick aunt.

"Fine. Fine. We'll be glad to resume our trade upon your return. Give your Aunt Helen our best wishes for a speedy recovery." The man's attitude was so generous that guilt robbed her of speech.

At the hotel, Mabel scrambled around like a harried hen. Mitch was nowhere to be seen, so Lucy carried her wares down to the cold storage herself. Afterwards, Mabel handed her the payment envelope and Lucy explained the need for her impromptu trip.

"I'm going to have to adjust some menus without your deliveries." Mabel stepped away to stir one of the large pots on the stove. "But we'll make due. You hurry back as soon as your aunt is feeling better." The woman crossed to some cinnamon loaves cooling on the wooden table, wrapped one in a kitchen cloth and handed the loaf to her.

"Here, you take this to her. I'll be praying for her speedy recovery." She returned to the stove to stir the pot again.

"Thank you so much." Lucy wished she could tell Mabel how much the Tylers would enjoy her baking. It felt so strange, this yearning to share secrets with a friend. Why had it taken so long to open herself up? She wondered if her relationship with Renzo had anything to do with the change. Well, there'd be plenty of time during her trip to ponder that.

She searched for something safe to say to Mabel. "I hope Mitch hasn't gotten into any mischief. It's not like him to leave you high and dry, is it?"

Mabel opened the oven and bunched up the front of her apron to rotate the pans inside. "No. He's been acting mighty strange the past couple days." She returned to her stirring. "It's been hard on him, since his pa died. Lord knows it's a big pair of shoes he's trying to fill. He's just going through a rough patch."

"Well, you've done a good job raising him." Lucy stepped forward to give the woman a reassuring pat on the shoulder but ended up hugging her instead. Real friends did that. And for the first time, Lucy realized her home encompassed more than a few buildings on a plot of land.

Minutes later, she sighed with relief as she headed down Main Street. No one had questioned her story. It's too bad they'd all find out once her trip came to light that she was a liar. But she had to do what was right. The futures of Emily and her children depended on it.

As she approached the sheriff's office, she spotted

Charles Hopper coming out the door. Lucy's heart skipped a beat. He looked in the opposite direction and she clucked at Gertie, vainly hoping they could pass by unnoticed. But with no other traffic to speak of, he rushed down the steps and trotted alongside the cart until he could grab hold of the horse's bridle.

"Whoa, there." The docile animal immediately obeyed.

Lucy scanned the street for onlookers, speaking through clenched teeth. "What do you think you're doing?"

Ignoring her, he looked back over his shoulder toward the building. "Sheriff Tate! I've got her."

Every nerve in her body flared. "You said I had until tomorrow." The coward didn't look her way.

Sheriff Tate hobbled through the doorway and out to the edge of the boardwalk. What had Charles told him?

The lawman's blank expression gave nothing away. "Mrs. Neels. Would you be so kind as to join me in my office?" Although worded as a request, she could tell saying no was not an option.

She nodded even as Charles robbed her of the choice by turning Gertie toward the rail. Two women stared from the walkway outside the Farmer's Bank, so she pasted on a smile and raised her chin as if her stop was a social call.

"You lowdown double-crosser," she muttered to Charles as she passed.

Sheriff Tate gestured her in ahead of him. "Please, have a seat," he said, making his way to the desk.

Seeing his crutches made her think of Thomas. How long could she be delayed before he would know something was wrong and try to make it over to his place?

The sheriff leaned against the desk and crossed his bad foot over his good one. The door closed, but not before Charles snuck inside. He fidgeted with the hat in his hands until he noticed all eyes were on him.

He opened his mouth to speak, but Sheriff Tate beat him to it. "Charles, here, says he was over at your place this morning."

She met the sheriff's gaze but said nothing in response. She'd have to think carefully before she spoke.

"Said he heard a number of hushed voices coming from inside your barn." The sheriff's scrutiny was her biggest enemy. "He also said that he heard a baby's cry."

"That's a lie." She glared at Charles. What was he up to? Why hadn't he said he'd seen Emily and the children with his own eyes? And that Mildred had, too? Why was he altering the facts? Was he trying to protect himself from blackmailing her should the truth come out? She wished she could show him for the lying coward that he was.

Well, there was no evidence of the Tylers being at her place now. Charles and the sheriff could spend all afternoon in her barn and they'd come up empty-handed.

"Sheriff Tate, this is ridiculous. The only person, other than me, who has been in my barn is Thomas." She wouldn't say anything that might get Renzo into trouble.

"Mr. Hopper must have heard me speaking with Thomas when I took him his breakfast this morning." She could hear Charles shifting his boots on the floor but didn't look over at him again for fear of calling him every filthy name she could think of.

Charles, the snake, mumbled something then cleared his throat. "I tell you, there was another woman's voice besides hers. And a baby crying."

She crossed her arms, trying to inspire the sheriff's disbelief. *How am I going to get out of this?*

The evil rat took a step forward. "Those slave catchers have been hanging around for weeks, bothering honest citizens like me and my wife. While I understand Mrs. Neels' compassionate female nature, it's our duty to inform those men that their runaways are at her place. The sooner we do, the sooner they'll be on their way."

The sheriff nodded, while her head throbbed.

She clenched her teeth. What kind of game was Charles playing? He probably would like to see the slave catchers leave, but that wasn't what this was all about. There had to be some selfish reason for him to be going back on their deal, for the life of her, she didn't know what it was. Fear mixed with a double dose of confusion.

I have to get them away. She stood. "I'm not going to sit here and listen to this man's preposterous accusations for one more minute. Good day." She stepped toward the door, visually challenging Charles to stop her.

His startled gaze went past her shoulder. "Aren't you supposed to arrest her, Sheriff?" Charles sounded like a child who'd tattled on a sibling.

The window of the door darkened, and her heartbeat accelerated as Carl Mays entered, forcing Charles off to the side. Sheriff Tate said something rude under his breath.

I have to get out of here.

Mays glanced over her before addressing the sheriff. "I understand you have news for me?" His large form blocked the door so there was no chance of escape.

Sheriff Tate uncrossed his arms, eying Charles. "And who delivered this message?"

"Some boy rode out to my camp. Said the sheriff knew where my fugitives were."

The sheriff refocused on Charles. "Hopper, was that your doing?"

Charles straightened, but the perspiration beading on his upper lip belied his confident stance. "Well, I thought you might need some help since you're lame and Deputy Ross is covering a lot of territory. So when I came into town I gave some boy a half dime to fetch this fellow for you."

Mays waved a hand in the air. "It don't matter who told me. Have you got them in a cell?"

"No one has actually *seen* them yet." Sheriff Tate said. "Mr. Hopper seems to think they're hidden in Mrs. Neels' barn."

Mays's gaze whipped to Lucy. "I knew it. I knew you were hiding them."

If looks could melt flesh and bones, she'd be a puddle seeping through the gaps in the floorboards.

She turned to the only marginally friendly face in the room. "Sheriff, I really need to be heading home. I have animals depending on me. If you'd like to drive out and look around my farm, that's fine. You'll find no one there but Thomas and my livestock."

Charles cleared his throat. "Now that this fella's here, I'll head on home." While all three gave him sneers of various degrees, no one objected. "I am sorry about this Mrs. Neels." He tipped his hat and scurried out the door like the frightened skunk that he was.

Mays crowded her but spoke to Sheriff Tate. "I want this woman locked up." He tucked his thumbs under his gun belt. "She's been harboring fugitive slaves and law says she should be arrested and tried."

"Now see here, Mr. Mays." Sheriff Tate said, straightening, "I've yet to be presented with any evidence of Mrs. Neels' guilt."

"You got that fella's say-so. And if you don't hold her until I get to her place to search, she'll warn them off."

She didn't have time for this. "Sheriff, I can drive behind your rig." She glared at Mays. "Where I couldn't possibly move anyone or *warn them off.* But I need to get back home."

"No. She's got something up her sleeve. I say lock her up."

The sheriff moved closer to Lucy. "Mr. Mays, I really don't think that's necessary.

"Well, I want some time to fetch Fred and Gil. That way we can surround the place before she can scatter them by shouting a warning."

It could take all afternoon for Mays to round up his friends. Thomas might try and set off with them himself if she was gone that long.

Panic welled up inside her. She shoved Mays back, catching the big man off-guard, and grabbed the door handle. "I'm going home. Follow me if you like."

But Mays quickly regained his footing and grabbed her. "Not so fast."

With her arms pinned at her sides, she could only wriggle and kick at him, trying to get away. Suddenly, it was as if she'd been sucked into the past. She was drowning in memories of Emmett's beatings. But she'd survived each one. Even the last. She was stronger now, and unlike then, this time she'd fight.

"Let me go, you bastard." She squirmed and kicked her feet. She threw her head back, hoping to catch him in the mouth. She tried to pinch him, but the band of his arms tightened with her struggles. Kicking and flailing were her only options but she wouldn't, couldn't give up.

"Calm down, Mrs. Neels," the sheriff said.

Mays grunted as her heel finally connected with his kneecap. "Damn it, woman." The arms around her tightened. It got harder to breathe.

Sheriff Tate's face wavered in her vision and his voice faded in and out with undistinguishable words. Her hands tingled on the verge of numbness, doubling her panic. How could she get away? She had to at least warn Thomas. But her fury and desperation had surpassed the point of her regaining self-control.

A growl of rage rattled from her lungs and then suddenly everything went black.

Chapter Twenty-One

Renzo opened the door to find Lucy's limp body in the arms of Carl Mays. "What the hell did you do to her!" If it weren't for the fact that Lucy would hit the floor, Renzo would have grabbed him by the throat and choked the life out of him. He lifted her out of the man's arms, scanning her for injuries.

Killing Mays was still a very real possibility.

"Renzo," Sheriff Tate said with a stern voice. "She fainted is all. Mrs. Neels became hysterical."

Renzo gave an angry chuckle. "Lucy doesn't get hysterical. She gets angry, but not hysterical. Now what the hell is going on?" He'd expected her to be angry and fearful, and maybe pacing inside a jail cell, but for God's sake not unconscious.

"Mr. Mays simply restrained her when she tried to leave."

He gave Mays a murderous glare and pushed his way past them, carrying her to one of the two cells in the back room. Sheriff Tate hobbled behind him so there'd be no privacy once she came to.

As his ragged breathing slowed, guilt pounded in

his head. Would she ever forgive him for the nightmarish situation he'd placed her in? He only hoped that after all was said and done, she'd consider it a fair price for getting the Tylers to safety. Renzo twisted through one of the cell doorways and laid her on the cot.

Kneeling next to her, he rubbed one of her hands. "Lucy. Can you hear me?"

Her eyes fluttered open, and Renzo leaned in, wishing to hell that Tate and Mays weren't as close as shine on new leather.

"Renzo?" She put a hand to her forehead.

"It's me. You're at the jail. Sheriff Tate is right here." He hoped she'd know they weren't able to speak freely. "He said you became overwrought and fainted."

The confusion cleared from her eyes. "They won't let me go home, Renzo. You know how upset Agnes gets when I'm late for her milking." Good, she wasn't admitting anything. She may not know what he was up to, but as long as she kept up the innocent routine, the plan could work.

He helped her into a sitting position but couldn't bring himself to let her go. "What the hell is this all about, Sheriff?" He was still mad as hell about the slave catcher's hands being on her, but he also needed to sound unaware about what was happening.

"Charles Hopper was in. He thinks Mrs. Neels is hiding those runaways in her barn."

Renzo knew the sheriff would be weighing his every reaction since he'd been to her place daily.

Here we go. "Hopper's mistaken, or trying to stir up trouble for Lucy since Thomas is staying there. I've been inside her barn to visit Thomas and, I assure you, except for some barn cats and a cow, he was very much alone."

Mays huffed. "All this talk is a waste of time. I'm going to search her property. From the tip of the weathervane, to the bucket in her well." He left the back room.

"Hold up just a minute there, Mr. Mays." Sheriff Tate went after the slave catcher.

"I have to get out of here," Lucy whispered to Renzo. "I moved the Tylers to Thomas's barn, but I'm certain those men will search there again once they finish at my place." The glass pane of the front door rattled as it slammed.

"I know. I spoke with Thomas earlier and-"

"Renzo," Sheriff Tate hobbled back into the room. "We need to go, son. Mays has already left to round up his friends." His attention switched to Lucy as he approached the cell door. A large key on a ring jingled from his fingers. Her heart thudded as if trying to break free from the confines of her chest. Eerily similar to how she felt about being locked in this cell, with its iron bars.

"I'm sorry Mrs. Neels. But so Mays can't claim you did anything to interfere, I'm going to detain you. Just for a couple hours, until we get this mess cleared up." He leaned on his crutches and pulled the cell door half closed. "Let's go, Renzo."

When Renzo backed away, broaching no argument on her behalf, she battled memories of betrayal and confinement. *Stop it. That was Emmett.* Those insecurities had nothing to do with Renzo. He had known about the runaways and hadn't turned them in. No, she would trust that he would somehow warn Thomas before it was too late. She clasped the bars as the sheriff turned the key in the lock.

Renzo gripped her hands. "I'm certain you won't be here long. Once the sheriff sees that these charges are unfounded, we'll get you right out."

"That's right, Mrs. Neels," Sheriff Tate agreed. "I'll send for my wife. She'll see to any needs you might require."

And then both men were gone. She sank back into the cot, gripping its musty pillow to her chest.

A couple of hours, not two days. She wouldn't let old fears suffocate her. This is nothing like the smoke house. It's clean, I have somewhere to lie down and there are people who know where I am. Unfortunately, three-quarters of Rush Crossing's population would know before the supper dishes were clean and stacked.

A tear trickled down her cheek. It was a relief not to have to squelch them. After all, there wasn't anyone here to see. Lucy's throat constricted. Oh, how she wished Wink was here to rest his big head on her lap.

Renzo and the sheriff watched Mays and the Greenley brothers circle into position as they approached Lucy's place. Tate reined in his wagon in front of the barn while the three slave catchers closed in from the other directions. Renzo tied Terra to the rig and came around to help Tate to the ground.

"This goddamned gout. I've about had it," the sheriff grumbled. "Let's see what all the fuss is about." He gestured with his head toward the door, and Renzo opened it. They stepped inside just as Mays stormed through the back door, revolver drawn.

"Thomas?" Renzo called, knowing good and well that the man was nowhere in earshot. "Are you here?"

Mays crossed to the cot, kicking it over with the toe of his boot. "You don't see him, do you?" Wood shavings littered the ground and writing supplies sat abandoned on the crate. The leather bound Bible was missing.

"I'll check the outhouse," Renzo offered. He didn't want to see how they upended everything looking for people who weren't here.

"Yeah, like they'll all fit in there?" Mays smirked and went to search the stalls.

As Renzo returned Mays was holstering his gun and Gil was coming down the ladder from the loft.

"No sign of them. But since Washington ain't

here, I bet he's stashing them somewhere else." Mays turned to his partners. "We need to go check his place again. He's probably moved them there."

"What about the house?" Renzo asked. Every minute he could stall would bring them all closer to dusk. And darkness was crucial to the illusion.

"Well, why the hell didn't you look already?" Fred asked.

Pummeling the man would be physically satisfying, but the plan called for him to appear to be helping them. "Seeing as I've been courting Mrs. Neel, I didn't think it likely that you'd believe me when I say there's no one hiding inside."

Sheriff Tate hobbled to the door. "I'll check the house. That leaves the other out buildings to you all." He looked back at Mays. "I have I feeling I'm going to be issuing my deepest apologies to Mrs. Neels, so take care not to destroy any of her property. If you do, I *will* hold you responsible."

They split up and searched each outbuilding.

"Nothing," Tate said when they all met up again. Renzo suspected Charles Hopper was going to get an earful from the lawman about making false accusations. "Now unless any of you found evidence of those runaways, I'm headed back to town to release Mrs. Neels."

Gil snorted and spit. "Just because they ain't here don't mean they weren't."

Mays nodded to his companions and they mounted up and trotted off as if they'd been told what to do next. "You mark my words, she's involved," he said. "Meanwhile I'm going to search Washington's place." Without a backward glance, he headed toward the trees.

"Renzo," Tate said, "I know you're even more anxious than I am to free Mrs. Neels, but I think it would be best if you're there when they search Thomas's place."

"You're right. His barn escaped one disaster, but I wouldn't put it past any of those three to drop a lit match."

And if Thomas's spacious new barn was destroyed, Charles might go back on his end of the bargain.

"I wouldn't put *anything* past them at this point," the sheriff said.

Renzo felt the same. "Sheriff, I need to ask you to do something that might not make much sense. When those three don't find their runaways, my guess is they'll be fuming." Hopefully he'd run them on a wild goose chase for at least the next hour. "I'd like to know that Lucy isn't driving back here by herself. If you could hold her until I can bring her safely home, I'd be grateful. Maybe get her to eat something?"

Tate puffed out his cheeks. "Son, you didn't see that woman when she realized she couldn't just push her way out of my office. She's not going to sit down to a meal. Those bars are the only thing that's keeping her there." They reached the rig.

Renzo helped the man up onto the seat and handed up his crutches. "Then keep her locked in the cell. Tell her we're still searching the woods and she can't leave until we get back." He loosened Terra's reins and mounted.

Tate shook his head. "You're going to need a bucket of water to cool her off once you get there."

In any other situation, he might laugh at the image. But he knew that a bucketful wouldn't be nearly enough to cool Lucy down when he saw her next.

Renzo tied Terra in a small clearing and made his way through the trees along Thomas's drive just as the slave catchers had done at Lucy's. He wasn't about to give Mays any reason to drive him off the hunt. The sun hung low in the sky, and he had to study the ground carefully for a quiet path. About fifty feet from the clearing, he heard the Greenley's ahead. Neither one heard him draw near. Not trusting that they would share their plan with him Renzo paused behind a tree trunk to eavesdrop.

Fred watched the barn through the trees. "Ha. After all that bitching about making sure that mutt didn't smell us, it catches Carl."

Gil dug the tip of a knife into a sapling, gouging it over and over. "Yeah, and after the way that damned dog bared its teeth at me yesterday, I wanted to be the one to send it to Hell."

Renzo rubbed his fist, barely able to control his fury and remain silent. He wanted to pound all three of them into a bloody pulp, but the success of his plan depended on sticking to it. Avenging Wink's murder, while mentally satisfying, couldn't hold a candle to the Tyler's successful escape.

"Carl don't even know for sure that it's dead. He had to high-tail it outta there once he fired so he couldn't follow to make sure."

"It's dead all right. You can bet money on that. Hey, here he comes." The two made their way out of the trees.

Renzo waited a minute then emerged from the trees as if he'd just caught up with them. "Sheriff Tate sent me to help."

Mays narrowed his eyes. "Just don't be getting in our way." He cocked his chin. "Go on around that side and meet up with Fred in the back. Wait for my signal and don't make any noise."

They split up, and Renzo circled the barn. When he met Fred near the back door, they drew their guns and waited.

"Now!" Mays yelled.

Fred burst through the door first, as if a band of murders rather than a mother and her children might be hiding there. Inside the barn, Mays and Gil waved their guns as they ran from stall to stall. Renzo couldn't allow himself to dwell on how the three would treat helpless prisoners for fear he'd just shoot the three of them and be done with it.

"See anything?" Mays called.

"Not yet," Fred said, holstering his revolver and heading up one of the ladders to the hayloft. "Gil, go up the other ladder and meet me in the middle." The other Greenely ran to the opposite side and ascended.

Stalling for time, Renzo made a show of poking a hay pile with a pitchfork, hoping Mays noticed and ordered the brothers to do the same up in the hayloft. They wouldn't need much light to follow the tracks from the crutches. Not if these fellows were halfway decent at tracking.

Someone whistled from the loft. "Hey, Carl. Guess what I found?"

Mays pointed his gun up at the loft. "Did you find them?"

Gil appeared at the edge of the loft, a small bundle of cloth hanging from his fingertips. "Naw. But this here's proof they've been here. And the piss is still wet." He tossed it down to the ground.

Mays kicked dirt over the cloth. "Get down here. Everybody outside. Let's pick up their trail outside."

They hadn't bothered to check before storming the barn. Renzo knew the only tracks close to the building would be theirs, but he also knew where to *find* the runaways' tracks. Mays went out the front and Renzo headed out back. He walked toward the woods, spotting the trail immediately but didn't call out until Fred headed his direction.

"I found them." Renzo knelt and pointed to the markings, his excitement genuine. "I bet these round ones are from crutches. And look at all the footprints. The small ones must belong to the children." It sickened him to see Fred's eyes light up as he squatted to examine the prints.

Mays ran up and leaned down. "That's Washington all right. I followed those all the way from her place." He looked back toward the barn. "Sneaky bastard must have swept them away with a tree branch or something."

"They're on the run, boss." Fred stood and hitched a thumb over his shoulder in the direction of the setting sun. "But it's going to be hard to follow their tracks in the dark.

And in order to get to the river before it was too dark, they needed to get moving. Renzo stepped under the cover of the trees, itching to move but knowing he had to let them do the tracking.

"You've been through here the most, Gil. If we go straight that way, where does this woods take you?" Mays asked.

Gil spit in the dirt. "There's a stream not too far in that runs down to the Hickory River. From there it's about a half mile to the Ohio. If you cross through the stream and go over the hill it's another mile to the next farm."

"Let's find that stream. I've got a feeling they're headed that way."

Mays passed Renzo and took the lead. The undergrowth made it more difficult to see the tracks, but the leader moved at a good pace. Renzo had wondered if he'd have to fight to stay toward the front of the pack, but the Greenleys seemed content to bring up the rear. Soon enough the trickling of moving water signaled their proximity to the stream. At the bed the trail of prints went right into water.

"Deputy Ross, I'd say it's about time you got those fancy boots dirty," Mays said. "Cross over and look downstream along the bed for tracks. Gil, go upstream. Fred and I will check this side."

Renzo waded through the water and headed downstream. They still had a half mile to cover, and with only the sliver of moon tonight, timing was crucial for success.

"I can't hardly see anything," Fred complained. *Where are those tracks?* After a moment he spotted them. "Here, they're headed this way," Renzo called. He started off at a trot, and the others hopped over downed branches and patches of undergrowth to keep up.

Mays met Renzo's pace on the other side. "Faster," the leader called. After a minute of running, Gil and Fred lagged behind. Good, Renzo needed to get there first. If only Mays would drop back, but the man was in better physical condition than his men.

Soon the sound of the moving water grew louder. Renzo knew the confluence of the stream with the Hickory River lay just ahead. The banks of the widening stream grew steeper, forcing him to slow. He heard Gil slip and fall in the mud behind him, but Mays picked up speed. As if he knew how close they were to their prey.

The stream bed dropped off suddenly and Renzo had to grab hold of a sapling and swing past it to keep from falling into the water. He saw Mays slip and go down on one knee, but he righted himself quickly. They ran faster now, the rushing water of the Hickory drowning out the sounds of their pounding feet.

Renzo pushed through his fatigue, knowing he needed to be the one to spot the apparent runaways. He cleared the trees at the confluence of the river and scanned the opposite side of the Hickory. Gil fell again somewhere behind and let out a string of curses.

It was almost full on dark, and Renzo widened his eyes looking for the little boat.

"Over there." Mays yelled, and his arm shot up.

Shit. Renzo glanced over at the other two slave catchers then searched in the direction Mays pointed.

There. Dark shadows broke the surface of the water two-thirds of the way across. A tiny rowboat. He made out darkly clad figures huddled inside. One tall with a hat and three smaller. It was them. Someone in the boat pointed in their direction and screamed, but the flow of the water drowned out the voices.

"Damn it, we can't let them get away." Fred

yelled.

The slave catcher raised his gun, and Renzo's heart almost stopped. He drew his gun and fired across the water.

Chapter Twenty-Two

"Mrs. Neels, you should sit down and rest. You're going to wear holes in the soles of your boots." Anita Tate sat outside the cell, knitting. The sheriff's kind-hearted wife had been trying, without success, to distract Lucy with idle chit-chat. "Are you certain you won't eat any of your supper?" Mrs. Tate had brought a fine chicken and dumplings meal which sat untouched on the tray.

Still pacing, Lucy shook her head and absently rubbed her aching back. What a time for her monthly flow to begin. Thankfully Mrs. Tate had been able to provide her with some supplies. Although she hadn't really expected the Lord to grant her a second chance at motherhood, her heart ached to have had the daydream ripped away while she was locked in jail.

"I don't understand how it can take so long to look around." Besides, how could she be held accountable for anyone found wandering around in the woods? Would the slave catchers have gone all the way to Thomas's place and searched it, too? She prayed Renzo had prevented that from happening.

Lucy heard the front door opening and rushed

forward to grasp the bars. The sheriff's crutches clunked across the floorboards and he came into view. Although she hadn't heard any other footsteps, she strained to see past him. Did he have the Tylers in custody or had Thomas managed to escape with them? Was Renzo here?

"Am I free to go home now?"

"No and yes," he said, handing his wife the keys. "If you would, Anita."

Mrs. Tate unlocked the door and wrapped a comforting arm around Lucy. "Are you going to be alright, dear?"

Lucy met the sheriff's gaze. "I take it you believe me now?"

He looked as wretched as she felt. "I apologize, Mrs. Neels, for holding you so long. I hope you understand that I didn't have much choice." Not only was she worried about Thomas and the Tylers, but the strain of telling lies all day long had her worn through.

"I understand." No use scolding the man for doing his job. Especially since she *was* guilty. "I just want to get home." She hurried past them, thanking Mrs. Tate for everything. But just as she reached the front door, Gil Greenley burst through the door. She backed away, unwilling to chance that he would try and grab her as Mays had. She braced herself for news of the family's discovery.

"Sheriff!" Gil called, not giving her more than a cursory glance.

Sheriff Tate hustled in from the back room. "What is it?"

"We spotted them in a rowboat on the Hickory River."

A wave of dizziness hit her and she leaned her hip against the office's desk for support. Then Renzo stepped in the open doorway behind Greenley, and something in his lifeless eyes made her stomach plummet. If they'd escaped, he'd look more confident.

Gil hitched a thumb over his shoulder. "Your

deputy here shot and killed Washington."

Her knees wobbled and she grabbed the edge of the desk.

No, I must have heard him wrong. She held her breath and looked to Renzo, waiting for his denial.

He stepped closer to the Sheriff. "I was just trying to stop him. I didn't mean to kill him."

The room wavered before her eyes.

Mrs. Tate's arm slipped around her once more. "Perhaps you should sit down."

Lucy blinked everything back into focus. "This can't be."

"Are you certain he's dead?" Sheriff Tate asked.

"Unless he's a real good swimmer with a bullet in his chest," Gil said.

A bullet in his chest? It wasn't possible. Renzo couldn't have done what this man accused him of.

"This has got to be some kind of mistake. Renzo wouldn't shoot Thomas." He couldn't have shot her best friend.

Renzo spoke to the sheriff. "My aim was off. It was an accident."

Why wasn't he looking at her? Why wasn't he telling her this was all a huge mistake? But the answer stabbed her heart and propelled her forward. She swung with all her might, slapping his face.

His head snapped back and his hand went to his injured cheek.

"How could you? Thomas was the kindest man I ever met. And you pretended to like him." Despair slammed into her with unexpected force and she barely recognized her own shaky voice.

Renzo met her gaze. "I did like him. He was a fine man. As I said, it was an accident. I want you to know how very sorry I am for all of this." He turned to the sheriff. "I'm responsible. I was the one who fired."

"That leaves us out of it," Gil said. "Them

runaways have probably floated ten miles down the Ohio by now." He took a step toward the door and then swept his gaze over everyone. "I still say she had a hand in this whole business." Then he left as abruptly as he'd arrived.

The walls felt as if they were closing in on Lucy even more than when she'd been locked in the cell. She had to get out of here. Away from all this hurt, to what she knew. Her animals. Solitude. She prayed that the Tylers had evaded Mays. But, Lord, the cost. Thomas was dead. How could Renzo betray her trust?

"Tell me this is a mistake," she pleaded.

Without answering, he met her gaze with one so guilty, chills tingled down her arms to her fingertips. She reached to pull at a coat front that wasn't there then dropped her hands in defiance.

No, I won't be weak ever again.

"Lucy, please forgive me." Renzo reached for her hand.

She slapped it away. "Go to hell," she said, then walked out, head held high.

Renzo watched Lucy walk out the door. He'd never been prouder of anyone, and yet his chest ached. Definitely love. Only love could make her scorn cut this deeply.

"I'm going to leave you two alone." Emily Tate gave her husband a reassuring pat on the arm and a moment later the door shut behind her.

With an exhausted sigh, the sheriff maneuvered himself to his chair. "Well, if this hasn't been one helluva day."

The man's weariness ate at Renzo's conscience. It would be such a relief to share the truth. And although he suspected the sheriff would be an ally, assuaging his guilt wasn't reason enough to put that theory to the test.

"As much as it pains me to say it, Renzo, I'll need your gun and your badge."

Surprisingly pained to hear it, he unhooked his gun belt and laid it on the desk. He tugged the badge from his vest, amazed at how such a miniscule task required such a Herculean effort.

Tate took the star in his hand, his fingers running slowly over each letter. "You know, I was hoping I might convince you to stay on permanently. But now..."

Sheriff Tate would soon find out Renzo hadn't killed anyone, but damned if it didn't hurt like hell having everyone believe he was responsible for Thomas's death. He glanced through the window at the darkness outside, replaying Lucy's last words in his mind. He winced. Never had he wanted a woman's love more, and she hated him. Hated him enough to wish him an eternity with the devil.

He rubbed his chest and turned his gaze to a light bobbing on the opposite side of the street.

Mitch stood in a recessed doorway, holding a lantern. He must have been waiting for Lucy to leave town. The boy hustled across the street. His clothes were clean and dry but his neatly combed hair was damp. Hopefully Tate wouldn't wonder about that.

"Sheriff," Mitch called as he burst in the door. "I have a message for you." The young man panted. "Me and my brothers were fishing down at the mouth of the Hickory when all of a sudden, what do you know? Mr. Thomas Washington comes swimming up to the bank in all his clothes."

"What?" Renzo feigned surprise and then his breath caught in earnest. Mitch had missed washing away a spot of the soot he'd darkened his skin with. Renzo met the young man's gaze and gave him a pointed stare. Then he scratched at the same place below his own ear, hoping Mitch would understand. The young man ducked his chin and discreetly swiped it away with his cuff.

The sheriff came to the edge of his chair, not bothering to mask his excitement. "Was he injured?"

"No, his leg seemed fine." Mitch quirked his

brow. "I thought he was laid up with a broken leg."

"Well, I'll be." A Royal Flush grin spread across Tate's face.

Renzo let his jaw go slack, pretended to be speechless with relief.

"Was he just pretending to have a broken leg?" Mitch shrugged. "I don't understand. Anyway, he told me to tell you that he'd been thinking about moving to Cincinnati for a while now. Said he'd sold his farm and was real sorry he hadn't stopped by to say goodbye in person."

Tate stood, looking at Renzo. "You said he was still hobbling around on crutches."

"He was, just yesterday. It appears Thomas fooled us all, including Lucy." Why not reinforce her supposed innocence in all this? "He even had me help him choose the branches to make his crutches."

Tate pounded him on the back. "Well, son, I've never been so glad to hear that someone's not a crack shot. I sure didn't relish the thought of charging you with murder."

Chapter Twenty-Three

Lucy made it home through the spotty moonlight. She checked the barn to make certain Agnes had been taken care of, just as Sheriff Tate had assured her. She stroked the cow's soft ear and, avoiding Thomas's makeshift quarters, bid her goodnight.

She summoned what remained of her energy and rounded the front of the house, needing to confirm whether anyone had yet laid Wink to rest. She held her lantern high. There. A mound of loose dirt disturbed the dusty strip of yard just in front of the porch. Tomorrow she would transplant some lilies to the spot. Such a loyal friend deserved a proper tribute.

She said a brief prayer over his grave and went inside. Her dry eyes burned from the combination of grief and the strain of managing the cart over the dark road. Without bothering to light a lamp, she undressed and slipped into her nightgown. Although hunger gnawed at her belly, she couldn't summon the energy to walk back to the other room. Instead, she crawled into bed and let exhaustion drag her into a deep sleep.

Much too soon, The Sheik's cock-a-doodle-do

signaled the morning. She'd have to depend on routine to carry her through the hours until she could once again slip away into oblivion of sleep. Washing and dressing in the coming light, Lucy made her way to the breadbox. Inside, on top of what remained of the towel-draped loaf, was a folded piece of paper. Puzzled, she pulled it out. Her gaze flew over the page and paused on the signature.

Thomas. He'd written her a note before he'd left. She hugged it to her chest, almost joyful, until she remembered that this was the last message her friend would ever have written.

Dear Lucy,

There isn't much time but I wanted to leave you with some assurance that we are all fine.

She closed her eyes. At least her dear friend had been hopeful during his last hours.

Seems I can't bring myself to say goodbye to Emily and the children. Lucky for all of us, your Deputy Ross can think on his feet. He came up with a plan to help us travel north, while at the same time, making sure you aren't implicated. Just for a while, we need the slave catchers to think I am dead so they will move on. But all is well, child. I will be nowhere near the river when Renzo fires his gun high over the heads of our impersonators.

The paper rattled in her hands. Although she had been paying close attention to the text, she stopped to reread the last sentence. Could this be? She held her breath and read on.

If everything goes according to the plan, Charles Hopper will be getting you thrown in jail. But just for a short while. Hopefully, you'll be released by tonight and my farm and new barn full of hay will satisfy the man's lust for more.

I'll write once we arrive in Canada and I get my new family settled. I hope you can forgive me and Deputy Ross for leaving without proper goodbyes. You were right about him, so forgive him for whatever uncomfortable circumstances this plan puts you in.

Take it from an old man who thought he'd die alone, be strong and open to risking love.

Ever Your Dearest Friend,
Thomas

Lucy dropped into a chair and read the note twice more to make sure she hadn't misunderstood. It had all been planned? He was alive! She breathed out the tangle of grief and helplessness that had bound her lungs as effectively as a coil of thick rope. Thomas was alive, and Renzo had only pretended to kill him in order to get Mays and the Greenley brothers to move on.

Renzo. Her heart thudded with the memory of her spiteful words. He'd stood there silently, letting everyone believe him a murderer. She'd accepted the story as fact almost without hesitation. And how had she repaid him for sacrificing his good name to protect others? She'd slapped him and scorned him to hell. Oh, how he must loathe her. He'd accused her once of not really knowing him, and she'd proven it yet again.

Oh, God. She glanced at the paper in her fingers but her vision blurred with unshed tears. Thomas's ending words confused her. What did he mean by being open to risking love? Although Renzo had offered marriage, he'd only done that out of obligation. And to think that she'd actually been considering his proposal. He'd probably thanked his lucky stars a hundred times since last night that she hadn't accepted yet. And now that she'd driven him away, he'd be free to follow his heart's desire with other women. She fisted her hands, crushing the edges of the paper.

A knock instinctively brought her to her feet, and she ran to the door, throwing it open.

"Lucy." Mildred Hopper's free hand went to her bosom. "My goodness. I didn't expect you to answer quite so quickly."

Lucy didn't think to hide her disappointment. She'd hoped to find Renzo standing on the other side of the door, impossible as that was. Thomas's letter said Renzo was assisting their little band on their journey north.

"Mildred." She looked past the woman's shoulders expecting to see her devil of a husband.

"I'm alone." Mildred's gaze was uneasy. Perhaps she, too, felt confounded about yesterday's events. Lucy backed up in wordless invitation, and Mildred stepped inside. "I wanted to check on you, to see if you were all right." The statement—or ones very similar to it—had crossed the woman's lips hundreds of times the previous two years. Normally Lucy would have rolled her eyes, but this time, her heart listened. Why was it she'd never sensed the woman's sincerity before? Mildred's tone and piteous facial expression were as they always were. What was different? She sifted back through a filter of mundane memories.

Was it she, rather than her neighbor, who'd changed? Mildred's soft touch on Lucy's arm brought her gaze up and somewhere, deep in her mind, a door opened. The woman's concern had always been genuine, not the habitual melodrama she'd always assumed.

"Perhaps I could sit and we could talk for a spell. You've been through quite an ordeal and I want to help."

Long-standing habit taunted Lucy with subconscious jeers. *Tell the busy-body to mind her own business and leave you alone.* But during the past weeks, a sense of inclusion had been growing inside her which made it easier to ignore the whispers.

She crossed to the chairs in front of the cold, brick hearth and sat.

Mildred joined her. "First off, I need to apologize for Charles." She reached across and rested a hand on top of Lucy's. "I made him tell me what he'd said to you. I was stunned." She shook her head. "And ashamed. Please believe me when I say that the man I married would never have done such a horrible thing. And I told him so." Mildred sat back in her chair.

"When I first met Charles, he was so tender and sweet. He doted on me as if I was a princess." She smiled.

"We were so anxious to start a family. He would have made such a wonderful father. But it just never happened. And as the years passed, it was as if he replaced his desire for children with other things."

Lucy knew what it was like to desperately want a child. And it had only been two years since that dream had been ripped from her. What would another thirty years have done to her?

"What are you saying? Has he agreed not to blackmail me?" Her fingernails dug into her palms. Now that the Tylers were on their way north and she'd been cleared of suspicion, was blackmail even possible?

Mildred pulled out a handkerchief and dabbed it at the corners of her eyes. "Charles won't cause you any more trouble. We had a long talk before the deputy showed up yesterday and I think he's truly sorry for what he did."

If so, it probably had more to do with his wife's disappointment than any belated onslaught of scruples.

"Why didn't he tell Sheriff Tate that you two had seen the runaways here? He just said that you heard voices and suspected I was hiding them."

"That was Deputy Ross's idea. You see, he came to the house and confronted Charles."

"He did what?" Lucy's throat burned thinking about all of Renzo's quick planning and all that he'd sacrificed.

Mildred put her hankie back in her pocket. "The deputy arranged everything. And *I* told Charles that if he didn't agree to follow the deputy's plan to the letter, he could just drive me to the hotel because I wasn't going to spend the rest of my life with a blackmailer."

Lucy caught her breath, never suspecting Mildred would show that kind of backbone to her spouse.

"The idea was for you to be incarcerated, but only temporarily. I'm sorry. I'm sure that was terribly unpleasant, but Deputy Ross said it needed to be long enough for Mr. Washington and that poor woman and her children to get away. That way, you are cleared of any wrongdoing, and those evil men are gone. Hopefully, for good."

Lucy rose and crossed to the mantle. She toyed with a candle stub, wishing she could see into the future and know they'd all escaped safely. And Renzo. He'd planned it all in such a way as to clear her name. And tarnish his. Why would he make such a sacrifice for her? Unless? Unless...Was it possible that his feelings had been deeper than he'd admitted? But why wouldn't he have said so? No, that was her wishful thinking again.

She brushed the wax from her hands, shifting her thoughts to their escape.

"But how could Thomas travel? His leg wasn't fully healed."

"He took one of our big wagons as partial payment for his land. Didn't you notice that his team was gone?"

Lucy shook her head. "I was so tired when I got home, I forgot all about them." With a wagon Emily and the children could bed down in it during the day.

"And don't worry about them not having enough to eat. I filled four bushel baskets with food."

Lucy smiled. Thanks to Renzo, the Tyler's journey would be much easier than the trek they'd have undertaken with her. She fished in her pocket for her own handkerchief.

"Don't worry." Mildred's gentle hand on her shoulder was her undoing. Lucy turned to the older woman and without hesitation, went into her open arms. "Shh. It's all right. They'll be fine." Mildred patted her back. "Mr. Washington knows what to do."

A bursting dam of emotions washed away Lucy's voice, and after quiet minutes, the motherly comfort of Mildred's crooning made her realize there was no need to reply.

Chapter Twenty-Four

Four Weeks Later

Bess Anderson leaned on her broom outside the front door of the mercantile and called to Lucy. "Don't forget about quilting at Mabel's on Saturday afternoon."

Lucy waved and managed a smile, wondering how long the dear group of ladies would put up with her uneven stitches and jagged curves. But deep down she knew. As long as it took for her to get the hang of it. Mabel, Bess, Mildred and the others had been an incredible help throughout the lonely days since Renzo had left. While she mourned driving away the man she loved, with the support of her new friends, the days were becoming easier to manage.

She reined in Gertie in front of the post office and retrieved the one piece of mail waiting for her. There was no name with the return address, but she recognized Thomas's handwriting and ripped open the envelope as soon as she got outside, devouring the first news she'd had from him.

He and Emily were married, and all three children

were thriving. They wanted her to come visit them in Canada, but a long trip like that was unlikely. Still, she could and would be diligent with her letter writing.

His letter made no mention of Renzo. Had he stayed long once they'd made it to Canada or returned home? Perhaps she should ask the sheriff—who thought Renzo had left town that night for Philadelphia—if he had his address. Now that she knew Thomas, Emily and the children had arrived safely she should write to Renzo and apologize for what she'd said.

Lucy refolded the paper, stuffed it inside her pocket and headed home. The drive seemed different each day, what with more and more leaves changing to brilliant yellows, oranges and reds. But even the shifting beauty of the countryside couldn't take her mind off of Renzo and the sacrifice he'd made for all of them. He hadn't had the opportunity to share his plan, and knowing her own tendencies, she might have insisted on going along. At least her violent reaction had given the plan an extra measure of credibility. Oh, but the anguish on his face when she'd cursed him to hell. It was probably too much for a man to forget.

She turned Gertie down the drive and almost dropped the reins. A familiar horse grazed in front of the house, and her chest tightened as she saw Renzo. Holding his hat in his hands, he rose from one of the rockers.

Lord, help me. She didn't know whether to jump down and run to him, or tuck her tail between her legs. Her parting words had been filled with such despair and anger, she'd never expected to see him again. But here he was, and even if she couldn't throw herself into his arms, she could drink in his tall form, dark curls and square, handsome jaw.

She reined in by the porch.

"You're back."

"Yes." He just stood there staring at her, his words and actions giving her no clue as to what he was thinking.

She couldn't move. What a time for her muscles to revolt.

"Aren't you going to get down? Gertie's going to get mighty confused." His smile, the one that said he was entirely too sure of himself, robbed her breath. He crossed to the cart and extended his hand. Miraculously, her legs moved and she accepted the hand down. Then, she stood there memorizing each of his features.

"Can we sit?" he asked, gesturing to the pair of rocking chairs. He opened his mouth to speak then closed it again, dragging a hand through his hair. "I knew this was going to be difficult, but seeing you, knowing what I've put you through. I'm sorry sounds so inane."

He's sorry? "What are you talking about? Because of you the Tylers are free and Thomas is a husband and a father. Not only that, but I still have my farm. I'm the one who should be apologizing to you for the way I spoke to you that night."

He leaned toward her and is hand covered hers. "No. You reacted as any true friend would. I'm just sorry for the anguish you must have gone through." He gently laced his fingers between hers and she gripped them back. "For making you think Thomas was dead. For being locked up in that jail cell. But I couldn't think of any other way to keep you safe from the slave catchers, and get them to leave."

"How can you think any of those things outweigh what you did for Emily and the children and Thomas?" She bit her lip, remembering her hurtful words. "Your plan was brilliant. And compared to the danger all of you were in, my discomfort was nothing."

Which wasn't the whole truth. Her heart had been aching for weeks.

"I'm glad." He released her hand and stood.

Don't go. She rose too. "There is something about your plan I never understood and when I asked Mildred, she didn't know. If Thomas and the Tylers weren't the ones you were shooting at, then who was?"

He grabbed one of the wooden posts, tested its strength then met her gaze. "Understand, I was desperate and didn't have any alternatives."

She gripped the armrests of the chair, not liking the sound of that.

"It was Thomas's scarecrow and the Wilcox boys."

She gasped.

"Now before you chastise me, I want you to know that they're all excellent swimmers."

If Mabel ever finds out she'll take after him with an iron skillet.

"Mays and the Greenleys wouldn't have killed anyone. They wouldn't get their bounty if they did. But I could shoot, and the boys knew I'd aim high and wide. We'd gone over the plan. They knew exactly what to do."

Lucy couldn't believe they'd been willing to take the risk. All of them. But since the Tylers escape was over and done, what good would it do to admonish him for enlisting the boy's help?

She went to the post next to his and leaned against it. "Did you have any trouble? Hiding that big wagon and the horses during the day must have been difficult."

"We didn't need to hide. We traveled during the day."

She straightened. "I don't understand. Thomas insisted that I was only to travel only at night.

"We all dressed like Quakers. You know how some of the strict Quaker women wear those huge brimmed bonnets and gloves. Of course, James had to be a girl, but he took it in stride."

She smiled at the image of James in a bonnet and dress. "And Thomas?" Surely you couldn't pass him off as a Quaker woman.

"Thomas is a free man with papers saying so,

remember? He was just an injured traveler that we picked up along the way."

Of, course. It was a good thing they'd had Renzo and his quick thinking. With her leading the way, they'd have been caught for sure. "So you didn't have any trouble?"

"One close call, but nothing I wasn't able to talk us out of."

She grinned. "*That* I can believe." The man could sell snake oil to a preacher. "I got a letter from Thomas today." She pulled it from her pocket.

Renzo nodded. "He said he'd write to you as soon as they'd found a place."

"So you didn't stay with them once you crossed the border?" Where had he been? For the first time since she'd laid eyes on him, she took note of his apparel. His hat, boots and clothes were covered with dust, and she couldn't ever remember seeing him in greater need of a bath. "Where have you been since then?"

Somber eyes met hers. "I've been in Philadelphia."

He'd gone home. Of course, why wouldn't he? But why had he come back? Then she realized. For the same reason he'd proposed. He'd come back to see whether she was with child.

"I had lots of time to think about things on the way to Canada."

Like whether he could go through with a marriage if she was expecting. Problem was, now that he'd come back, Lucy wanted him to ask her again so she could accept. She loved him so much. She'd do whatever she could to make him love her back.

"You know I was angry with my father for lying to me. That it was part of the reason I'd left Philadelphia."

She took a step forward, remembering their talk the night before he'd left. She hoped that one day he'd feel comfortable enough to tell her about their dispute. His willingness to do so now sparked some hope that they might be able to have a future together. "I knew you'd had an argument."

"I overheard something that I shouldn't have and it hurt so much that I took off."

She rested a hand on his sleeve, wanting to offer comfort but not wanting to interrupt.

"On the day we had our picnic I told you that *I'd* been told my father's parents died before I was born."

"I remember."

"Well, the truth is, my grandmother wasn't dead."

Why would his father have lied about that? "Did you know her?"

His eyes crinkled at the corners and he looked out over the yard. "She lived with us."

"I don't understand."

"My father's mother was the woman I knew as Nanny. She helped my parents raise Roberto and I from the time we were born."

But why would his father's mother be known as the nanny rather than a family member? "I still don't under-"

"Neither did I," he said, swinging away and returning to the chair. "It was because Nanny was mulatto."

Lucy sat next to him. It *would* be something unusual—even in a big city like Philadelphia—for a prestigious white family to admit their family included someone with Negro blood. "And you thought that because your father kept his mother's identity a secret, he was ashamed of who she was?"

Renzo's head shot up. "Yes, but how did you know I wasn't the one who was ashamed?"

"Because I know you. I *really* know you." Her gaze held his. "I saw how you treated Thomas. And all that you did to keep the Tylers safe and help them gain their freedom. To you, skin color is simply another physical characteristic, like blue eyes or curly hair."

Renzo drew in a long, full breath and a smile spread across his face. "You don't know how much better I feel, hearing you say that."

"Tell me about her." Nanny must have been incredibly special.

His amber eyes crinkled at the corners. "Well, in a way, she's the reason I first noticed you."

An elderly mulatto woman? "What do you mean?" She *had* always wondered why Renzo had taken notice of her.

"Your voice. The tone, the accent. It reminded me of hers."

"I didn't realize you were so sentimental." And Lord help her, it made him all the more appealing.

"You're both very determined women, too," he paused, "but that's where the similarities ended."

"Oh?"

His smile turned sheepish. "Promise you won't get too angry?"

She agreed, even though she had a feeling what he was about to say wouldn't be that bad.

"Well, at least you know the reason I kept coming back wasn't because you plied me with sumptuous meals."

When understanding dawned, she didn't bother to suppress a chuckle. Perhaps later today she'd make him eat those words.

"I suppose I can understand why Nanny's family connection was kept a secret from the community, but why weren't you and your brother ever told?"

A sad humph escaped his lips. "I asked myself the same question a thousand times after I found out. I assumed it had been my father's idea, but as it turns out I was wrong."

"So you finally let your father explain?"

"Yes and no. Nanny did some of the explaining herself. You see, she'd written Roberto and I a long letter and instructed my father not to give it to us until one year after her death." Renzo sounded so worn down Lucy wanted to wrap him in her arms and absorb his sadness, but no one could relieve someone else's pain.

"Her letter explained so much. She told us what her life had been like with my grandfather." Renzo rubbed his beard-stubbled chin. "They met in Boston. My grandfather had put everything he had into building Ross Shipping, so she was afraid he'd lose it because of her. It took months before my grandmother agreed to marry him. He finally wore her down, but she held fast to one stipulation. That their marriage be kept secret."

"To outsiders, she would be the housekeeper and cook of a wealthy businessman whose wife preferred traveling in Europe to living in America. And when my father came along, they moved to Philadelphia and she became the nanny. My father took after grandfather in appearance, so if anyone ever suspected Nanny was his mother they never spoke of it.'

Renzo sifted a hand through his hair once more. "I guess my Italian heritage came in handy, explaining away our dark complexions and untamable curls."

"And your eyes? I've never seen anyone with your amber color." She'd adored his eyes since that first day at the mercantile.

"Until now, I'd never known where the color came from. I guess we can assume that one of Nanny's parents was responsible. Unfortunately the story of *her* heritage will remain a mystery. She never told my father about her life before she arrived in Boston, but because of her accent I suspect she came from the same area you were raised."

"So your father knew she was his mother?"

"Oh, yes. She wasn't that much of a saint. He says that in private she loved being called Mother. They were a very normal family when no one was around."

"So keeping the secret was her idea and not your father's?"

"Yes, although Father insisted my mother be told before they wed. He didn't want to enter into a marriage keeping secrets from his bride."

Lucy's hands curled closed in her lap. Would Renzo ever really be able to forgive her for keeping secrets from him since the first day they met? "Do you really think anyone would care about your grandmother's Negro heritage?"

"Oh, I've painted a picture of Philadelphia as a very progressive city, and it is. But there are still plenty of people in my parent's circle who would look down on them if they knew. That's why Nanny didn't want us to be told. She was afraid one of us might accidentally say something or come to her defense in a way that would give away her secret."

"Well, I'm glad that you and your father have made peace."

"I am, too." He breathed out a long breath. "I've always looked up to him, and it was eating away at me to think he hadn't been proud enough of his own mother to acknowledge her. Family is everything."

Lucy shifted in her chair. Was this the reason he'd come back? To sacrifice his future by proposing to the woman he thought might be carrying his child. She may be determined to marry him, but she wouldn't mislead him ever again.

"Renzo, I'm not pregnant."

He studied her for long moments. "And that disappoints you?" His expression was impossible to read.

"Yes and no. Any baby is a wonderful gift from God."

He shifted from his chair to kneel at her feet. "Lucy, I'm not here because there might have been a baby." His gaze trapped hers and something began to simmer in her belly. "If you're barren-"

"I'm not," she said. "I lost a child the night Emmett died."

He studied their stacked hands. "I'm so sorry." A quiet moment passed between them. "During our journey, Emily told me how you delivered Lilyann the night of the thunderstorm. That must have been very difficult."

She thought back to that miraculous night. "It was, but looking back, I think it helped me move past my own hurt."

He bent and kissed her hand. "That's good. But Lucy, children aren't why I'm here."

The butterflies took wing in her stomach. "They're not?"

"God, no. I mean, if there was a child growing inside you, I'd be thrilled. But that's not why I came back."

Her heart hammered.

"Lucy, didn't you believe me when I said I loved you?"

Her breath caught. "What? When?" she asked. She believed him, but how could she have missed such a thing? She began to suspect her hearing loss was the reason she's missed the most important declaration one person can make to another.

His brows rose. "When? Our last night together. Don't tell me you don't remember."

They'd snuggled and talked, but she'd been so tired. She scooted forward to wrap her arms around his neck, tears blurring her vision.

He loved her.

"Renzo, I didn't hear you."

He hugged her back. "How could you not-"

She set him away so he could see her tug on her lobe. "I'm deaf in this ear." His eyes widened. "Usually it's only an issue when I can't see. I didn't intentionally decide not to tell you, it just never came up."

He took her jaws in his palms. "Are you saying you weren't listening when I poured out my undying love for you?"

She looked at him askance. "Is that what you did?

Poured out you heart?"

His eyes crinkled at the corners once again. "Well, maybe I whispered the sentiment. But I meant it. I do love you, Lucy. I wouldn't have taken you to bed if I didn't."

She laughed, pulling him back into her embrace. Then he stood, tugging her up with him.

He kissed her temple. "Does this mean your answer is yes?"

She knew it would take a lot of training on her part to make herself the kind of woman Philadelphia's society would accept, but if it meant they would be together for the rest of their lives, it was a price she would happily pay.

"Yes. Although it's going to be a pretty big job, helping me transform myself into someone you'll be proud of. But if you're willing to try, then so am I."

He snapped her back to arm's length so fast her teeth rattled. "What in the world are you talking about?" he said. "I'm immensely proud of you just as you are." He rubbed her upper arms. "I wouldn't change one hair on your head."

Didn't the man care about his social status? "So your society friends won't mind that I've milked cows, weeded vegetable gardens and mucked out stalls?"

"Other than your opinion, I really don't care about anyone else's. Frankly, I'm surprised they matter to you."

Her love for this man just continued to deepen, but his standing in society shouldn't have to suffer for it. "Well, I don't relish the thought of people thinking less of you because of me. People might not want to socialize with someone like me."

"And is that what you want? To try and fit into society?"

"I want to be with you, even if it means moving to the big city."

He picked her up off the ground again. "Lucy,

you'd be bored out of your mind. You're used to being busy with more than shopping and sipping tea. No, I've already decided to move to Ohio and take up farming with my wife."

She hiccupped with shock. Would the surprises this man threw her way never end? "Could you be happy away from your family and the big city?"

"No question about it. You know, this past month I believe I missed Agnes, Gertie and The Sheik almost as much as I missed you."

She tightened the circle of her arms. "Oh, Renzo, I love you. I've loved you since the night you choked down that awful chicken."

His mouth found hers and they kissed, hungrily at first, but then they calmed to eager brushes of lips and tongues.

"Let's go find a preacher," he said against her lips. "I want to make love to you so much it hurts, but before you change your mind I want to make you my wife."

She was about to tempt him into reconsidering the order of those events when hoof beats interrupted. They turned to see Charles Hopper galloping down the drive as if he was being chased by the devil himself. He slowed in front of the house, but didn't dismount.

"About time you got back," he said to Renzo, then switched his attention to Lucy. "Mildred says come quick."

"What's the-"

But Charles swung his horse around and spurred it on.

"I take it you're on speaking terms with the Hoppers?"

"Come on." Lucy climbed up onto the seat while he untied Gertie's reins. She turned the cart and started down the drive, wishing Gertie had a bit more of Terra's speed.

"Since when do you ride to the Hopper's rescue?"

He propped a foot up in front and gripped the board behind her back.

"Mildred and I have formed a friendship over the past few weeks." She wouldn't spoil their newfound happiness with tales of heartache while he was away. Besides, she was worried that something had happened to her friend. Damn, Charles, for not telling her what was the matter before he took off.

"And here I was worried about how you'd be getting along with a man who tried to blackmail you into selling the farm."

She flicked the reins with a bit more force. "Oh, you were right to be worried. If it wasn't for Mildred laying down the law with Charles, I might have shot him by now."

Renzo's tone softened and he stroked her back. "You don't suppose she's hurt, do you?"

Lucy's pulse raced. "I don't know. I hope not."

Renzo scooted closer and wrapped his arm around her waist. At the Hopper's farm, she spotted Charles waving from the barn.

"Mildred?" she called a minute later as she and Renzo ran through the door.

"Shhhhh," the Hoppers said in tandem.

Seeing the two of them hale and hearty, leaning over a half-wall, Lucy halted. Renzo almost sent her flying forward, but he grabbed her arms and pulled her to his chest.

"What in the world is going on?" Lucy said.

Mildred rushed to her and grabbed her hand. The older woman's face glowed with a childlike smile. "Come and look." She tugged Lucy over to the divider and they peered over the top.

Lucy squealed into her cupped hands.

Butterbean, the Hopper's big yellow dog, lay licking a coppery brown, newborn pup. Six others, four of them the same brown and two yellow, were latched onto their mother's swollen nipples.

From behind her, Renzo chuckled. "Well, I'll be. I think this solves the mystery of where Wink was running off to." His hands settled on her shoulders.

"I guess so." She was itching to hold one of the freshly bathed pups, but Butterbean might not appreciate her interference.

"Of course, you'll have pick of the litter," Charles said.

"And what if I want more than one?" she said.

"As long as you leave the majority for Butterbean," Mildred said, still focused on the litter. "Every mother needs children to love."

"Don't worry, Mildred." Lucy turned into Renzo's arms. "I think two pups will round out our family quite nicely."

Epilogue

As Lucy bent over to lift the roast out of the oven, Renzo admired her backside. Could he convince her to skip dinner and go right to bed? He didn't' think he'd ever get tired of making love to his wife. Since they'd married his life was complete, full and happy in every way. She hummed out of key, unaware of her tin ear. Her apparent happiness made his heart swell.

"What did your mother have to say in her letter?" She set the platter on the table and slapped his hand as he tried to snitch a bite before she sat and they said the blessing. He'd been overjoyed to find out Lucy was really an excellent cook after the unpalatable trick she'd played on him. And it was a damned good thing he kept busy with chores, repairing the outbuildings and his plans for expanding the house. Otherwise he'd find himself as plump around the middle as Sheriff Tate.

"She's anxious to meet you and said they'll be expecting us for the Christmas holiday."

She went back to the stove and dished up mashed potatoes. He silently pulled a small piece of beef off the roast, chewing covertly. Studying her busy profile in one of the new day dresses he'd insisted she buy made his mouth water in a different way. And that new corset had done wondrous things to her already enticing breasts. She had needed to live so sparingly, he'd had a difficult time getting her to purchase a few new clothes. But if he knew his mother, she would drag Lucy to every lady's shop in Philadelphia when they visited.

A tugging at his trouser leg made him look down. He backed his chair away from the table to pick up Fink, their male puppy. His sister, Blink, lay curled in a blanket-lined crate in the corner.

"Fink, we hit the nail on the head with your name." The rowdy pup squirmed in his hands, trying to get a closer sniff of roasted beef.

"Don't you think Blink's name fits her?" Lucy set the steaming bowl of potatoes on the table.

"Not as well as this little fellow." He set the pup back on the floor. "Oh, I forgot. Mother also mentioned that Elizabeth's parents found her."

His wife pursed her lips at the mention of his wandering ex-fiancé. "How nice for them."

He grabbed Lucy's hips as she made to turn away and pulled her onto his lap. She wrapped one arm snugly around his shoulder but held her nose in the air.

"Lucy, I told you I never had any serious feelings for Elizabeth." He leaned in and nibbled her neck.

She wrapped her other arm around him and sank back into his hold. "I know. I supposed it is silly of me to be jealous of her when I'm the one you married."

He kissed her firmly on the lips for such a sensible reply. "That's right. You're the one I fell head over heels in love with."

"And you don't regret staying in Rush Crossing?"

She loved their farm, but he hadn't been able to convince her that *he* considered it his home as well.

Perhaps this would prove it. "Not at all. You know, Sheriff Tate told me he's thinking about retiring